D0627477

HAVE YOUR TICKET PUNCHED BY FRANK JAMES

A JEMMY MCBUSTLE MYSTERY

HAVE YOUR TICKET PUNCHED BY FRANK JAMES

FEDORA AMIS

FIVE STAR
A part of Gale, a Cengage Company

Farmington Hills, Mich • San Francisco • New York • Waterville, Maine
Meriden, Conn • Mason, Ohio • Chicago

LIBRARY OF CONGRESS CATALOGING-IN-PUBLICATION DATA

Names: Amis, Fedora, author.
Title: Have your ticket punched by Frank James : a Jemmy McBustle mystery / by Fedora Amis.
Description: First Edition. | Farmington Hills, Michigan : Five Star, a part of Gale, Cengage Learning, 2019.
Identifiers: LCCN 2018039838 (print) | LCCN 2018041377 (ebook) | ISBN 9781432851941 (ebook) | ISBN 9781432851934 (ebook) | ISBN 9781432851927 (hardcover)
Subjects: | GSAFD: Mystery fiction.
Classification: LCC PS3601.M576 (ebook) | LCC PS3601.M576 H38 2019 (print) | DDC 813/.6—dc23
LC record available at https://lccn.loc.gov/2018039838

First Edition. First Printing: May 2019
Find us on Facebook—https://www.facebook.com/FiveStarCengage
Visit our website—http://www.gale.cengage.com/fivestar/
Contact Five Star Publishing at FiveStar@cengage.com

Printed in Mexico
1 2 3 4 5 6 7 23 22 21 20 19

I dedicate this book to Damon,
the son who has always been the joy of my life.

ACKNOWLEDGMENTS

I owe a debt of gratitude to the wonderful people at the Missouri Historical Society Library, as well as both the St. Louis City and County Public Libraries. Without their maps of 1897 St. Louis and their microfilmed newspapers, I'd still be confused about the what's, who's, and where's. I also thank St. Louis itself for being the heartland's bustling center of commerce, culture, and crime in 1898.

I owe a big round of applause to my Sisters in Crime. Their unstinting support made me believe I could write a mystery, and their ceaseless prodding made me prove it.

AUTHOR'S NOTE

Although this Victorian whodunit is the fictitious product of my fevered brain, I've borrowed some real people and events from the past.

FRANK JAMES

Alexander Franklin James. (January 10, 1843–February 18, 1915)

During the Civil War, Frank fought under CSA Major General Sterling Price at the Battle of Wilson's Creek near Springfield, Missouri, (August 10, 1861) and at the siege of Lexington, Missouri, (September 12–20, 1861). He later became a bushwhacker under Bloody Bill Anderson and participated in the Centralia, Missouri, massacre (September 27, 1864). Anderson's men stopped a train, robbed the passengers, and murdered nearly thirty of them; most were unarmed federal soldiers on leave.

Frank James, along with William Clark Quantrill, formed Morgan's Raiders—some fifty guerrillas under Marcellus Jerome Clark, better known as Sue Mundy. The gang surrendered at Samuel's Depot, Kentucky, on July 26, 1865, and all were paroled.

Between 1870 and 1876 the James-Younger gang ranged from Kansas to Kentucky and from Minnesota to Texas robbing banks, holding up stages, and sticking up trains. Robbing trains brought them popularity with common folk because railroads were generally despised for price-gouging. The M-K-T (Missouri-Kansas-Texas, better known as the Katy Line) charged farmers more to ship their wheat to market than the wheat was worth.

The James boys' legend grew with help from dime novel authors and journalists who glorified them. St. Joseph *Gazette* editor John N. Edwards compared them to the Knights of the Round Table.

Pinkerton actions brought the James boys even more sympathy. Detectives sneaked up to the James-Samuel home and tossed a flare lamp through a window. It exploded and killed nine-year-old Archie Samuel. Frank's mother, Mrs. Zerelda Samuel, suffered such injury to her right arm that it had to be amputated. Later they tortured and killed Doctor Samuel, Frank's stepfather.

For three years Frank and Jesse lived under assumed names with their wives and children in places like Nashville, St. Louis, and even Kansas City, less than forty miles from their home town of Kearney, Missouri. They hid in well-populated places. As Frank once remarked, "Most people look alike in the city."

Railroads offered a $10,000 reward for information leading to the capture, dead or alive, of either Frank or Jesse.

After Jesse's death at the hands of the Ford brothers, Frank surrendered to Governor Thomas T. Crittenden at Jefferson City on October 5, 1882. He stood trial at Gallatin, Missouri, and Muscle Shoals, Alabama—acquitted for lack of evidence both times.

When he was a free man, Frank worked as a shoe clerk and as a starter at the race track at St. Louis Fairgrounds Park. The title *Have Your Ticket Punched by Frank James* came from a promotion run by the Standard Theatre in St. Louis, where Frank served as doorman in 1898. Frank's arrest in St. Louis is my complete fabrication. After Jesse's death, Frank was an exemplary, law-abiding citizen. Frank was also quite the Shakespearean scholar, thanks to his minister father, a graduate of Georgetown College of Kentucky. Robert Sallee James wanted his sons to be well educated.

Frank toured with Cole Younger in the unsuccessful "Cole Younger–Frank James Wild West Show." During his later years, Frank returned to the James-Samuel farm, where he charged visitors fifty cents apiece for tours.

SASSY AND TONY

Tony von Phul (Yes, it's pronounced "von fool") and Sassy Patterson were real people. Both were St. Louisans, though their story played out its tragic ending in Denver thirteen years after the setting of *Have Your Ticket Punched by Frank James*. Sylvester Louis "Tony" von Phul was a famous balloonist and rake about town.

In 1900, twenty-year-old Isabel married drunk and abusive shoe salesman John E. Folck and moved to Memphis. "The Butterfly" returned alone to St. Louis in 1906. She lived at the Jefferson Hotel, built in 1904 for World's Fair visitors. "At midnight, things begin to wake up" at this posh new hotel—just the place for Sassy.

For her second husband, Isabel "Sassy" Patterson Folck turned practical. She married rich Denver businessman John Springer. But marriage didn't keep her from writing steamy letters to von Phul—which she later regretted. She enlisted the help of handsome Denver admirer Frank Henwood to retrieve the letters.

Henwood confronted von Phul in Tony's rooms at the Brown Palace Hotel—and von Phul roughed him up. Henwood came better prepared later when he drew a gun on von Phul at the Palace's Marble Bar on May 24, 1911. Frank Henwood shot and killed von Phul. In the melee, he also killed bystander

George Copeland.

Henwood was tried twice, convicted, and sentenced to death, but the governor commuted the sentence and later paroled him. Springer divorced Sassy, and the notoriety followed her. She died alone and penniless in New York in 1917.

MORE GENUINE BITS OF POP CULTURE FROM THE MAUVE DECADE OF THE GILDED AGE

The City of St. Louis adopted the Bertillon system on May 19, 1897. The goal of the system was to discover criminal type. To that end, police measured ear and nose length—as well as the length of the middle finger.

Storm Queen boots cost $1.38. Plays were often double-cast to make them more impressive. The Mizzou football team got in trouble for going all the way to Mexico City without permission in 1896. In 1879 Doctor Joseph Lawrence and Jordan Wheat Lambert invented Listerine in St. Louis as a surgical antiseptic. It was not a rousing success until the 1920s, after some genius invented a "disease" Listerine could cure— halitosis, a fancy made-up name for bad breath.

Under the leadership of Julius Lesser, the Jewish fair took place during Thanksgiving week, 1898, and it ended with paper streamers thrown in their Confetti War on the Saturday after Thanksgiving.

Mary Institute really did present a matinee program on Thanksgiving Day, November 24, 1898; and there really was an honest-to-goodness cussing Japanese lady acrobat at the 1898 St. Louis Hebrew Charity Fair.

CHAPTER ONE

St. Louis, Missouri
Thursday, November 17, 1898
One Week Before Thanksgiving

"I can't breathe. Just think. We're about to meet the famous outlaw himself—Jesse James."

"Calm down, Sassy. Jesse James is dead. The ticket taker we're about to meet is his brother, Frank James."

"But he's a famous outlaw, too, isn't he?"

"Yes. He's the most famous living outlaw in America." Jemima McBustle rolled her eyes. Could anybody but Sassy Patterson have a head so pretty or so empty? Jemmy couldn't help envying Sassy's careless optimism. Sassy could do as she pleased. She wasn't torn between a family pushing her to marry well and the career she felt born to.

"Do you think Frank James will rob us?"

"No, I think he'll punch our tickets."

"If that famous outlaw speaks to me, I'll faint dead away. I had to sweet-talk my escort into letting me hold my own ticket. I would absolutely swoon if I'm not allowed to hand the great outlaw the ticket myself."

Jemmy shuddered from a gust of cold air and pulled her borrowed fur capelet snugly around her shoulders. She pulled up the collar to warm her neck with its silky softness.

The pair stood in line in the outer lobby of Crystal Palace Theatre on a chilly November evening. The foyer smelled of

13

floor wax with drifts of perfume from well-dressed ladies and gents.

"*You* don't faint over men. *They* faint over you." A wave of jealousy washed over Jemmy. She couldn't help it. With glossy, dark hair and cheeks that needed no rouge to be rosy, Isabel "Sassy" Patterson always looked as though she'd stepped off the pages of a Gibson Girl calendar.

Sassy giggled. "Just think—Jesse James's brother, Frank James, in person. Rumor has it he's murdered seventeen men. And that doesn't count the ones he killed during the War Between the States."

"Ssshh. If our escorts and my aunt and uncle hear you, they'll take us straight home. We wouldn't see the show or Frank James either."

"My old shuffle-shoon is deaf as a block of salt and half as handsome. He has only one saving grace—enough money to make a girl almost forget what an old fogy he is."

"My Aunt Delilah has perfect hearing. You'd be wise not to upset her. If you're fond enough of money to marry an old codger like Dr. Wangermeier, she's your best bet. I call her matchmaker to the white-haired, well-to-do old men of St. Louis."

"Heigho, Dearie. You're old fashioned. I don't have to marry a man, rich or otherwise, to get what I want from him."

Sassy told the truth. She had amassed an impressive collection of expensive jewelry. Garnering gems came as easily to her as fluttering her long, dark eyelashes. How did she do it? A simple ploy worked wonders. When escorted by a man of means, she wore no jewelry at all. She let her elegant neck and her smooth white bosom do the asking for her. Rich men who brought no presents to their second appointment never enjoyed a third.

That night she wore only tiny seed-pearl earrings. Her rubies and sapphires stayed home in velvet-lined boxes from Jaccards. Diamond baubles were reserved for balls—to be admired by spirited young men who danced well. Whether they were rich was entirely up to them.

Circumstances had brought the two young ladies together. Jemmy didn't actually like Sassy, but fate kept throwing the two girls into each other's company. They were born in the same year—1880. More to the point, they were outcasts—too fast for the proper debutante crowd. St. Louis society considered Sassy a loose woman—even though she wore her corset as tight as the snobbiest blue nose could wish. Powerful matrons deemed her less than nice because she accepted expensive gifts from men who weren't her betrothed.

Society took even less notice of Jemmy. She labored at a regular job and got paid for it.

Sassy was like no one else in St. Louis—in the Americas—in the world. She could never be picky with girlfriends, or she would have had none at all. But with the opposite sex, she was a tyrant. Next to her, Nero seemed docile as one of Bo Peep's sheep. She insisted the man for her would have the money of J. P. Morgan, the physique of Sandow the Strongman, the fashion sense of Beau Brummell, and Don Juan's legendary way with women.

Trouble was she could find no one man with all those attributes. She did the next best thing. She found one suitable representative from each group and somehow managed to keep them all balanced against each other. Renowned juggler Paul Cinquevali could keep in the air a piece of paper, a bottle, an egg, and a cannonball. Sassy was equally adept at keeping her exotic assortment of suitors aloft.

That night Sassy fairly glowed in rose satin, which elegantly matched the blush in her cheeks. Dark hair upswept and adorned with rose quartz teardrops, she turned heads from the moment her escort handed her down from the carriage in front of the theatre.

"Look, Skeezuck, look. 'Have your ticket punched by the legendary Frank James.' " Sassy pointed to the words on a banner pasted in upswept diagonal across a play poster.

"I see it. Stop beating on my arm. And don't you think I'm a little old to be 'Skeezuck?' " Jemmy loathed the nickname. In fact, she loathed Sassy's habit of sprinkling cutesy lines from children's poems into every conversation.

"No one ever grows too old for monkeyshines. I'd die of boredom if ever I did."

The pair had become so ensnared in their own conversation, they arrived at the ticket taker's stand unawares.

"Young lady, may I verify your ticket?" The man spoke— Frank James, none other than celebrated train robber and brother to the legendary Jesse James. Handlebar mustaches sprinkled with gray gave him a distinguished air.

Jemmy held out her ticket for him to punch while Sassy stood with mouth open. "Miss, may I have your ticket? I promise not to keep it." Frank James tilted his head expectantly.

Jemmy pulled Sassy's hand, the one holding the ticket, up to meet Frank's hole punch. *Snick.* It was done. Jemmy eased Sassy into forward motion. Just then Sassy found her voice. "I'm charmed to meet you, Mr. James."

"And I, you, miss. If we do meet again, why, we shall smile."

Jemmy steered Sassy past the ticket taker's stand.

"You don't have to yank my arm out of its socket."

"Yes, I do. You can't start a conversation in a theatre queue. People are trying to come in from the cold."

"What a lovely thing he said to me. Shakespeare, wasn't it? He's famous for quoting Shakespeare."

"The line is from *Julius Caesar.* Said by an assassin who's about to commit suicide."

"You rob the moment of all joy, you naughty Skeezuck."

"My name is Jemima. Stop calling me 'Skeezuck.' And stop pouting. You're not in kindergarten."

"I promise to stop calling you 'Skeezuck' if you'll help me at intermission."

"I know that tone of voice. It means trouble."

"Don't be silly. We'll have a great lark. If you help me get backstage, I'll introduce you to a fellow with the biggest muscles you ever saw."

"Let me guess. You're sneaking away to meet your mystery strongman. He's the person you came to see, not Frank James. After all, Mr. James must be past fifty—and not rich, or he wouldn't be a theatre ticket taker."

Sassy stuck out her lower lip in a pretty pout. "I wanted to see Mr. James, too."

Jemmy shook her auburn tresses and gave in. No doubt Sassy would land both of them in trouble. Of course, they could generally extricate themselves. Two smiling pretty girls who knew how to work their wiles could be mighty persuasive to males of all ages.

The party of six entered Mr. Erwin McBustle's loge box. The gentlemen seated the ladies in front, then took their own places on the second row. Jemmy's Aunt Delilah produced her opera glasses to investigate the crowd. "We're in good company tonight. Mayor Zeigenhein and Boss Butler are two boxes down."

Aunt Delilah Snodderly McBustle, wife of Mother's brother-in-law Erwin McBustle, was a fine figure of a Victorian lady "of a certain station and of a certain age." Beyond plump and somewhere between imposing and obese, she looked exactly like what she was—one of the leading ladies of St. Louis society. Dressed all in bronze satin, she resembled the statue of Thomas Hart Benton in Lafayette Park.

Jemmy handed Sassy her own opera glasses. Sassy would want to gawk at Ed Butler. Naturally, she would not have remembered to bring her own theatre glasses.

She whispered in Jemmy's good ear. "Boss Butler does look the tough customer. How exciting!"

Aunt Delilah reveled in organizing outings and people. When she learned Jemmy was assigned to review the play, she took charge. Auntie Dee obtained yet another in the parade of escorts deemed suitable for Jemmy to marry. Auntie and Mother never ceased their efforts to marry off Jemmy and make her "comfortable for life."

Tonight's old coot was the color of yesterday's oatmeal. He smelled of formaldehyde and cigars. What's more, he had less personality than a dead catfish—and the looks to match. *Could Auntie Dee possibly believe I'd marry a dwarf who's a good thirty years older than I?*

Aunt Delilah's theatre party had come to see *Uncle Tom's Cabin.* Harriet Beecher Stowe's anti-slavery story had outlived its author, not to mention her intentions.

Before the Civil War, the melodrama provoked high emotion. A half-century later, the new version provoked more laughter than outrage. During the 1880s companies piled on the humor and theatrics to meet the tastes of a new audience. By 1898, the play's message had been made tolerable even in a volatile state like Missouri.

The new bigger and better version offered two special features to delight St. Louis playgoers. The producer double-cast the play. Two Elizas crossed the river on moving ice floes, two little Evas died, and two Gumption Cutes trounced four hissable villains in Scene Two.

The second modern innovation yielded even greater spectacle. Local boxing star Quisenberry Sproat played slave chaser Tom Loker in the first act and Simon Legree in the second. He remained mute the whole time. The *bona fide* actor Tom Loker-Simon Legree spoke all the lines. Sproat's real job was to keep control of twenty-seven baying hounds. The dogs created enough barking to satisfy a hundred 'possum hunters as they scrabbled across the stage in Scene Two.

Two Eliza Harrises alternated lines to open the scene. They started by wringing their skirts made wet from crossing the Ohio River from Kentucky. *Must have slipped from one of those ice floes.* The slave Elizas ran away to save their sons from the Arthur Shelbys. The Master Shelbys meant to sell Eliza's boy-Harrys down the river along with two Uncle Toms.

Two husband Georges arrived. A brace of Gumption Cutes offered horses for the six Harrises to escape to Canada. The speaking actor Tom Loker entered. Beside him came boxer Q. B. Sproat with more than two dozen hounds pulling at their leashes. The howling, bawling canine mass was supposed to race across the stage in hot pursuit of the runaway slaves.

Something was amiss. Midway across the stage, Sproat began to totter, then slipped down on one knee. Leashes slithered through his fingers, one or two at a time. The rest of the dog pack bolted. In less than a minute the whole theatre erupted in canine chaos.

Freedom made the dogs delirious with joy. They leaped off the stage and did what dogs do: raced up and down the aisles, jumped in tuxedoed laps to lick gentlemen's faces, and clawed gashes in taffeta gowns as they charged across ladies' laps.

A young girl of about eleven, wearing rust-colored velvet and white leggings, stepped into the aisle and flung her arms wide open to a liver-colored bloodhound. The exuberant dog ran at her—up and over. The pair sprawled backwards against a row of seats. For a moment the two looked like a gigantic brown cockroach with too many legs.

The dog scrambled over the girl's head to land square in the pompadoured hair of a society matron. In his frantic effort to escape, the hound's paws tangled in her tresses. Off balance, he fell upside down in her lap. The creature yelped and thrashed with paws still tangled in her hair. All those seated nearby came to her aid. Still, it took some moments before they extricated his feet from her hair—but not from her hairpiece.

Once freed, the dog hightailed it up the aisle. From time to time he stopped and gnawed at the sausage-shaped roll of brown wool the lady had used to augment her hair. Anyone who didn't know better would think the mutt was chewing at a turd. He burst out the door without ridding himself of the lady's hair rat. The lady herself covered her head with a lacy hanky. She held her chin high as she marched off to the powder room. Her haughty stare dared anyone to snicker.

A black and tan coonhound leapt from the stage and landed on a chubby dame in the first row. She beat the creature's nose with her fan. The result appalled everyone. The dog stood stock still in shock while he turned her light blue skirt into a soggy pool of dark blue satin.

One bluetick hound, too mixed up and excited to choose a direction, ran in circles on stage. That was the only dog easy to catch.

In moments, Frank James and other front-of-the-house employees raced in to help. Gentlemen patrons from the orchestra seats had already corralled most of the canines. At length, cast members led the creatures off stage. The theatre returned to a semblance of calm. Time for the show to go on—but it didn't.

Quisenberry Sproat lay deathly still on the stage apron.

CHAPTER TWO

November 17, 1898

The portieres at the back of the loge box opened to reveal Frank James. "Which of you gentlemen is Doctor Delmadge Wangermeier?"

Sassy's escort stood. He was a shriveled fellow of about sixty. His pinkish-tan scalp peeked through his white, wispy hair like a boardwalk through a white picket fence. Jemmy thought he probably read Plato in ancient Greek.

His voice sounded like an ungreased pulley. "I would have come to the stage, but I saw two excellent physicians go to the aid of the fallen actor."

"I've come to fetch you in your other capacity."

"If you'll forgive me, ladies, gentlemen." The doctor followed Frank into the hall behind the boxes. Sassy followed him. Jemmy followed Sassy.

The other three had to straggle along behind. As the girls' chaperone, Aunt Delilah was obliged to accompany them. Uncle Erwin and Jemmy's escort had no choice but to traipse along as well. True gentlemen would never leave ladies unattended.

Jemmy itched to go because she smelled a story for the *Illuminator*. She had not produced paper-selling stories for over a month.

A pack of guard dogs couldn't have kept Sassy in her chair. Doctor Wangermeier was acting coroner for the city of St. Louis. If a theatre official summoned him in his "other" capacity, there

21

could only be one reason. Quisenberry Sproat, Sassy's strong-man with the amazing muscles, was dead.

Frank James ushered the party of six downstairs and through the theatre along the far aisle. On the way towards the stage, he answered questions from Doctor Wangermeier. At least, that's what Jemmy imagined.

She trod on Frank's heels in an effort to hear, but hundreds of theatre patrons made far too much noise. Excited babble coursed through the hall.

"Did you see that hound with the hair rat?"

"It was all I could do to keep the filthy mutt from—"

"I didn't dare laugh. After all, she's my mother."

Not many outings could match tonight's outlandish goings-on at the Crystal Palace for first-rate gossip and good clean fun.

The group paused to listen to an announcement by Patrick Short. The dapper manager stepped in front of the red velvet curtain and raised his hands to quiet the audience. "Ladies and gentlemen, I apologize for the mishap and the delay. The dogs have all been rounded up, and we will recommence the play shortly. I beg your indulgence for a few minutes longer. To reward your patience, the management invites you to complimentary champagne in the lobby at intermission. Once again, let me express my deep gratitude for your forbearance."

Dr. Wangermeier took no notice of the train of people behind him until they arrived backstage. He scowled. "McBustle, old chum, why on earth didn't you keep everyone in the box? The last thing I need is to have this mob underfoot."

Aunt Delilah answered for her husband. "My dear Doctor, we would never be so ill-mannered as to desert a member of our party. If you are unable to see the performance, we feel it our duty and honor to accompany you."

The doctor frowned. "I'm going to examine a dead man, not dance a schottische. A death scene is no place for ladies."

Sassy wheedled. "Don't scold them, dear Doctor. It's entirely my fault. They came because they couldn't have stopped me at pistol point. I so very much longed to see you in action. Would you deprive your little Sassy of her one and only chance?"

She batted her lush, dark lashes. Doctor Wangermeier visibly melted. "But my dear . . ."

"I promise not to faint. I'm begging to accompany you. I'll lock myself in my room and pout for days if you deny me."

"And what about her?" Dr. Wangermeier nodded in Jemmy's direction. "The sight of a dead man may well offend a young lady's delicate sensibilities."

Aunt Delilah murmured into the doctor's ear. "My niece writes for the St. Louis *Illuminator.* You may have seen her byline Ann O'Nimity."

The doctor's head shot up. "My word. A woman wrote those lurid stories? A female brain producing such vulgarity quite amazes me, Miss McBustle."

"I've stopped a train robbery and seen a body crushed by a rockslide. I am hardly likely to faint at the sight of a dead actor."

The doctor waved his hand in defeat. "Come along then, all of you. I take no responsibility for your nightmares."

Frank James led them down a spiral staircase to dressing rooms in the basement. The place smelled of sawdust and fresh paint. *Thank heavens it doesn't smell like a moldy cave. It would take a pair of draft horses to get me down under St. Louis again.*

On one side of a long corridor were at least a dozen doors to dressing rooms. The pair of Tom Loker-Simon Legrees shared the men's star suite.

Inside, trunks and furniture had been pushed aside to make way for the body on the floor.

Quisenberry Sproat lay on his back, eyes closed as if he'd stretched out for a nap between acts. Frank James borrowed the exact words from Shakespeare: "He dies, and makes no sign."

The surviving Tom Loker stood beside the body, arms folded as if ready to offer a funeral sermon. The young actor's golden good looks stopped Jemmy cold. The worry lines on his forehead only added to his appeal. He could have posed for a statue of blond Adonis.

Without bidding, the actor launched into a description of the previous twenty minutes. "Out of the corner of my eye, I saw Sproat fall to one knee. I thought he probably got twisted up in the leashes, so I turned back to help. That's when he started sweating and gagging like he was about to disgorge his supper."

Red faced, Tom Loker interrupted himself. "Pardon me, ladies, I should have thought of a more genteel way to say it."

Aunt Delilah offered a feeble smile as she fanned her face. "Quite all right, young man. Plain speaking is the order of the day."

The doctor snapped, "Yes, yes, man. Get on with it. The ladies knew what they were getting into—and are quite *free to leave* whenever they wish."

"He was breathing fast when he began letting go of the animals. I started to chase after the dogs, but he grabbed my arm. His hand was cold. I think he said he felt dizzy. I'm not sure because his words were slurred. Then his head hit the floor."

Tom Loker stood in silence with all eyes watching him. The doctor prompted, "What did you do then?"

"I nodded to the stage manager to bring down the curtain, but he didn't. Too busy giving orders about the dogs, I suppose. A few actors came out on stage. We got hold of Sproat's arms and legs and started to move him into the wings. He seemed to rally. He waved us off and tried to sit up, but then he collapsed and stopped breathing altogether."

"How did he get down here to this dressing room?"

"The stage manager said we had to get him out of the way so the show could start up again once all the dogs were caught."

"My word, why bring him down here? Why not go to the alley door while someone telephoned for an ambulance to take him to the hospital?"

Loker dropped his head in embarrassment. "It sounds quite silly now. But I think we brought him to his dressing room because we wanted him to be comfortable—in his own place."

"If you wanted him to be comfortable, why did you put him on the floor?"

"Some watery ooze was seeping through his shirt. We didn't want to spoil the chaise longue."

"Let's see his back."

Uncle Erwin and Jemmy's escort helped Loker turn Sproat over onto his stomach. Pink-red diagonal slashes ran across his white shirt back in random pattern.

"I don't have my physician's bag. Does anyone have scissors?"

Tom Loker fished around in his make-up kit and produced a pair of shears. Dr. Wangermeier knelt down, pulled up Sproat's shirttail and made one snip through the hem. He took the cut pieces in both hands and pulled. The shirt ripped clean to the collar and fell aside, exposing Sproat's back.

Sassy gasped and ran out of the room. Aunt Delilah fanned with increased fury. Uncle Erwin's face took on a green cast, and Jemmy's bland gentleman swooned in a heap over Sproat's legs.

The stink could make a vulture gag—like spoiled fish doused with spruce-oil liniment.

Tom Loker pulled Jemmy's escort off Sproat's legs and helped him to the door.

Jemmy put her hanky over her mouth and bent over Sproat for a closer look. Slashes of red flesh and white bone crisscrossed his body. A dozen or more gashes wept pink ooze from the boxer's raw back. Someone had flogged Quisenberry Sproat.

Dr. Wangermeier called to Tom for a measuring stick.

"The costume mistress always wears a tape measure round her neck. Will that do?" The doctor's nod sent Tom off to find her.

Dr. Wangermeier addressed the escorts. "Gentlemen, I'd be obliged if you would see to the ambulance. And please take the ladies elsewhere now their morbid curiosity has been satisfied."

Jemmy's escort was still sitting on the floor in the doorway with his head tucked between his knees. Uncle Erwin helped him stand. Aunt Delilah alternated fanning his red face and her own as the trio shuffled out. Only Jemmy and the doctor remained.

Jemmy said, "I'd like to be of assistance if I may."

"I intended for you to leave with the others."

"There must be something I can do here."

"My word, a young lady with the stomach of a coyote."

"A hospital nurse must see such sights every day."

"Very well, then. Find a handkerchief to tie up his valuables after I empty his pockets. Then gather up every cream and liquid and powder in this room—and I mean every single one. Find some container to hold them. When that actor fellow comes back, have him identify everything that belongs to Mr. Sproat. I plan to take it all with me tonight."

"Yes, Doctor." Jemmy found a theatrical trunk bearing the initials *Q.S.* Inside was a change of clothes, pistol, riding quirt, tin of Cloverine salve, bottle of Watkins Liniment, and flagon of laudanum. To those she added everything from the dressing table.

"Dr. Wangermeier, did someone horsewhip this man to death?"

"Unlikely. Too young and healthy. A hundred lashes can be a

death sentence, but not fourteen—at least not right away. The lesions can fester. But then sepsis would be the killer—not the beating itself."

"What killed him then?"

"Even if I knew, I wouldn't tell you. My word, that's no information belonging in the newspapers. It's my job to inform the police, not the yellow news trade."

"I'd never reveal information you asked me to withhold. I promise. What do you think was the cause of his death?"

"I'll know more after the autopsy. Come see me then. For now, just write that the man collapsed on stage. Don't mention the lashing, or I'll never tell you anything more."

Tom Loker returned with the costume mistress's tape measure. The doctor measured the welts and wrote their dimensions in a notebook. Jemmy took notes in her own little book.

Tom stared at the newly vacant dressing table. "Where did my things—my makeup . . ."

"Dr. Wangermeier requested me to gather up all of Mr. Sproat's possessions and add them to the contents of his trunk. It will go to the police."

"Most of the things on that dressing table belong to me. You have no right to take them, Doctor."

"You'll get them back in due course."

"May I at least have the greasepaints and powder? I need to make myself up for the next act."

"Go ahead. But put them back when you're finished."

Tom grumbled but did as he was told.

The doctor picked up one of Sproat's hands to examine the fingernails. "Miss McBustle, if you want to be of use, fetch some stage grips to move the body and take the trunk to my carriage. I can do no more here. And, Miss McBustle, kindly offer my regrets to Miss Patterson. I will be unable to transport her home. Also please convey my appreciation to your uncle.

Tell him I regret I must prevail upon his good nature to attend Miss Patterson. I hope he doesn't find it an undue burden."

"I'm sure they'll all understand and forgive your absence." Jemmy tucked her notebook in her reticule. "Mr. Loker, where may I find the stagehands."

" 'Tom' will do. There's always a grip by the saltwater rheostats."

Jemmy raised her eyebrows. "Saltwater . . ."

"Tubs of salt water with electric bars to pull up or down in the water. That's how we dim the lights. This theatre is fully electrified, you know."

"I remember some containers. I thought the water was to put out fires."

"Not much danger of fires. The Crystal Palace has a fire curtain—a roll-down curtain of asbestos, the latest thing."

Jemmy pulled on her gloves.

Tom said, "The man at the rheostats wouldn't be able to leave his job. None of the hands would. You'll have to get front-of-the-house people. If you'll wait just a moment, I'll take you myself—point you to Mr. Short's office."

When Tom Loker turned around, Jemmy stepped back in surprise. Her foot landed on a Sproat shoe. She would have been the second person to fall on the poor dead boxer if Tom hadn't grabbed her hand and pulled her toward him.

She shuddered at the transformation greasepaint and powder had wrought on the dashing young actor. With his gleaming hair hidden under a ragged slouch hat and his elegant chin dirtied with black beard stubble, he looked the very incarnation of brutality. Jemima McBustle found herself in the arms of Simon Legree.

CHAPTER THREE

November 17, 1898

"Miss McBustle, ready with your review of *Uncle Tom's Cabin* so early? You must not have stayed for the whole show." The St. Louis *Illuminator*'s night manager leaned across the counter to collect her story.

"I have something much better. Front page news."

"Mr. Hamm warned me not to use your stories without proper verification." The man clearly belonged with other creatures of the night. His skin was the color of a peeled banana, and his eyes bulged watery blue with pink rims. Jemmy thought an hour of sunlight would turn him the color of rare steak.

Jemmy stood her ground. "I've brought four of St. Louis's leading citizens. They'll swear to the truth of the strange events at the Crystal Palace Theatre tonight."

"Said events would be?"

"Quisenberry Sproat died on stage."

"The man is a boxer. He never laid claim to be an actor insofar as I know." The manager smirked to punctuate his little joke.

"I'm not speaking in a figurative sense. The man died in fact. This very night, Quisenberry Sproat died on the stage of the Crystal Palace Theatre."

"Might rate the front page if factual." The night editor raised his eyebrows in the direction of wealthy warehouse owner Erwin McBustle.

"Quite true. Verified by the coroner in our presence."

The night editor pored over a test pull of the morning edition's front page. "Miss Ann O'Nimity—" The night editor smirked again.

Jemmy cringed. *Someday I'm going to give Mr. Hamm a piece of my mind. How could he hoodwink me into that awful name? How could I let him get away with making fun of me?*

"I can give you two half columns on the top right if you can have them ready to set in"—he looked at the big Regulator clock on the wall—"twenty-six minutes."

"Done and done."

"One more thing. Have you a headline?"

"Lashed Actor Dies." The instant the phrase popped from her mouth, panic struck. She shouldn't have mentioned the whipping. She'd promised Dr. Wangermeier on pain of being banished from his good graces and his store of information.

I've done it again—let my instincts run rampant over common sense and good judgment. When will I learn to think before I open my yap?

Jemmy backpedaled. "Make that 'Local Boxer Dies on Stage.' "

"I'll use the first one—snappier."

"But Mr. Hamm says to always use the local angle."

"What Mr. Hamm says is law during the days. I'm in charge at night."

"But the coroner personally asked me not to mention the beating."

"The coroner should know better than to trust discretion in a female."

"I beg you . . ."

"You now have twenty-three minutes to write the article."

Jemmy made a mad dash two floors up and began pounding on her new Remington typing machine. Her fingers struck seven mistakes in the first sentence. She clenched her teeth and reached for a pad and pencil instead.

Her mind raced. Should she lay out the story of a sensational death in front of a live theatre audience? Dr. Wangermeier would never forgive her, never give her information for a follow-up.

Should she focus the story on runaway dogs? Blame the night editor for the headline? After all, he had complete control over headlines. Perhaps she could tell Dr. Wangermeier Aunt Delilah had blurted out the news without knowing the coroner had asked for secrecy.

The budding journalist in her knew she shouldn't dilute the story—or lie to the coroner either. But what else could she do?

When she handed in her story, the night manager perused it and frowned. "Kind of tame after the buildup you gave."

"Print it. It's factual, and it will scoop every other paper in town."

"Excuse me, folks. I'm off to the linotype."

When Jemmy's escort and Uncle Erwin McBustle put on their top hats to leave, Aunt Delilah noticed one of the group was missing. "Where did Miss Patterson go?"

Jemmy said, "If she'd come to the third floor press room, I would have known. Iron steps make a terrible racket."

Aunt Delilah moved toward the exit. "Perhaps she didn't get past the second floor. We'd have seen her if she were still here on the first floor."

"Indeed, the second floor is the place to look." The trio climbed wooden stairs to a room filled with gigantic black machinery. They found Sassy admiring an ink-stained young man in a leather apron. His biceps swelled when he hoisted a roll of paper to his shoulder. She looked suitably impressed as she followed him.

Aunt Delilah's voice cut through the smell of ink and acetone. "Miss Patterson, we are leaving now."

31

"Of course, Mrs. McBustle. I was just fascinated by . . ."

"We know, Miss Patterson. You are always fascinated by . . ."

The next morning, Jemmy felt the full weight of Suetonius Hamm's displeasure. "The night manager must be a lunatic. He gave you one-sixth of my front page. Do you deliver exciting details of a well-known young athlete about town who mysteriously died while performing on stage? Did you find out enough about the man to know he had been arrested for killing a man in the boxing ring? Well, did you?"

"If I may explain—"

"No, you may not explain. What you wrote defies explanation."

"Please, sir—"

"This city hungers daily for the news we bring them. You furnish not news, but dogs spoiling ladies' hairdos." He whacked his own balding head with the offending newspaper.

Hamm turned toward the window and stood rocking from heel to toe, hands clasped behind him.

"Mr. Hamm . . ."

The instant Jemmy found her voice again, he stopped her cold. "*Diem perdidi.* I have lost a day. Do you know the cost of losing a day in the newspaper business? Of course you don't."

He whirled toward her and smacked the paper down on his desk. "The immortal gods continue to conspire against me. I do not know why Hermes should look down from newspaper heaven and heap gifts upon you. Why couldn't the messenger of the gods cast his magic wand on my real reporters from time to time? But no, the old trickster sees to it that you are the one present when calamity strikes."

With both fists on his desk, Hamm thrust his face mere inches from Jemmy's. "You, who are a novice—you, who don't belong in a reporter's job because it can be dangerous and ugly—you, who are a female!"

Jemmy edged toward the door of his office.

"Come back here." He pointed to the spot in front of his desk. "Get a decent follow-up, or I'll have exactly what I need to prove to Mrs. Willmore that you do not deserve your job at the St. Louis *Illuminator.*"

"Is there anything else?"

He pushed his glasses up and rubbed his eyes with thumb and index finger. "Bring me a headache powder and a glass of water."

Jemmy left the office red-faced. No one had ever spoken so harshly to her in her entire life. One thing made the dressing down a little easier. Her assignment would take her out of the building and away from office gossip.

Jemmy approached the one person who might be able to help her: the sports reporter. "I know you heard what Mr. Hamm wants. Sidewalk vendors probably heard it on Poplar Street. I'd be grateful for anything you can tell me about Quisenberry Sproat."

Autley Flinchpaugh was a former boxer, and he looked it. One side of his head sported a splayed-out cauliflower ear. His humped nose tilted permanently to the left. The compressed bones of his oversized hands made them next to worthless for writing. He composed stories in his head and dictated them to the staff typist.

Flinchpaugh offered his handkerchief. Jemmy dabbed her eyes.

He said, "Give me a few minutes, and I'll have the basic facts put in a file for you."

Armed with information from the sports desk, Jemmy donned hat and coat. Around her neck, she wrapped the white angora muffler her little sister Merry had knitted as a Christmas gift. Its soft warmth cheered her, but only a little. She slipped downstairs and out into a sunny, crisp day to unearth the lowdown on Quisenberry Sproat.

Two trolley rides and a brisk walk took her to 20th and Salisbury, across the street from Hyde Park. She looked up at the facade of the North St. Louis Gymnastic Club, where Sproat had trained as a boxer. The sign over the main doors read "Turnverein Halle."

Auburn-haired Jemima McBustle embarked upon the unthinkable. She dared enter the no-woman's-land of the Northside Turner Hall.

She stayed just long enough to get booted out.

She did manage to survey the gym. The main room stood two stories high with a gallery running around the second floor. The floorboards smelled of linseed oil and liniment.

On the first floor, one wall held racks of parallel wooden rods. A roped ring of raised canvas took place of honor near the far wall. Barbells with weight disks on both ends and leather medicine balls littered one corner.

Two young men lunged at each other with épées near the front windows. She could see only three men.

"No ladies allowed." An older man in short pantaloons over wool tights stopped hitting a sandbag hanging from a cross-beam. His paunch resembled an apron full of potatoes dangling below his belt.

"I write for the *Illuminator*. I'd like to speak to someone who knew Quisenberry Sproat."

"I'll see you to the door." He tossed aside his leather gloves with the fingers cut off.

"Was Mr. Sproat here yesterday?"

"I'll answer no questions asked by the likes of you." He took her arm roughly and rushed her out the door.

Jemmy had never been so ill-treated by civilized males. In the space of three hours, two men had bullied her. The first bellowed her into tears. The second laid hands upon her and threw her out into the cold, cold street. She stood on the sidewalk in front of Turner Hall trying to find her dignity. She swallowed hard to force down the lump of frustration in her throat.

From the side of the building, one of the fencers strode towards her as he pulled on a coat. "Miss, I'd like to apologize for Medley. He was Sproat's manager. Perhaps that will excuse his ill treatment of you."

"I wish I had known he was so close to Mr. Sproat. I must have seemed unfeeling and selfish."

"I don't think Medley has much use for ladies."

"It was very kind of you to explain Mr. Medley's rudeness."

"I have another reason as well—something you might find interesting."

"Was Mr. Sproat at Turner Hall yesterday?"

"Couldn't say. I wasn't."

"What can you tell me about him?"

"Not much. I just joined the Hall two days ago. Didn't ever see Sproat in person."

"Then why did you stop your sword fight to talk to me?"

"To bring you these." He fanned picture cards of a well-muscled, handsome young man. Jemmy stared at them. Yes, they were Quisenberry Sproat naked. Well, some had his private parts covered with fig leaves like the miniature statue of David she'd seen in Mrs. Nanny's sporting house. But some of the photographs showed the man altogether in the altogether. "One dollar each."

Jemmy blinked and peered at the cards even more closely. She marveled at Sproat's bulging muscles—so unlike the saggy lumps of flesh they'd been in death.

"Do you expect a whole dollar apiece?" She took the cards in hand to examine them in greater detail. She'd never seen a man naked as a peeled cucumber. Jemmy lived in a house of women.

"Cards of sportsmen cost a penny. Some are free inside tobacco packets."

"Not cards like these—of such a fine specimen of manhood and so recently deceased."

Jemmy dug in her reticule and came up with a quarter. "This is all I have."

He took back the totally nude pictures but offered her to choose among four others. In one, Sproat semi-reclined on a couch with one hand balanced on an insolent knee. He wore the sandals and helmet of a Roman gladiator with sword hilt strategically placed below his belly button.

The second displayed a rippling-muscled back view with Sproat as Atlas holding an oversized globe above his head. The third showed him in caveman stance, holding a great club and wearing a leopard-skin loincloth. The last showed him wearing Mercury's winged hat and sandals—and naked but for a fig leaf.

She lingered over the gladiator pose but chose Sproat as caveman. It was less daring, and easier to explain if the need arose. The swordsman sauntered back to Turner Hall.

Jemmy sat on the steps poring over the image. At the sound of boots tapping wooden sidewalk boards, she tucked the card in her reticule.

"What are you looking at that is so fascinating you won't come in from the cold?" Sports reporter Autley Flinchpaugh tipped his hat.

"I'm surprised to see you here."

"I came to help. It occurred to me that you would not receive a warm welcome at the Turner Hall. Tell me what you want to know. I'll ask them for you and remember their answers."

"It's not so simple."

"Why not?"

"What they say tells less than what they do. I have to see how they act—decide whether they're telling the truth—whether they're hiding something."

"Don't you think I can do that?"

"You wouldn't know what to ask next."

"Please, excuse me then." He tipped his hat again and started up the steps.

"So, you intend to steal my story."

"A story you can't get is not your story. But my beat is sports—not sudden death. If a prominent boxer died of a wishbone stuck in his throat, I would write an obit for the *Illuminator* and the wire services. Sproat was a nationally known pugilist."

Jemmy fixed him with a stony glare. "So that's what you call poaching my story. An obituary."

Flinchpaugh sighed. "To prove I'm on the up-and-up, I'll help you get your story. After work, I'll take you to the tavern where these fellows drink on Friday nights."

"I'm supposed to attend *Uncle Tom's Cabin*. Last night I saw only the first two scenes."

"I've never known a critic who couldn't pan a play after the first ten minutes."

"You're looking at an honest reviewer. I always stay right through curtain calls."

"My offer is only for this evening. I have to be at a boxing match tomorrow night. Will the theatre review wait another day or two?"

"I suppose so. Mr. Hamm can't despise me more than he already does."

"Care to make a small wager on that?"

"After the morning I've had, you can't cheer me with jokes."

"Then let me cheer you with a round or two of good German lager. The more men drink, the more they'll tell you what you want to know, especially if I'm there. They trust me."

A date with homely Autley did not appeal, but a story to redeem herself did. "Thank you. I'll meet you a little after six at the trolley stop on Washington."

"Far enough from the *Illuminator* so the staff won't see? Good thinking. And here's something else to prove I'm rooting for you—the address of Sproat's mother, if you'll get me something heartwarming about his childhood."

"Deal." Jemmy took the paper.

"Until this evening then. If you'll excuse me, Miss McBustle. I have an obituary to prepare." Flinchpaugh tipped his hat one last time and strode up the steps into Turner Hall.

Deep in thought, Jemmy began walking.

"Please, ma'am, would you like to buy a pencil?"

Startled, Jemmy took two quick steps backward.

"Sorry, ma'am, I didn't mean to fright you."

Jemmy looked into the wide, brown eyes of a frail Negro child of ten or eleven. She wore no hat or earmuffs, just a threadbare coat and blue mittens with one thumb sticking out. "Why, you're the girl with pigtails tied with blue checked gingham—the girl who sells hot pretzels in front of the newspaper where I work."

"That's a good place for selling, but now I have to stay near home—got to tend my mama. She's poorly."

"I'm sorry to hear that. I hope she feels better soon."

"Ol' man winter make her cough—and he just gettin' started."

"I see you've changed from pretzels to pencils."

"Pretzels is better, but I got no way to keep 'em hot. Pencils don't need heat—and they supposed to be hard."

Jemmy reached into her reticule but found no money—just a card of a semi-nude boxer. She sighed. "I wish I could buy all of your pencils, but I don't have even one penny."

The girl bowed her head and turned away, but not before Jemmy saw a single tear slide down her cheek.

"Wait a minute. You ought to be more warmly dressed for work outside in the clutches of Old Man Winter. Here." Jemmy took the angora muffler from around her neck and wrapped it around the little girl's.

"I cain't take your throat warmer. Mama don't allow no charity."

"Surely you don't think I'm giving this scarf to you. No, no, it's just a loan. Your mama couldn't object to a little loan, now could she? I fully expect you to return the scarf to me promptly on the first day of May, 1899. Mind you, it better be properly mended and laundered, too."

The girl's pigtails bounced as she dipped a neat curtsy and said, "Thankee kindly, ma'am." She smiled as she wrapped the muffler around her ears. "I'll have it for you all done up nice the first day in May."

Jemmy watched the girl smiling as she walked toward a lady in the park. The girl's story made her think about her own mother. What if Mother Belinda McBustle felt poorly? Even with three sisters, would Jemmy be able to run Bricktop? Would the borders leave? Would Jemmy have any hope of becoming a stunt reporter?

It's true. I'm no more than a single illness away from poverty— not even my own illness. What if Mother should . . . ?

The minute Jemmy became sentimental about Mother, she remembered the woman's tyranny. Mrs. Belinda McBustle, widow, expected a full accounting of Jemmy's time. This very night she needed good reason to be away from her mother's boardinghouse and her mother's prying.

If Father were still alive, he wouldn't cage me in the way Mother does. He was ahead of his time, and he believed that women have rights and brains. He didn't hold with private girls' schools. He wanted me to graduate from a coeducational school. While he lived, he sent me to Peabody School, St. Louis Branch High School No. 3.

Jemmy brushed a tear from the corner of her eye. The tornado of 1896 had destroyed both school and father. The cyclone blew sheltered Jemmy into a rough and gruff world. Every day, she had to make choices, overcome fears, and suffer harsh reality. Jemmy blew her nose, turned up her coat collar, and set her jaw.

CHAPTER FOUR

Friday, November 18, 1898

"Ma'am, I'm Ann O'Nimity from the St. Louis *Illuminator*. Are you mother to Quisenberry Sproat, the famous boxer?"

A faded woman in a wrapper of washed-out pink roses pushed back a lock of graying hair from her sallow forehead. She reminded Jemmy of wallpaper discolored from years of exposure to the sun. "He's not here, miss, but I expect him directly. You're welcome to come in and wait."

Jemmy's heart flip-flopped in her chest. *Could it be his mother didn't know?* Jemmy took a deep breath and faced an appalling burden. She would have to break the tragic news to the man's own mother.

She clasped the woman's arm and steered her to the kitchen. "Why don't you sit at the table while I make you a nice cup of tea?"

"I don't like tea. Never have."

"Cocoa then, or coffee. I could make either."

"I've always liked cocoa." The woman put her head down on the table next to a quart milk bottle filled with dark liquid. The handwritten label bore the words "Q's Cordial." Jemmy smelled it—licorice. Then she understood. Mother Sproat was soused. More accurately, she was in a haze born of homemade laudanum elixir.

Jemmy looked in every cupboard but found no cocoa—just a tin of Arbuckle's.

"Coffee is all I can find."

The woman snored softly.

As the aroma of perking coffee began to warm the kitchen, Jemmy poked around the house. The Sproat half of the two-family flat included parlor, dining room, kitchen, and back porch on the first floor. The second floor sported a balcony and three spacious bedrooms. The farthest back belonged to Quisenberry Sproat.

Jemmy wrote down the dates and titles on his boxing trophies. In his wardrobe, she found handsomely tailored suits of clothes all neatly brushed and pressed. In his chest of drawers, piles of white linen underwear and stiffly starched shirts gleamed in immaculate white.

She touched his soft-soled boxing boots, shook out his black wool boxing singlet, marveled at how short his white boxing tights seemed compared to her own legs. Her hands trembled when she touched real leopard skin—the very loincloth he wore in the picture she'd bought.

Her heart beat faster when she sifted through the contents of his desk. She read a letter from Miss Mabel Dewoskin demanding money. She found a paper bag filled with perhaps a dozen brown curls tied with gold ribbon.

She picked up a stack of some twenty trading cards. Scrawled across his picture were these words:

To Helen, the best girl a man ever had,

I'll be yours forever,

Q.B.

The next card in the stack bore exactly the same handwritten words—and so did the one after that and the one after that. Only the names changed—Hannah, Julia, Martha, Isabel, Ermintrude.

A crash downstairs interrupted her snooping. She replaced

the curls but stuffed the letter in her reticule. Still clutching the cards, she scurried down the stairs. Back in the kitchen Mrs. Sproat had fallen from her chair. Jemmy found her snoozing peacefully on the linoleum.

Jemmy prepared two coffees and eased the woman back into her chair. "Thank you, my dear. I came over all dizzy for a time. I'll be better directly."

"Drink a little coffee. It always clears my head."

"How strange. I don't remember brewing it."

Jemmy took a deep breath and fixed her mind on the sad task. "Mrs. Sproat . . . it is Mrs. Sproat, isn't it?"

"Yes, Mrs. Emmeline Sproat, widow."

"It breaks my heart to bring you such sad news, but your son, Quisenberry, passed away last night."

"Q.B. isn't here, but I expect him directly. You're welcome to stay if you like. I've been hoping a nice girl might stop by."

Jemmy took the woman's hands in her own. "Q.B. won't be coming back. He's with the coroner."

"I suppose he spent the night with one of his lady friends, but he always comes home next day for clean linen."

"Q.B. won't be coming for fresh clothing. He's gone to meet his maker."

Mrs. Sproat looked blank.

"Yes, ma'am. Your son is deceased."

"That's what the police told me last night, or maybe this morning. Is it still morning?"

Mrs. Sproat had known her son was dead all along. Feeling tricked—and less guilty about stealing Sproat's letter, Jemmy let go of the woman's hands. "Would you like to talk about Q.B.?"

"Q.B. isn't here. I expect him directly though. You're welcome to wait."

"Perhaps you could tell me about the lady friends you mentioned. Do you recognize any of these names?" Jemmy spread the trading cards on the table.

"Never met a single one—just smelled perfume on his clothes. One wears Jicky—very hoity-toity. I don't understand the fuss. Smells like gin and oranges to me."

"Do you recognize any of these ladies?"

The woman shook her head in the negative.

Jemmy drew the cards into a pack. "Perhaps your son has enemies."

"My boy? No, everybody loved him. That's why he was never home—always out with friends."

"Yesterday, someone beat him badly. Would you have any idea who might do such a thing?"

"He got beat up some by his friends—in the ring, I imagine."

"This wasn't from boxing. He had lashes from a whip on his back."

"You'd better go, now. I have to do his laundry directly."

"Please, Mrs. Sproat, just one more thing. A little story from his childhood. My colleague wants something nice, something nostalgic, for your son's obituary."

"Let me put my head down and think about it. I'll come up with something directly."

Jemmy shook the woman's shoulder. "The story—about Q.B.—tell me the story, please, ma'am."

"I remember now. Quisenberry must have been seven or eight. Someone told him Frenchmen eat snails and call them some fancy name . . ."

"*Escargot.*"

"That's it, *escargot.* So he washed off a garden snail and swallowed it down. I tried to get him to bring it back up.

"I said, 'Frenchmen don't eat the shells.' He wouldn't try to throw it up, though. He said he liked to feel it crawling around in his stomach. Ever since, when any little thing hurts him, he blames the snail. 'Dang snail playing pick-up sticks in my head,' he'd say. Or, 'Look what that snail did to my right eye.' "

Jemmy didn't know what use Autley Flinchpaugh would have for the snail tidbit, but at least she'd remembered his demand.

Miss Mabel Dewoskin was easy enough to find. She'd printed her address at the bottom of the letter ordering Quisenberry Sproat to send her money. Jemmy arrived in the lobby of a hotel that had seen better days. It reeked of unwashed cuspidors and musty disappointment.

"I'm a friend of Miss Mabel Dewoskin. Would you be good enough to give me her room number?"

The desk clerk looked up from reading a dime novel to greet her. The man must have slathered his scalp with Macassar oil. His too-long hair left greasy patches on the shoulders of his gray linen jacket. Jemmy thought his signature probably took the shape of a dollar sign.

He wrote something on a slip of paper. "I'm not accustomed to dispensing information about our guests." The clerk stalled, waited for a tip.

Requests for bribe money annoyed Suetonius Hamm. He personally grilled the reporter who had to resort to paying for information. He often refused to pay. Jemmy did not look forward to those sessions. Still, she would have obliged if she'd had money. Jemmy vowed to learn to read upside down.

"Sir, I've come on an errand of mercy. Miss Dewoskin's fiancé has passed away." Jemmy dabbed the corner of her eye with her lacy hanky. She reached for the paper.

He placed his palm over the paper and moved it toward her.

Jemmy grabbed the hand and shook it—while neatly slipping away the paper. "Oh, thank you, sir. I'm certain Miss Dewoskin will be more than grateful."

She wondered whether crime reporter Amadee Boudinier could have accomplished such a slick trick—and gotten away without paying.

While Jemmy climbed four flights of stairs, she imagined her conversation with Miss Dewoskin. Was she a mother-to-be, heavy with the offspring of Quisenberry Sproat—perhaps already a mother to his love child?

Half expecting to hear the sound of a squalling baby, she rapped gently on the door to 405. No answer came. She rapped again. "Miss Dewoskin, may I please speak with you?"

She pounded harder. "Miss Dewoskin, I have something I believe you'd like to see."

A head in rag curlers popped out from a door down the hall. "Stop that pounding. Most of the people who stay here are actors. We don't get up until two or three in the afternoon."

Jemmy pounded again. "Miss Dewoskin, I'm sorry to wake you, but you really must speak with me."

The woman in curlers clomped to Jemmy in wooden clogs. "Who do you think you are? Making a racket and ignoring me. I've a good mind to—"

"I really must speak with Miss Dewoskin."

"If she were in her room, she'd have answered by now."

"Would you know where I might find her?"

"You might try the kitchen."

"Is Miss Dewoskin a cook?"

The woman in curlers smirked. "It may not be food, but you could say she cooks."

"Thank you, ma'am. I take it the restaurant is downstairs."

The woman in curlers scratched her armpit. "Take the restaurant. Take anything that isn't nailed down, but take yourself out of here."

Back on the first floor, Jemmy walked among bare tables to the back of the hotel. In the kitchen a woman was pouring boiling water into a five-gallon sauerkraut crock. The steam released liquor fumes that stung Jemmy's nose and made her eyes water.

46

"Miss Dewoskin, I'm Ann O'Nimity. I write for the St. Louis *Illuminator.* May I have a word with you about Quisenberry Sproat?"

Jemmy noted the woman's unearthly appearance from the rear. Scraggly gray hair drooped down her back. The mottled gray tail of some creature waved out from her skirt hem. A fleeting thought passed through Jemmy's head. *Might this gray-tailed hag be an escapee from the netherworld stirring a cauldron of hellfire stew?*

No wonder the man at the front desk wanted money. He surely knew Jemmy was lying. This was no dewy-eyed ingénue trapped by a mistake into motherhood. The clerk must have had a good laugh. The only fiancé Mabel could attract would have to be blind and without a working nose.

The woman turned around. Jemmy hardly thought it possible, but Mabel was even uglier in the front. Her face looked gray and streaked—like a corn-shuck doll dragged through fireplace ashes. She might have been a hundred years old, for all Jemmy could tell. Her skin was not just wrinkled; it was furrowed with deep crevices from lips to chin.

"Are you aware Mr. Quisenberry Sproat died last night?"

"News travels faster than a greyhound in the theatre world."

"Then perhaps you know something about the suspicious circumstances of his death."

Mabel shook her skirts and kicked at the creature with the tail. It skittered out from her skirts with a high-pitched *Mrooow* and ran to hide behind one curved foot of the iron stove. All Jemmy saw was a grayish streak, but she supposed the animal was a smallish housecat.

"Why should I tell you anything about Q.B.?"

"The authorities might be interested in your 'cordial making.' "

"What I do is not illegal."

"Not in itself, perhaps, but city health inspectors might find reason to stop your little manufactory in a hotel restaurant."

"In case you hadn't noticed, they already have. They closed this restaurant two years ago for the public welfare. The owners didn't even try to reopen. They had a close call with fire when one of the residents tried to cook with an alcohol burner in her room. Now the owners let residents use the kitchen—for a fee, of course."

Jemmy noticed that only two of the room's cabinets had hasps and padlocks. Newspaper tacked inside the glass door hid the contents of the upper. China cups, food tins, and boxes were plain to see inside all the others. *What's inside that one Mabel doesn't want seen?*

Two lower cabinet doors stood open. Jemmy moved closer to note the labels of big apothecary jars on a shelf—opium, camphor, benzoic acid, oil of anise, glycerin. Another shelf was filled with gallon liquor jugs. Miss Dewoskin seemed to have everything needed to make paregoric. Mabel shut the doors and padlocked them.

"How well did you know Quisenberry Sproat?"

"You're not the police, though you beat them here. Quite enterprising, I'd say."

"Were you friends?"

"Enterprise. A fine word. You have an enterprise—getting information. I have an enterprise—making an excellent product to sell."

"I didn't come to buy elixir."

Mabel thrust forward a brown bottle so Jemmy could see it. The handwritten label bore the words *Harvest Cordial.*

Jemmy shook her head. "I have no money, not even trolley fare."

"A trade, then. That fancy hat with the ostrich feathers."

Jemmy touched the soft fronds. "I couldn't trade this. My

48

dear friend Annie made this hat especially for me. Besides, I can't go out in a public street without a hat—bareheaded—in winter. No, I can't trade it for liquor—not that there's anything wrong with your cordial."

Mabel danced the bottle side to side as further enticement. At length, she set it on the table and stuck her hands on her hips. "If you won't help me in my enterprise, I can't think why I should help you in yours."

"Perhaps a certain letter you wrote might give you a reason."

Mabel began a slow walk, steely gaze boring into Jemmy. "Give me the letter."

"You don't think I'm foolish enough to bring it with me, do you?"

"Get it. Then we can talk."

"First we talk. If I'm satisfied, I'll see you get the letter."

"And if you're not satisfied?"

"The letter goes to the authorities."

The woman raised her hand as if to smack Jemmy's face with a big wooden ladle. "I have nothing to say but this: if you go to the police, you'll regret it. Get out. Get out now!"

CHAPTER FIVE

November 18, 1898

Mabel Dewoskin took a step toward Jemmy.

Jemmy began to panic but tried not to show it. She took a slow step backwards.

The creature crept out from under the stove and ducked its head under Mabel's skirts. *That pair suit each other to a tee. That's the ugliest feline I've ever seen.* The calico cat's fur spiked out in dirty gray, black, and orange tufts.

Jemmy backed out through the swinging doors. She muttered under her breath. "Heavens in a handbag. I almost ended up in a wrestling match with one of the hags from the Salem witch trials."

Jemmy's afternoon fared no better than her morning. She discovered nothing useful for writing a proper follow-up on the Sproat story. She had information enough for an obituary, but the sports reporter was writing that. She sat at her desk, barely tasting her meatloaf sandwich, as she thumbed through Flinchpaugh's file on Sproat.

Tucked in the folder along with basic biography were a number of clippings. They chronicled Sproat's prowess in the ring. "Sproat Wins Tenth Bout in a Row." "Sproat Defeats Benson in Chicago."

But then came the eye openers. "Sproat Kills Struckhoff." "Sproat Arrested in Death of Struckhoff."

Seeking clues, she pored over the articles. They raised more questions than they answered. Quisenberry Sproat and Vincent Struckhoff fought a contest in June. The pair were evenly matched. The fight went on for twenty-seven rounds before Struckhoff simply lay down on the canvas and refused to get up. The ring official declared Sproat the winner. Crowds cheered him on his way to the locker room.

When Struckhoff's corner men tried to rouse him, they found no heartbeat. No obvious reason presented itself. What caused the man to die?

Could concussion have ruptured something in his brain? That seemed unlikely. The exhausted pair had spent the last six rounds dancing about. They either slogged around looking for openings or grappled with each other until the referee stopped them. Sproat hadn't landed a punch for half an hour.

Did the young boxer's heart give out? Not likely. Struckhoff was twenty-two years old and a trained athlete. The coroner ruled it "death by misadventure."

Still, the St. Louis County sheriff arrested Sproat and kept him in jail until his arraignment. The judge dismissed the case for lack of evidence. Sproat was free, but with a cloud over his head. The *Illuminator* dubbed him "Sproat the Slaughterer." That was the last of the clippings. He apparently hadn't had a bout since June—five months ago. Did Struckhoff's death kill Sproat's career?

Questions rumbled through Jemmy's head all afternoon. She spent two hours writing an article on a local author. Mrs. Kate Chopin had read aloud her stories "A Night in Acadie" and "Polydore" at the Chart Club months earlier. The unpreoccupied Jemmy could have pounded the piece out in twenty minutes.

Getting ready to leave the office, she looked for her muffler for a full minute before she remembered she'd given it to the little pencil girl. She sighed. Mother would accuse her of being irresponsible. Merry would be cut to the quick because Jemmy had been careless with her gift. Jemmy felt the weight of everyone's displeasure heaped upon her head.

All of a sudden, everything changed. On her way to meet Autley, an idea struck like a bowling ball knocking down all ten pins. She clenched her fists and screamed through her teeth. The people waiting at the streetcar stop inched away but darted anxious glances in the direction of the screeching female.

"Did Quisenberry Sproat kill his career when he killed Vincent Struckhoff?"

Jemmy asked the question out loud just as Autley Flinchpaugh arrived at the corner of Washington and Broadway. "Did Struckhoff's death kill Sproat's career?"

Flinchpaugh set his lips in a thin line of disapproval as the pair boarded the northbound Broadway trolley. "Greetings to you, too, Miss McBustle."

"Well, did it?"

"When one door closes, another opens."

"Meaning?"

"People like vicarious excitement. They flock to blood sports to watch other people suffer—so long as they don't have to take the beating themselves."

"I don't understand."

"Marquis of Queensberry Rules govern all bouts at Turner Hall and all legitimate bouts. That means no unfair punches like kidney punches or rabbit punches to the back of the neck. No stomping on feet or grinding eyes. No kicking a man when he's down or between rounds when he's not expecting it. The referee can stop the action if he sees fit. That's boxing on the up-and-up.

"Other, word-of-mouth-only fights are no-holds-barred. The referee has no power to enforce safety. As long as the pair keep getting up off the mat, the fight goes on."

"Bare-knuckle fights."

Flinchpaugh nodded. "St. Louis fisticuff fights are well attended and pay better than boxing with gloves. So what if no one would give Sproat a legit match? Plenty of back-alley money to be made. Of course, after Struckhoff died, Sproat could have made a living from selling photographs and locks of hair alone. That's how popular his notoriety made him with the ladies."

Jemmy felt a pang of regret. She'd missed her opportunity to swipe one of the hero's gold-ribboned curls. Then she gave herself a silent tongue lashing. Stealing is wrong—even in small amounts or in ways no one would notice—like a certain letter in her reticule.

Inside Boedke's Rathhaus, Autley chose a big round table in the center of the room. Cherry-cheeked barmaids hustled to keep up with demand. One named Marta sloshed a half-dozen Anheuser lagers in glass steins onto Autley's table. He nodded to Jemmy to take one. Jemmy didn't like beer. The bitter taste and the skunkish smell offended both tongue and nose. Still Jemmy smiled as she picked up the stein, waved a toast in Autley's direction, and took a tiny sip.

Jemmy wondered what was to become of the other four steins. She didn't have long to wait. Within five minutes, four burly men plunked themselves down and began to swill the beer.

Autley greeted them with a raised stein. "Gentlemen, I'd like you to meet Miss Jemima McBustle. Miss McBustle, these gentlemen are the notables of the northside boxing world.

"The good-looking fellow with the split lip is Handsome Harry Benson, lately come from Chicago. Harry has a heck of a right cross. Please pardon my salty language.

"The other three are his corner men: Amos Medley, Harry's Manager; Deke Whicher, his trainer; and Bud Whicher, his cutman."

Jemmy nodded to each in turn—and recognized the one

called Amos Medley, the man who'd booted her out of the Turner Hall.

Medley said, "Pleased to meet you, Miss McBustle. I'm glad Flinchpaugh finally brought you out of hiding. Nothing makes me happier than to drink a toast to such a comely young lady." He raised his stein. "To the lovely Miss McBustle."

If Medley recognized her as the woman he'd bodily ejected from the Turnverein Halle that very morning, he didn't show it.

While the men took long pulls from their steins, Flinchpaugh said, "Amos, my man, you wasted no time finding another fighter to replace Sproat. One day to bring Harry all the way from Chicago—must be a record."

"Not at all. Harry has been in town four months. He's poised to be the next St. Louis city champion. He's already bested every comer on the north side."

"Don't change the subject. You can't tell me you ditched Sproat at the height of his popularity. I saw him in a bare-knuckle contest not two weeks ago. The three of you were in his corner."

"Does some law I don't know about keep me from managing more than one fighter?"

"I've never known a good manager with a big stable."

"Not so. Everybody knows I'm the best manager in St. Louis, and you just said I owned both Sproat and Harry Benson."

"Perhaps Sproat was looking for new management and let you go."

"Perhaps he wasn't as good a fighter as he thought he was."

Jemmy found the grit to ask her own question. "Does one of you have a bullwhip?"

The four looked at each other, slopped down the rest of their beer, and left the table—with many "Thank you's" to Flinchpaugh for buying the round.

"As a reporter you have the subtlety of a sledge hammer.

You'll never get an answer to your whip question now. How could you possibly be so foolish?"

Jemmy deserved the scolding. *What made me do it? Frustration, I guess. I have no control, no place in this world of violent men. I've been an outsider every day since I decided to be a stunt reporter. Still, I've never beat my head against so hard a wall as in the Turner Hall and in this tavern.*

An accordion player struck up the "Champagne Polka." Flinchpaugh said, "Had enough? Maybe you'd like to stick around and try again. Won't get far, though."

"Polka with me. Handsome Harry is on the dance floor. When the musician calls 'Change partners,' take his."

Flinchpaugh offered a wry grin but stood and offered his hand.

Right on cue, Flinchpaugh spun Jemmy into Harry's arms. The polka left her breathless, but Harry had plenty of wind. "What are you doing with that ugly fellow? You deserve better, much better."

"What you lack in finesse you make up for in forwardness."

"I'm not a fellow to waste time. When I see something I like, I go after it—whether it's in the ring or on the dance floor. Dump old pig puss and come with me. I'll take you places you've never been."

Before Jemmy could answer, the "Change partner" call swung her into the arms of Amos Medley. "Don't fall for Harry's sweet talk. He may be handsome, but he's a rakehell with women."

"He seemed quite the gentleman to me."

Medley gripped her fingers until she winced with pain. "Harry doesn't have energy enough to box for me and to cavort with low women at the same time."

"I beg your pardon. I most certainly am not a low woman."

"Prove it. Stay away from Harry."

The next "Change partners" call swooped her into the arms

of one of Harry's corner men. "I've never met a cutman before. What does a cutman do?"

"Tend cuts and such. Rinse 'em off, wipe 'em down. A little alum to stop bleeding. Keep 'em on their feet."

Jemmy laughed. "When I first heard 'cutman,' I thought it meant you cut the fighters."

"Aye, we sometimes do that to 'em, too."

The accordion player finished the polka with a grand flourish and launched into "The Band Played On."

Amos Medley jostled Harry aside. He grabbed Jemmy without the courtesy of asking her to waltz. "I want your promise not to cozy up to Harry."

"I'll give my word not to flirt with Harry on one condition."

Medley gripped her back. "I don't like conditions."

"I don't like strangers bossing me around."

"I'm not going to let a woman ruin Harry, too."

"Did a woman ruin Quisenberry Sproat?"

"When she was in the room, Sproat couldn't keep his mind on anything important, like winning a fight. Nearly got him killed. High-hatted him when she found a new beau. Sproat pined. Couldn't be bothered to train for weeks on end. Just when he'd got back the old ambition, here she'd come again to bedevil him another time."

"What was the name of this woman?"

Medley jerked her hard into his chest. A round cylinder bulged in his breast pocket. It felt like a cold, fat poker against her breastbone. "Promise me to leave Harry alone."

"If you tell me what I want to know, I'd have no reason to seek Harry's company."

"I don't know her rightful name, but Q.B. called her 'Sassy.'"

All the questions she'd burned to ask Sproat's corner men vanished from Jemmy's mind. Could it be that Sassy Patterson had so bewitched Sproat that he botched fights?

A banging noise turned all eyes toward the center of the room. The accordion player stopped playing. A thickset bartender shot out from behind the bar with baseball bat in hand. He jogged over to Handsome Harry, who was cracking a fellow's head on a table. The fellow turned out to be Autley Flinchpaugh.

The barman gave Harry a small bat tap on the bean just to get his attention. Harry turned around with a puzzled look on his face. The barman stood back and took up a batting stance, but Harry's trainer and cutman pulled their man out of harm's way.

Medley raced over with Jemmy close behind. Medley gathered up Harry and the rest of the crew and headed for a table on the far side of the room.

The barman went back to his business. The accordion player launched into a lively "Beer Barrel Polka." The altercation was over.

Jemmy dipped her hanky in beer and used it to wipe blood from Autley's face.

"Why was Harry bashing your head on the table?"

"Did you get any information from Sproat's manager?"

"A little. Why did Harry bang your head on the table?"

"Handsome Harry seems quite taken with you. He apparently considers me a rival."

"He beat you up over me? I've barely said ten words to the man. We are not even acquaintances, much less sweethearts."

"Here's a lesson for you. Men often see what they want to be real instead of what is real—especially when women are involved."

"I think he broke your nose."

"Just what I need. My nose broken for the fourth time—and all for the sake of a girl who cares not a whit about me."

With a shock, Jemmy realized Flinchpaugh had motives other

than helping a colleague. The man was smitten. Either that, or he wanted to show his sports chums he could attract a pretty girl despite his homely face. Either way, Jemmy would have to be careful.

"You'd best go home and lie down."

"First I need a whiskey or some stronger anesthetic."

"The apothecary shops are closed, but I have an idea."

Jemmy walked straight over to Medley and tapped him on the shoulder. "Your boxer broke Mr. Flinchpaugh's nose. The least you can do is give him the paregoric I know you have in your coat pocket."

Medley's eyes bulged, but he turned the paregoric over to Jemmy without comment. Jemmy looked at the label. *A.M.'s Cordial.* She recognized the curlicues on the *C*. Amos Medley was a regular client of Mabel Dewoskin.

Back at the table, Flinchpaugh took a grand swig from the bottle and tucked it in his pocket. "That'll do me until I've seen you home."

Through two streetcar rides, Autley nursed his nose with Jemmy's hanky while Jemmy sat next to him, trying to think of something to say.

Autley broke the tension. "What did you find out?"

"Practically nothing. I bungled everything from the very start."

"Come now. You said you got a little something from Medley. Don't I deserve your trust? After all, I'm bleeding for it." Autley's voice sounded tinny and unreal.

"He bought the paregoric from Mabel Dewoskin, a woman I tried to interview today. I don't know what it means, but I guess I'll have to call on Mabel again."

"What do you mean you 'tried' to interview her?"

"She threw me out when I wouldn't buy paregoric from her."

"Perhaps I should come along—just to buy some. Not much

left in this bottle, and my nose will hurt worse tomorrow."

"You don't need to protect me. Mabel Dewoskin is all business. If I buy, she'll talk."

Autley fetched two dollars from his money clip. "That should be enough for a small bottle."

Jemmy took the money. "Did you discover anything?"

"Perhaps."

"Are you going to tell me?"

"Not yet. It may be nothing."

"I told you what I found out."

"And I appreciate your honesty. But we may be entering dangerous territory. I want to be better prepared than I was tonight."

Autley left her at the door to Bricktop. She'd dutifully invited him in, but he declined. "I wouldn't want your mother to see me with blood on my shirt. That would make a bad first impression."

Jemmy muttered to herself, "Heavens in handbag. Does Autley Flinchpaugh expect to meet my mother? Why on earth would this man I barely know want to meet my mother?"

Jemmy had little time to mull the question over. Waiting inside the hall at Bricktop, Mother said, "Jemima Gormlaith McBustle. Where is your muffler? Do I smell beer on your breath?"

CHAPTER SIX

Saturday, November 19, 1898

Saturdays at Bricktop demanded a flurry of activity. The whole house had to be dusted, bed linen changed, rugs beaten, floors polished, gas lamp chimneys washed, kitchen scrubbed, and necessaries scoured. And still to be done were the daily chores of slops emptying, ash removing, coal supplying, and cooking, serving, and cleaning up after three meals for thirteen or more people.

Mother issued weekly assignments and personally saw them completed to the letter. Gerta, the efficient German cook, scrubbed the kitchen. Mother allowed no one but herself to shine the waxed floors. Sixteen-year-old Miranda, better known as Randy, grumbled about a recent change in routine. She enjoyed beating the rugs—a job well-suited to her volatile temper—a job Mother forced her to turn over to the new maid of all work.

In fact, Dora wasn't exactly new. She had been the boarding-house's laundress for months. Prosperity returned and spirits lifted when Merry's hand-painted sign

Room to let

Inquire within

disappeared from the first-floor parlor window. Rent-paying guests filled all six second-floor bedrooms. Mother could afford to hire Dora full time.

Mother assigned Randy the more genteel and tedious job of changing bed linens with Nervy, the youngest McBustle sister, Minerva. After that, the pair dusted an incalculable number of whatnots.

As punishment for Jemmy's sins of the night before, Mother set her to scrub the necessaries. Mother made Jemmy's job disagreeable but quick. After all, Jemmy had become a newspaperwoman, a person without a real day off.

Jemmy's out-of-the-house job rankled Mother, but she'd stopped her loud protests. Lately, she'd hunkered down and devoted her energies to helping Aunt Delilah find Jemmy a respectable husband.

Mother entrusted the task of taking down and cleaning the gaslight lamps only to patient and ever-careful Merry. But on this particular Saturday, the sweet fourteen-year-old left the family short handed. Esmeralda "Merry" McBustle's shaky hands dropped a lamp chimney from a hall sconce. The glass shattered on the hardwood floor just in front of Jemmy as she walked with her scrub bucket toward the first floor necessary.

Trembling and teary-eyed, Merry slipped down the ladder. "Oh, Jemmy, what have I done? If you'd taken one more step—I hate to think—"

Mother rushed in from the dining room. She needed only one look at Merry to see all was not well. A quick palm to the forehead confirmed her suspicion. "I thought you looked peaked at breakfast. Why didn't you tell us you felt poorly?"

"On Saturdays everyone must work so hard. I didn't want someone else to have to do my work, too."

Mother was not known for being soft on herself or anyone else. But she visibly melted in the face of Merry's selflessness. "You foolish girl. Come to my room. You must go to bed."

"Please, Mother, I won't break any more glass. My hand

61

slipped a little. You must let me pay for the one I broke. I've saved enough money to replace it."

"You're talking nonsense. It's the fever. I'm putting you in bed right this minute. You must have rest, and I must prevent the remainder of the household from contagion. We can't have everyone ailing—not with Thanksgiving dinner less than a week away. It's your duty to get well, so to bed with you."

Mother escorted Merry off to the maid's room behind the kitchen. Mother McBustle had claimed it for herself when she turned Bricktop into a boardinghouse after Father died. All four daughters and both workers occupied the ballroom-turned-dormitory on the third floor.

Over her shoulder, Mother cast a few words to Jemmy. "Clean up the glass, then fetch Merry's nightie. On the way, tell the others to stay away from her and to be extra careful. I'll clean the lamps myself, and you can help with the floors. Have Randy fetch the doctor."

Jemmy could not get away until past eleven. She didn't reach the *Illuminator* until past noon. She was about to sit at her splintery pine desk when her immediate supervisor, Miss Turnipseed, sashayed to Jemmy's desk with her hand out.

"Your review of the Crystal Palace Theatre's *Uncle Tom's Cabin,* if you please."

"You'll have it Monday."

"It needs to be submitted today."

"I'm seeing the play tonight."

"You were supposed to see it Thursday."

"I did go to the theatre, but I saw only the first two scenes—in fact, only part of the second scene. A man died onstage. Silly me. I thought his death would be more important news than a description of little Eva flapping up from her deathbed on angel wings."

"Spare me your excuses and your sass. What am I to use in

'Critic's Corner'? A genuine newspaper journalist—"

"I know, I know. A genuine newspaper journalist always has other resources to rely upon."

"At least you acknowledge I'm right when it comes to the world of journalism."

"I have just what you need, Miss Turnip—Miss Belle Buckley. A review of Mrs. Kate Chopin's latest book. A story collection called *A Vocation and a Voice*. I wrote about her story 'The Falling in Love of Fedora.' I also have reviews of 'An Egyptian Cigarette' and 'The Kiss,' if you'd prefer. Of course, you may consider those stories too racy for our sedate St. Louis society."

"I have no qualms about reviews of improper material. I have qualms only about improper reviews."

"Another bit of wisdom I'll take with me to my grave. And I'll have the "Uncle Tom" review by the end of the play tonight."

No sooner did "Belle Buckley" Turnipseed leave than Hal showed up to continue the badgering Miss Turnipseed started.

"Fancy meeting you here. I was beginning to think you'd been fired for never coming to the office."

"I spend most of my time out in the city, gathering news."

"What a coincidence! Gathering news. That's exactly what I'm supposed to be doing. What's more amazing still—I'm supposed to be gathering news with you. Have you forgotten that I'm your photographer?"

Suetonius Hamm had hired Harold Dwight Dwyer because he had red hair and worked cheap. Apparently Hamm thought anyone with red hair would look enough like Jemmy to pass as her brother—not that anyone would leap to said conclusion in this case. Unlike Jemmy's unblemished pale skin, all six feet of Hal's gangly body sprouted freckles. Jemmy could read him like a newspaper galley. His baby-mouse–pink ears turned bright red when he grew mad or embarrassed. That minute, his ears glowed the color of cherry juice.

"I had to pretend you and I were working out of the building together yesterday and the day before. Where have you been?"

"Interviewing ladies—some of them in their nether garments. None of them would have talked to me while you were taking their pictures."

"Have you forgotten? I'm also your bodyguard."

"I don't need my body guarded against a couple of old women." Jemmy failed to mention that one of the old women had threatened her. She also conveniently forgot her undignified ouster from the Northside Turner Hall.

"So you want me to get fired. Is that it?"

"Of course not. When I find the right thing to photograph or when I need guarding, I depend upon you to the death—or dismissal, whichever comes first."

"I need a job all the time, not just when you think you need guarding. Besides, you don't have the slightest common sense when it comes to your own hide. I've saved your bacon more than once, and you know it."

"Let's not forget—I've also saved yours."

"Right. We're a team."

"If you say so."

"I do. So tell me, what is our team doing today?"

"I don't know about the photographer half, but the reporter half is off to have lunch with a friend."

"Nothing to do with a story?"

"It might, but I do not need a photographer or a bodyguard. I need privacy to persuade my friend to tell the truth, the whole truth."

"At least I can give you a ride."

"On that hideous chartreuse bike of yours? Not likely. I'll take a streetcar."

"So what can I do?"

"You might ask your policeman uncle for information on the

Sproat death."

"And after I get it?"

"Bring it to me at the Lindell Hotel."

Jemmy rose as she handed her cape to Hal. He dutifully held it for her as she slipped into the brown wool and wrapped Father's old brown tweed muffler round her neck. The scratchy wool and the pungent smell of camphor made her cough. Still, she felt duty-bound to wear it. Mother insisted even a devil-may-care girl who lost her pretty muffler needed something to chase away drafts.

Hal stood with hands on hips as Jemmy smoothed her skirt. She tucked her notebook into her badger-fur muff and swished down the stairs. "Don't come before two thirty."

Jemmy had promised to meet Sassy Patterson for lunch at half past one. She had high hopes of discovering all the girl knew about Quisenberry Sproat.

The instant she saw Sassy in the hotel dining room, Jemmy should have abandoned her plan. Sassy was not alone. Three men attended her as if they were drones bringing honey to their queen bee.

Jemmy recognized two of them when the trio stood to acknowledge the presence of a new female. One was Sproat's boxing trainer, Deke Whicher. Another was Jemmy's former would-be suitor, a young scoundrel about town named Peter Ploog. Jemmy had found him appealing, until she saw him escaping from the fire at Mrs. Nanny's Sporting House—in his unmentionables.

The third person was no one Jemmy knew—a handsome fellow, tall and broad shouldered. He noticed her straightaway and waited not a minute for politeness sake. "Miss Patterson, aren't you going to introduce us to your charming friend?"

Sassy stopped batting her eyelashes at Sproat's trainer. "Jemmy, dearie, I'm so glad you're here. These horrible men have been telling such funny stories. My tummy positively aches from laughing."

The man with the rugged good looks broke all the rules of civilized introduction. He stuck out his hand to shake Jemmy's. Men were never supposed to touch a lady unbidden. Offering a hand was the lady's prerogative. A gentleman should feel honored if she held out her hand.

This man scoffed at social convention. "Miss McBustle. I'm Tony von Phul."

Sassy glared at him until he stepped back and withdrew his hand. "Heigho, my dearie, I'd like you to meet the overeager Sylvester Louis von Phul."

Jemmy hid a snicker behind her gloved hand at how altogether apropos it seemed to meet a mannerless man named "von Fool."

Sassy said, "With a name like Sylvester Louis, I've always wondered why you call yourself 'Tony.'"

"Two reasons. First, when I walk through a door, I always improve the *tone* of the establishment within."

Peter Ploog clicked his tongue and said, "The only way you could make a place more toney is by leaving it. Hello, Miss McBustle. Jemima and I are old friends. We attend the same church."

Von Phul put a hand on the table and leaned toward Ploog. "I can't imagine Ploog being acquainted with church—well, maybe a church mouse."

Ploog's words came with steel edges. "From what I hear, you're the one who is church-mouse poor."

Sassy put a hand over von Phul's. "Now, dinkey birds, mustn't go to bumpville in a nice place like the Lindell Hotel. If you want to set up a fisticuffs match, I'm sure our professional boxing trainer can accommodate you." Sassy patted Tony's hand. "Now tell me the second reason why you call yourself

'Tony' instead of 'Louis,' which I consider a perfectly good name."

Von Phul struck a chin-up pose. "Imagine this head in a bronze helmet with Roman brush atop. Now imagine this profile on a gold coin. I'm told I look just like Marcus Antonius. This head belongs on an aureus. That's a gold coin, for those of you who don't know Roman history."

Ploog offered a wry smile. "I know where your head belongs, but it's not a gold coin. In fact, it's not a place I could name in the company of ladies."

"If that's a joke, I fail to see the humor."

"Perhaps you and Marc Antony are a true match. I understand he owed buckets of gold aurei, just like you do."

Von Phul rose from his chair and began wrapping his napkin around his knuckles.

Sassy said, "Dinkums, dinkums. You boys must cease this bickering immediately. Else I shall leave and not speak to either of you for a whole week."

Ploog and von Phul said no more, just glared at each other when their eyes strayed from Sassy's pouty lips.

And so the onion soup was followed by fried oysters, which preceded savory shepherd's pie. As the party of five tucked into their apple crisp with cream, Hal arrived. He stood, hat in hand, staring at Sassy over von Phul's head. Ploog noticed first, then Jemmy, then Sproat's trainer. When Sassy looked up, von Phul turned around and stood.

"Have you business with anyone at this table, young man?"

Jemmy said, "Yes, Mr. von Phul. He has business with me. I'd like you all to meet my photographer from the *Illuminator*, Mr. Harold Dwyer. I do hate to leave such excellent company, but Mr. Dwyer and I have to get the news while it is still new. Please forgive me for dashing off in the middle of the meal. I know I'm unforgivably rude, but I beg your indulgence."

The pair said nothing until they reached the street. Jemmy read Hal's mind. "Pretty, isn't she?"

"Pretty doesn't begin to describe her. Just thinking about her brings a lump to my—throat."

"You'll have to stand in line—a line that grows minute by minute, man by man."

"A poor chap from Kerry Patch would never have a chance. I have eyes, though."

"Even that might not be wise. Tony von Phul was about to blacken both of yours."

"Might be worth it."

"Might be time to change the subject. Did you speak with your uncle?"

"He talked with Cyrus Struckhoff, Senior, the father of the man Sproat killed in the ring."

"This may sound strange, but I have a reason for asking. Could he have horsewhipped Sproat?"

"Not possible. The man is in a wheelchair. The police are looking for the boxer's older brother, Cyrus Struckhoff, Junior, and a few others."

"Do you know the names of the other suspects?"

"Only a couple. Sylvester Louis von Phul and Frank James."

"Sassy had been seeing Quisenberry Sproat. Von Phul is a jealous man who might resent a romantic rival. But why do the authorities suspect Frank James?"

Hal shrugged his shoulders. "Just the way police think. Always on the lookout for a way to bring down a famous outlaw."

"In any case, I want you to take me to the Crystal Palace Theatre. Be sure to photograph the leaded glass in front, the ticket taker's stand, the stage, and the dressing room, if they'll let you. I have a feeling those pictures may prove useful."

The pair climbed on Hal's ugly chartreuse tandem bike along with his ungainly wooden camera, tripod, and close to twenty pounds of glass plates. The twosome made quite a sight as they trundled off to the scene of the crime on a cold Saturday afternoon.

"Do you really think they'll invite us in to snoop around?"

"I can talk our way in—I hope."

CHAPTER SEVEN

Saturday Night, November 19, 1898

Aunt Delilah balked at rescheduling for Saturday the already-rescheduled-for-Friday theatre outing but finally agreed. She even managed to secure a loge box—at great cost and with supreme effort, as she informed everyone on several occasions.

When Jemmy opened her program, a slip of paper fell out. It announced that Tom Loker, the dog handler, would be played by Harry Benson. Handsome Harry Benson inherited Sproat's corner men and his acting job. She looked at Sassy and wondered whether Handsome Harry had inherited anything else that once belonged to Quisenberry Sproat.

This time, events on stage proceeded in apple-pie order—at least until intermission. No one died. No dogs hounded the audience. No corpse decorated the stage. But once again Frank James came asking for the coroner.

"Doctor Wangermeier, may I have a word in the hall."

The doctor set his champagne glass on the tray, pulled down his frock-coat lapels, and walked stiffly through the velvet curtains. Jemmy and Sassy crept after him.

Jemmy put her good ear to the gap between curtains. Aunt Delilah shot her a look that could have speared a catfish, but Jemmy ignored the warning.

The girls gave Aunt Delilah no choice but to join their conspiracy. When Uncle Erwin turned his head toward the eavesdroppers, Auntie Dee distracted him with a spill of champagne down his trousers.

The girls focused on the conversation in the hall, but background noise kept Jemmy from grasping most of the exchange. *I wish I had two good ears. Still, I guess scarlet fever when I was three could have left me deaf in both ears.*

From Frank James, she sifted out, ". . . apologize . . . bothering . . . dressing room . . . everything yesterday . . . some substance. Missing . . ."

And from the doctor: "Don't excite yourself, Mr. James. Miss McBustle . . . considering the nature . . . would have noticed."

New voices and shuffling feet blurred the conversation. Jemmy couldn't pick out another single word. "Sassy, do you know what they were talking about?"

Sassy answered with raised shoulders and a puzzled look.

The girls scrambled back to their seats as the doctor opened the portieres. His bottom lip scrunched his upper in an upside down smile. The action pushed in his chin until he resembled a pug dog.

"Miss McBustle, please recall Thursday night in Mr. Sproat's dressing room. Are you quite sure you placed every cream and ointment and liquid into the valise?"

"Yes, Doctor. Even the grease paint. Remember how the other Tom Loker objected?"

"Did you take note of anything that doesn't belong indoors?"

"I went through everything in the actors' trunks and looked on the floor and in the cupboard. I recall seeing nothing unusual. Perhaps if you could be more specific, I . . ."

"And would you be willing to swear as much in a court of law?"

"Of course. And now may I ask you why?"

"You'll find out in due course." He pursed his lips and smicked through his teeth. "I read your account of events in the *Illuminator.* Because you're female, I'm not surprised at your

71

lack of discretion. However, your lack of self-discipline appalls me. You swore to keep certain information hidden from the general public."

"Doctor, I'm as devastated as you are by that headline. It was entirely my editor's idea. I have no control over headlines. The article itself made no mention Sproat had been whipped."

"Your editor had to find out about the whipping from someone. Are you telling me that informant was someone other than yourself?"

Jemmy couldn't bring herself to lie, to blame Aunt Delilah—certainly not with Auntie Dee standing four feet away. She hung her head. "I suppose it is my fault."

"And it has cost you my good regard. Don't seek anything further from me. I refuse to divulge knowledge to someone incapable of keeping vital confidential information private."

Jemmy wanted to assure him she would take confidential information to her grave if he would only give her another chance. At that moment, an unwelcome and uncouth interloper chased away all hope of persuading him.

Heathcliff Smoot pushed aside the portieres with a great rattle of brass rings on brass rod. "They like to never let me in downstairs. Kept me waiting until intermission. I flat out missed the scene with all the hound dogs. That was the only thing I wanted to watch."

Aunt Delilah marched to Healthcliff's side and took his arm. "Dr. Wangermeier, Miss Patterson, I'd like you to meet my nephew, Heathcliff Smoot. He's the son of my sister Sophia and her husband, Elsinore, who recently moved to Seattle. Young Mr. Smoot, this is Miss Patterson and Dr. Wangermeier."

Jemmy shuddered when the doctor shook Heathcliff's hand. During the day Heathcliff sloshed buckets of Mississippi River water to wash away urine from the brick streets and alleys of the waterfront district. She wondered whether the doctor knew how unsanitary shaking the lad's hands might be.

A realization startled Jemmy. Auntie Dee had failed to provide her with an escort—until the arrival of Heathcliff the Hellion. *Heavens in a handbag. The drab little assistant coroner isn't here. I didn't even notice.*

Three months had elapsed between her grand debut and this evening. During that time, Auntie had invited St. Louis's richest, most eligible, stodgiest, and oldest men on various outings to meet the newly marriageable Miss Jemima McBustle.

Jemmy endured the parade of potential husbands to keep peace at home. Eventually Mother and Auntie Dee would have to conclude marriage was not something they could force. Jemmy paid little attention to those faded copies of aging businessmen.

She'd expected the same lackluster gentleman as on Thursday night. Her escort for the excursion was as close to invisible as a person can get. He was so devoid of personality, Jemmy once sat in his lap because she failed to notice he was already in the chair.

One look at Heathcliff made her long for a nondescript old coot like the assistant coroner. The last time Heathcliff had been bribed into escorting her, he'd managed to humiliate her in front of the handsomest man in the state. She'd regurgitated on Heathcliff's shoes.

Just looking at Heathcliff the Hellion made her stomach quaver. Worse had come to worst.

Of course, young master Smoot looked more presentable this time. He'd grown at least two inches but still did not quite fill out his tuxedo—probably borrowed from Cousin Duncan. Jemmy covered her nose with her hanky to protect it from the waves of bay rum pulsing from Heathcliff's face.

The boy's mouth opened in a wide grin to expose his crooked bottom teeth. They grew not in a traditional gentle curve but in the shape of a capital *W.* The whistle he produced through that picket fence could startle acorns out of trees and shatter eyeglasses at ten paces.

On this occasion, he exhaled the sweet, mournful sound of wind rustling through autumn leaves. He whistled low in the direction of Isabel Patterson. He stared at Sassy as if she were a cherry phosphate at Baker's Confectionary.

When he gave Sassy an exaggerated wink, Sassy retreated behind her fan. Aunt Delilah seated Heathcliff behind Jemmy on her right and Sassy on her left—as far from Heathcliff as possible.

Jemmy didn't need to peek behind her to know the boy was panting over the tendrils of dark curls caressing the nape of Sassy's luminous neck. Sassy didn't have to turn a finger or smile a single time. Even when she stayed cold as oysters packed in ice, she captured the heart of the thirteen-year-old piss-alley boy.

Jemmy turned back to whisper to Heathcliff. "Did you overhear what happened in the hall?"

He winked and grinned.

"Tell me."

"Pay attention to the play."

"Please tell me."

"You're scotching the fun of everyone at Aunt Delilah's theatre shindig."

"I have to know."

"Shush now. You're rude."

"Do I have to come back there and box your ears?"

"You're welcome to try."

Auntie Dee whispered, "Jemima, you may chastise Heathcliff after the play. Do turn around."

"I'll be quick. I promise."

Jemmy gave up threatening the boy in favor of a straightforward bribe. "I know what you want—money. I'll pay you."

"I might tell you one thing now. And more when you come up with, say, three dollars."

"Three dollars? I don't make that much money in three days."

"Two, then."

"Twenty-five cents."

"One dollar. That's my final offer."

"Fifty cents, or I'll find the information some other way."

"Deal." Heathcliff spit into his hand and stuck it out to her.

Jemmy declined to shake but said, "Deal. Now, what happened in the hall?"

CHAPTER EIGHT

Saturday Night, November 19, 1898, into Sunday, November 20, 1898

Heathcliff said, "Policemen arrested Frank James for the murder of Quisenberry Sproat."

Jemmy turned that line over and over in her mind. *Why arrest Frank James, of all people?*

After the play, the theatre party trooped to Tony Faust's restaurant for a late supper. While the others pored over menus and exchanged tales of other meals at the best restaurant in town, Jemmy wrote her review of *Uncle Tom's Cabin*.

When the waiter took their order, she was still distracted. "I'll have whatever Miss Patterson is having."

Before she'd finished the review, a platoon of servers arrived with dinner. When they lifted the covers from their dishes, savory aromas of garlic and roasted meat wafted across the table. Jemmy's mouth watered. She put her article aside.

Over beefsteak with bordelaise sauce, she tried to get Heathcliff's attention. Conversing with him should have been easy, since he was her escort. But the fellow who was supposed to hang on her every word and indulge her every whim had eyes only for Sassy.

Heathcliff sat sandwiched between Jemmy and Aunt Delilah. Three times Auntie Dee kicked him in the shin. Jemmy couldn't hear what she whispered in Heathcliff's ear, but she could guess: "Stop gaping at Miss Patterson. Your face looks like a pair of long johns with the flap down." Alas, Auntie had no power to stop Heathcliff from ogling the stunning Miss Patterson.

Neither did Jemmy's bribe for information. Nonetheless, she tucked the promised quarters into Heathcliff's hand and demanded fifty cents worth of information. "What else did you hear in the hall?"

"The police found new evidence in Sproat's dressing room." No sooner did the words leave his mouth than he leapt to his feet and reached across the vinegar caddy to give Sassy the pepper shaker. His hasty action wreaked havoc on the table. His arm brushed the wine carafe. The falling crystal splashed Chablis on Auntie Dee, though Heathcliff himself got the worst drenching.

"Not again, Heathcliff."

"How can you be so clumsy?"

"You must learn to pay attention to what you're doing."

"I can't take the boy anywhere."

"The boy will smell of fermented grape the rest of the night."

A troupe of waiters fussed around, dabbing up wine, offering clean napkins, and resetting the entire soaked tablecloth. Auntie Dee took Heathcliff aside and gave him a tongue lashing. Jemmy couldn't hear the words, but she knew the substance. She'd bet a week's pay Heathcliff had forfeited his good behavior bonus.

At length, the table gleamed with fresh dry linen, and dinner could resume. Heathcliff, though wine-wet, was just as obnoxious as before. He butted into every conversation with a new compliment for Sassy. He praised her eyes, her hair, her voice, even her discerning tastes. *Discernment? Sassy couldn't tell a peccadillo from an armadillo.*

Everything the boy did set Jemmy's teeth on edge. Still, she'd paid him and expected to get her money's worth.

"What else happened in the hall?"

"Not much."

77

Jemmy punched his arm.

"Ow. I've a good mind not to tell you."

"Give me back my money."

"OK, you win this one time, you great cow. The police found a jar of something in Sproat's dressing room."

"A jar of what?"

"They didn't say."

"Is that all?"

Heathcliff bobbed his head in a "maybe yes—maybe no" gesture.

"You little weasel. If you know why they arrested Frank James, you tell me this instant."

"Or you'll do what?"

"I'll think of something. Count on it."

"They found Frank James's buggy whip in the dressing room."

"Why would a buggy whip—Frank James's or anyone else's—be in Sproat's dressing room?"

"Doesn't she look swell?"

"How do they know the whip belonged to Frank James?"

"Has his name tooled on the handle."

"It wasn't there Thursday night."

"That's what Dr. Wangermeier said."

"But the police arrested Frank James anyway."

"Guess so. Isn't that a swell perfume she's wearing?"

Jemmy gave up asking questions of the infatuated boy. She had her fifty cents' worth. Barely aware of the pleasant company at the table, she alternated between silent pondering and writing her review through the rest of the meal.

On the way to the *Illuminator* to turn in her piece, she said even less. Auntie Dee prodded. "Jemima, dear, you haven't told us your assessment of the play. Did you find it enjoyable?"

To herself, Jemmy said, *Read my review tomorrow and you'll find out.* Aloud, she said, "Yes, Aunt Delilah. You've taken great trouble on my behalf. I'm deeply grateful."

Heathcliff popped in. "I thought it was double stupid. Why did they have two fellows playing Uncle Tom? One would have been stupid enough to bore everybody in the place."

Auntie Dee thwacked him across the knuckles with her fan. "When one's view has not been sought, one should keep one's opinion to oneself, especially if one cares to remain in the vehicle belonging to persons one might offend."

Heathcliff sank into a sullen silence, which lasted from that moment through Jemmy's turning in her review to the night editor and all the way to Jemmy's home. Heathcliff handed her down from the carriage and yanked her at top speed to the door at Bricktop.

"Did you found out anything tonight you haven't told me?"

"Maybe one more thing."

"What else?"

"Miss Isabel Patterson is the swellest girl I ever saw."

The next morning all during church, Jemmy mulled over events surrounding the death of Quisenberry Sproat. She sat through the pastor's usual "Bounty of the Lord" pre-Thanksgiving sermon without finding any real answers. The Sproat problem would have to wait. Even maids got a day off each week. And this was Sunday.

Jemmy looked forward to Sunday—a day when factories ceased blowing coal cinders into the air; a day when commerce was suspended and no beer trucks rumbled over the brick streets of St. Louis.

Young people treated themselves on Sunday afternoons. They whiled away the days with picnics in Tower Grove Park in the spring, boating trips on the Meramec River in the summer, ice skating or sledding down the big hill in Forest Park in the winter.

With the end of summer, fall in St. Louis tended to be less pleasure filled and more educational. That particular Sunday the Mercantile Library scheduled a speech by a famous police officer from France. His topic was anthropometry. The French system of criminal identification held great fascination for Jemmy.

At one o'clock, Hal called for her on his garish chartreuse tandem bike. As they pedaled up Broadway toward Locust, she probed for more information on the Sproat case. "Have you spoken with your uncle?"

"Took his picture with Frank James. Exclusive for the *Illuminator*. I think that will make Hamm happy."

"I guess you deserve to gloat a little. Does your uncle think Frank James killed Quisenberry Sproat?"

"He didn't say."

"But what do you think he thinks about Frank James?"

"Just that he was mighty happy to have his picture taken with the prince of bank robbers."

"Couldn't you pump him for a little more information?"

The edge in Hal's voice sliced like icicles in the frosty air. "Do it yourself. He'll be at the lecture."

The program promised the speaker would unveil a monumental step forward for police, a method to revolutionize crime control across the globe. Frenchman Alphonse Bertillon, Fiquette's teacher and mentor, had spent two decades perfecting his plan. Finally, he was ready to introduce the Bertillon system to the world. He sent Fiquette on an international tour to share the French secrets of criminal identification.

The Bertillon system promised recognition with odds of one hundred-forty-three-million to one that no two people would share the same results.

Fiquette was a petite, dandified fellow with a nasal voice and heavy accent. With dark hair parted in the middle and slicked down around a bald spot, his head looked like an eight ball on a pool table.

Jemmy watched Fiquette spend more than an hour taking measurements with tapes and calipers. Fiquette's secretary wrote down fourteen key measurements including foot size, nose length, ear lobe extension, and the more mundane height and weight.

Fiquette kept up a running commentary of the crimes Bertillon had solved. "Modern technology will one day catch more criminals than old-fashioned knocking on doors. The tide is turning even as I stand here today. The world's most noted criminologist, Alphonse Bertillon, is not and never has been a police officer. He began as a humble clerk."

Jemmy wondered why go to all the bother when a photograph would show exactly what the criminal looked like.

After the lecture, Hal's uncle invited the pair to police headquarters to enjoy a pumpkin pie and coffee reception for Fiquette and his secretary.

Jemmy tapped her pencil on her little notebook. "I find your identification system most intriguing. Might it not save time and effort to use photographs without those other measurements?"

Fiquette bristled. "I believe a Mister Thomas Byrnes in New York City had some success with his rogues' gallery. However, there is simply no comparison to the Bertillon system. What we do goes far beyond merely identifying criminals after they've committed crimes. We strive to identify the criminal type. Would it not be better to know which people are likely to commit crimes even before such people succumb to temptation?"

"Do you mean to imprison people for looking as though they might commit crimes?"

Fiquette didn't deign to answer. He simply stuck his nose into the air and stalked off to speak with the chief of police.

Hal said, "Thanks, Jemmy."

"What for?"

"Sticking up for photography."

She'd asked the question because photographs seemed the clearest, cleanest way to identify people. She had not intended to soothe Hal's feelings; but if he wanted to believe she was trying to make up for her earlier gaffe, she'd let him.

When Hal's uncle joined them, she asked, "What is your view of the Bertillon system?"

"Hogwash. Nothing will ever replace leather—shoe leather and sap leather—for getting to the bottom of crime."

"May I quote you?"

"Fourteen key measurements—what a waste of time. Police should be on the street preventing crime, not measuring snotty noses. The man is an idiot. In the demonstration today, he identified a pickpocket as a wife beater. What's more, the man he labeled as a potential bank robber was desk sergeant at the Lafayette Park station."

"May I quote you, and would you please spell your name so I can get it right in the paper?"

"Deputy Chief Michael D-W-Y-E-R. You may quote me if you leave out the cussing."

While Hal took a group picture of the dignitaries, Jemmy drifted through the open door of the office belonging to the chief of police. She itched to look in his files. Before she could open a single drawer, a white-gloved lieutenant took her elbow and steered her out of the room.

"Lt. Sorley O'Rourke, at your service. Let me show you our weapons wall. I hope you won't be too frightened. Some ladies swoon, so I hear."

Soon they were standing before a glass case containing a fearsome array of weapons fastened to a wall or propped up on pedestals. One section showcased firearms, from Gatling guns to pepperbox derringers and everything in between. At least twenty of them were homemade guns—some with handsomely carved wooden handles. Others were no more than lengths of pipe and bits of black rubber.

"Everything in the case was donated or confiscated from a criminal. Everything here has a story, Miss McBustle, a dark story."

"Which do you find the most intriguing, Lieutenant? It might make an interesting feature story. I am a reporter for the *Illuminator*, you know."

"Look at the case with the pair of dueling pistols—the case on the center pedestal with the horsewhip coiled below it. Miss McBustle, you are looking at the most famous dueling pistols in history—at least that's their reputation."

"Handsome weapons, aren't they?"

"Yes indeed, Miss. Fifteen inches long with silver fittings. Cursed pistols used to kill no fewer than eleven men. Fifty-six-caliber pistols—bigger and deadlier than the more usual fifty caliber. See the bullets in the lid of the case? Fifty-eight-caliber Civil War bullets. The entry point is the size of your thumb. The exit wound is the size of your fist."

"Why are these two pistols famous?"

"You are looking at the Pettis-Biddle dueling pistols."

Jemmy scribbled notes as he told the story.

"Spencer Pettis was an important man when Missouri was a brand new state in the 1820s. Has a county named after him. Just twenty-seven when he became Missouri's only member of the United States House of Representatives.

"He hated banks. The federal government took over all money printing during the Civil War. Before that, banks or insurance companies—anyone at all—could print up paper money that might or might not be worth something.

"Pettis was a Bentonite. He wanted hard money—money

folks could trust. Pettis spoke out against banks that didn't have gold bullion to back up every dollar they printed. In particular, he blasted the Bank of the United States, a bank owned by Nicholas Biddle.

"Nicholas Biddle's brother was stationed at Jefferson barracks. Major Thomas Biddle wouldn't sit still for insults to his brother. He called Pettis 'a dish of skimmed milk.' Pettis questioned Biddle's—er . . . manliness. The major would never let that pass unanswered.

"Early one summer morning Spencer Pettis was ailing. Major Biddle busted into his room at the City Hotel and beat him with that rawhide whip while the man was lying in his own sickbed."

The lieutenant nodded toward the whip on the pedestal. "By thunder, he would have beat Pettis to death if other guests hadn't come in to hold him back.

"A peck of Christian ladies couldn't have stopped those two from dueling. August 27, 1831, a thousand people gathered to watch the men and their seconds row to Bloody Island in the middle of the Mississippi.

"Biddle demanded they shoot from just five feet away—so near, the gun barrels could touch."

"Why so close?"

"Smoothbore flintlocks are so inaccurate, a fellow would be lucky to hit the broadside of an elephant at ten paces. Biddle and Pettis were serious about settling the score, and Biddle was nearsighted."

"It's hard to imagine both so eager to be killed."

"I heard that Pettis stooped a bit to make himself a smaller target, but Biddle's bullet killed him—slowly. He died the next day—at twenty-nine and still a bachelor. Pettis's shot hit Biddle in the stomach, so he lived a few days longer."

"Two men killed each other all because of a few insults. Why couldn't they forgive and forget?"

"They did forgive each other—when both lay dying."

"What did the newspapers say about the duel?"

"The newspapers praised it. Called Pettis noble and honorable. Spencer Pettis had a bang-up fine funeral, the biggest up to that time in St. Louis."

"I must say I do not understand why men fight duels."

" 'Death before dishonor,' so the saying goes. Some good came of it. In less than five years, Missouri put a law on the books against duels—made dueling a felony, even if no one was hurt."

"Do you know the year?"

"Indeed I do. 1835."

Jemmy peered at the pistols. "The placard calls them 'Church's amazingly accurate smoothbore flintlocks.' Who was Church?"

"Alexander Hamilton's stepfather, John Church. He brought from England this grand pair of Wogdon dueling pistols. He and Aaron Burr had already fought one duel with them—though neither was killed. Church lent them out for many duels, including, by thunder, the most famous duel ever fought on American soil. Aaron Burr killed Alexander Hamilton with one of those two pistols."

O'Rourke rocked on his heels. "Yes, Miss McBustle, Church's pistols are the star of our collection."

"And the whip. Is it the one Biddle used to horsewhip Pettis?"

"The very same."

"Does it have a curse, too?"

CHAPTER NINE

Monday, November 21, 1898

Jemmy hoped turning in two articles—a feature on the police department's wall of weapons *and* a review of Fiquette's lecture—would win her editor's good will. That didn't happen. Still, neither Turnipseed nor Hamm gave her a tongue lashing to start her day.

Buoyed in spirits by her not-overly-icy reception at the office and by the fresh start of a new week, Jemmy set out to interview the coroner. She feared he wouldn't speak with her. She was right. He sent his nondescript assistant to tell her so.

"Dr. Wangermeier says he's too busy to see you, and, even if he had nothing better to do than smoke a pipe and drink rye whiskey, he still wouldn't talk to you." The assistant wrung his hands. "I'm sorry for the insulting words, but he told me to quote him exactly. He said you'd know why."

Jemmy hung her head. "I do know why. I had hoped he'd forgive me, but I see my attempts to make amends are useless."

"I can't imagine what you did to set him against you. He's well known as a gentle and generous man. I'm sure he'll reconsider in time."

"Alas, time is a precious commodity, and I have none to spare."

"Might I be of assistance?"

"I'd be eternally grateful if you could confirm the cause of Quisenberry Sproat's death."

"Unfortunately, I cannot. The coroner hasn't listed the cause as yet."

"Then Sproat wasn't whipped to death?"

"No. The welts caused only a little bleeding, and they were too new to have festered. Dying from sepsis would take much longer—many days."

"Did the coroner suggest a cause of death?"

"No. But he's determined to find one. He mumbles to himself when he's working. Keeps saying, 'Young men, healthy as spring colts, don't just up and die.' "

"Do you have any ideas?"

"I hesitate to tell you because it is mere speculation on my part."

"Please, I promise not to use anything without your consent."

"I know very little, just that the coroner is trying to discover what kind of whip was used in the beating."

"Thank you. I'll keep what you've told me to myself—and I'll be back."

"Glad to be of help, Miss McBustle. I hope you and I might accompany Dr. Wangermeier and Miss Patterson to a future theatrical production—along with your aunt and uncle, of course. I quite enjoyed our last outing, despite my distressing attack of indigestion."

Not until that very moment did Jemmy associate this drab, gray soul with her colorless escort on the night Quisenberry Sproat met his maker. A journalist is supposed to take note of her surroundings at all times. *How could I be so mindless as to completely forget my escort at such a newsworthy event? And just now, why didn't I have the presence of mind to ask him one single question?*

With a clearer head, she found her way to the city jail. To her surprise, she had to make an appointment to interview Frank James. A handsome woman of middle years in a tan gabardine suit introduced herself. "I am Frank's wife, Anna. Today Mr. James is allowing only family members, agents of the press, and his attorneys. Admirers may come back tomorrow. I'd be happy to take your name and offer you a specific time."

Jemmy's press credentials surprised Mrs. James. "I can give you 1:15 this afternoon. Will that be agreeable to the representative of the *Illuminator*?"

With an hour to kill before the interview, Jemmy wandered across the street to a diner where police, lawyers, and newspaper men on the crime beat spent their leisure. Except for the scuffling of chairs on the wooden floor, the place fell silent. All heads turned in her direction to examine the only female patron in the place.

The sole empty table stood in the middle of the room. Jemmy marched there, plunked herself down, and peeled off her gloves.

Before the waiter could say a word, she said, "Bowl of beef stew and a cup of coffee as quickly as you can manage. I have an important appointment."

The server scuttled off to fill the order. Chatter resumed. Apparently the novelty of having feminine company faded fast.

Jemmy recoiled at the sight of the coffee. It looked like coal cinders in a mud puddle and tasted like ground-up walnut shells. With the addition of enough cream and sugar to coat a small dog, she turned it almost drinkable. The stew made up for the coffee. The fragrance of thyme and celery caressed her nose. The meat was tender; the carrots and onions savory.

She had lifted the spoon for a second mouthful when a figure loomed over her. "I'm surprised and delighted to see you here, Miss McBustle." The speaker was none other than the color-of-oatmeal coroner's assistant.

"Do sit down. I'm delighted to have a luncheon companion."

"Thank you, Miss McBustle. I hoped you'd invite me."

"Do have the stew. It's quite delicious. Though I'd avoid the coffee if I were you."

"I believe they make non-potable coffee in an attempt to sell more beer."

He motioned his order to the waiter and urged Jemmy not to wait. "Please don't stand on ceremony, Miss McBustle. I'd hate to upset your digestion with cold stew."

"You're most considerate. Has the coroner discovered anything since our last conversation?"

"Perhaps."

"Why do you think so?"

"He's having jars and bottles tested."

Jemmy already suspected as much. She'd packed up the jars and bottles herself. "What is he testing for?"

"I have no idea."

After Jemmy finished her food, she felt desperate to leave the restaurant. Good manners kept her in her seat while she listened to the bland man drone on.

"I wish to apologize for my inability to escort you on Saturday last. My mother is an invalid, and I was unable to find someone to stay with her."

"Your mother is blessed to have such a devoted son."

"I want to assure you I wished most desperately to attend the play, to see you again." He put his hand over Jemmy's.

"Put it out of mind. Family comes first." The smell of something sweetly cloying with an undertone of acid slid up her nose.

"But I have offended you."

"No, no. I've lost track of time and must rush to an appointment. I regret I cannot stay until you finish your luncheon." She slid her hand out from under his and pulled on a glove.

He stood with napkin in hand. "I hope you'll allow me to make amends."

Jemmy threw him a wan smile. She could feel him watching

her as she left.

Outside in the crisp November air, she shuddered. The memory of the same sweet-acid smell of embalming fluid brought back an undertaker's cellar. The vision of her grandmother—a horror she still had not the stomach to describe to her own family—made the evil coffee rise in her throat. Only by concentrating on Frank James could she keep from embarrassing herself. It wouldn't do to lose control of her stomach in front of the city morgue.

Back at the jail, Anna James was not in the place she'd held when Jemmy first saw her. Jemmy paced and fidgeted until she nearly lost her temper. She had raised her fist to knock on the warden's door when Mrs. James swooped in carrying a picnic hamper. "Sorry to be delayed, Miss McBustle. I was eating lunch with the Mister."

"Do the authorities allow you to bring him food?"

"They've been even more gracious. Mayor Ziegenhein himself provided this hamper filled with roast quail, German-style potato salad, corn muffins, apple cake, and a fine bottle of Riesling."

"A far cry from bread and water."

"Mr. James has no reason to dislike prison. Wardens always attend him kindly. In St. Joseph, he was allowed to spend untold hours conversing with his friends. On his first day there, five hundred people from Jefferson City came to visit him."

"No more than his due. The most famous outlaw in the nation, probably in the world, merits special consideration."

Mrs. James arched an eyebrow. "I'm glad you appreciate his qualities, though I'm appalled to hear him called 'outlaw.' My husband is a law-abiding, upstanding citizen. Please come with me."

Anna led Jemmy down cold corridors of rough-surfaced yellow limestone. She stopped at one branch and signaled the officer at the far end of the hall. He opened a massive iron door and waved Jemmy inside.

Jemmy had visited jail cells before, but none decked out like this one. Luxury abounded—Brussels carpet on the floor, one wall covered with family pictures, and one decorated with landscapes. The furniture could have graced the abode of a dapper man about town. It consisted of two upholstered chairs, a highboy desk and stool, a game table, and a bedstead with headboard of bird's-eye maple.

"Welcome to my current home, Miss O'Nimity. I believe that is your name?" He smirked almost imperceptibly.

"Ann O'Nimity is my pen name, Mr. James. My real name is Jemima McBustle. My real name is true and serious, not the stuff jokes are made of."

"If I offended, I offer an apology—a true and serious apology."

Jemmy looked around the room. "I was just admiring your quarters. Except for the stone walls, this room would not be out of place in a grand home in Compton Heights."

"Jails have always been kind to me while I awaited trial. I'm sure prisons would have been another matter had I ever been forced to spend time in one. Please have a seat and tell me what your readers at the . . ."

"*Illuminator.* The St. Louis *Illuminator.*"

"St. Louis *Illuminator* would like to know about Frank James."

"I was going to ask you if you have been well-treated, but I can see you have."

" 'What fates impose, that men must needs abide; It boots not to resist both wind and tide.' Words from the bard himself."

"An apt quotation. I've heard you're quite the Shakespearean scholar. Which play?"

"*King Henry the Sixth.*"

"If I may ask, how did a farm boy come by such education?"

91

"My father was an educated man, a minister of the church and a brilliant orator. A graduate of Georgetown College with honors and a master's degree. He held education in high esteem and was a member of the first Board of Trustees of William Jewel College. Naturally, he saw to the education of his sons."

"How interesting. And how surprising to find such scholarship in one reputed to be a criminal."

"Please remember I was tried twice but never convicted of any crime. I take umbrage at being lumped into the criminal class."

"Of course. I must choose my words more carefully. Might I ask how you feel about your current imprisonment?"

"Politics, Miss McBustle. Pure politics. The powers that be expect having Frank James in their custody to bring them importance and fame. What better way to seek money for more guards or new construction? What better way to launch a political career than to lure journalists like yourself to quote them in the newspapers? Pardon me if I sound cynical."

"Do you expect a quick release?"

"Not necessarily. I imagine they'll hold me as long as possible. Of course, they'll have to let me go sooner or later. I didn't kill Quisenberry Sproat."

"Have you any idea who might have beaten him?"

"No. I have no idea who might wish him harm. I met him only once, but I will say he seemed a brash young fellow—the type who would rather challenge than befriend the men he meets."

"Did he challenge you?"

"He made a coarse joke about outlaws who get away with murder."

"What did you do?"

"Merely suggested the obvious. If he believed me to be a murderer, he was flirting with the hereafter."

"Very shrewd. I've heard many tales of the James brothers' sharp minds. I confess I borrowed all my neighbor's dime novels. My favorite is the *James Boys in a Fix,* by D. W. Stevens. The cover shows you on horseback trapped in ropes slung between two trees. It had to be your likeness. The mustache is a true replica of your own."

Frank scowled. "Young ladies shouldn't read foolish trash riddled with lies."

"I apologize for offending. Still, the stories portray you as brave and heroic."

"Please, say no more about those cheap thrill books."

"I'd be remiss not to ask if the rumors are true. Did you kill seventeen men in cold blood?"

"No doubt I killed many more than that. I am proud to say I was a soldier for the South in the War of Yankee Aggression. That is the last question I mean to answer about my early days. Have you anything further regarding the case at hand?"

"After you put him in his place so cleverly, did Quisenberry Sproat stop making offensive jokes?"

"I believe so. I heard nothing more—not even from the backstage crowd. Perhaps you know their love of gossip."

"Could your threat to Mr. Sproat have caused the police to suspect you in his death?"

"Only if they're misguided. As I said: the man stopped his foolish behavior. What reason would I have had to take further action?"

"What words did you use? They may have been misunderstood."

"It would be unwise of me to air them in the court of public opinion. I won't help anyone use my own words to condemn me. Most particularly, I will not repeat to the press words uttered in the heat of the moment."

"I quite understand. How did your whip come to be found in

Sproat's dressing room?"

"The whip disappeared from my rig while it sat in an alleyway. Anyone could have stolen it."

"Is the whip the only actual evidence they have against you?"

"If not, they have yet to inform me."

"Who do you believe might have killed Mr. Sproat?"

"I know just one thing. I heard an argument as I walked by his dressing room. A female was screaming at him."

"Did you know he shared the room with another actor who also played Tom Loker?"

"Yes. I suppose some woman might have exchanged hot words with the other Tom Loker."

"Might I ask why you were in the basement where the dressing rooms are? Do ticket takers usually go there?"

Frank blinked his eyes a dozen times. "I visited one of the cast members."

"Which would that be?"

"I wouldn't care to involve anyone unless it becomes unavoidable." He stood. "And now I regret I must dismiss such delightful company as yourself. It's time for my next appointment."

"Have you any words for my readers?"

"Frank James doesn't, but Will Shakespeare does. Tell them I'm feeding on 'Adversity's sweet milk, philosophy.' *Romeo and Juliet,* act three, scene three."

Mrs. James had a message for Jemmy. "Before you leave, Mr. James's attorney would like a word with you."

Frank James's lawyer was a big man, round faced, barrel chested, and sweating despite the chill in the dank jail. Black eyes in a pink-red face reminded Jemmy of the watermelon feast on Labor Day.

"Pleased to meet you, Miss McBustle. Mrs. James tells me you write for the *Illuminator,* a splendid newspaper in a city filled with fine newspapers. The warden has offered me the conference room. I'd be grateful if you would accompany me. Mrs. James will come as well."

"I regret I must leave. We journalists have deadlines to meet. If you have information for me, please be brief."

"I merely wished to reassure you that Mr. and Mrs. James and I are confident he will soon be released. We will do everything possible to bring the true murderer to justice. I regret I cannot tell you the name of the culprit until the felon has been arrested. You see, Mr. James knows who killed Mr. Sproat."

Chapter Ten

November 21, 1898

The lawyer's words excited Jemmy to the point of frenzy. "Frank James knows who killed Quisenberry Sproat?"

"So he tells me."

"And the name of the murderer is . . . ?"

"He won't tell me."

"Have I permission to quote you in my article?"

"So long as you don't speculate any further. No naming names."

"Of course."

Jemmy left the jail with new purpose. Frank's lawyer had unwittingly given her the clue to scoop every newspaper in town. The place to go to uncover the truth had to be in the basement of the Crystal Palace Theatre.

On the trolley ride, she practiced a speech to convince the doorman to let her in. She didn't need it. With no doorman in sight, the unlocked stage door opened to her touch. When her eyes grew accustomed to the dim light, she slipped down to the basement.

In the "Tom Loker" dressing room, she turned a switch and thanked the management for installing electric lights. Mother McBustle had no faith in them, but Jemmy reveled in the liberation they brought.

Thomas Alva Edison freed everyone from the need to carry matches. Better still, the glass bulb that insulated glowing bits of metal also insulated people against man's worst horrors—the two opposite terrifying fears, fire and darkness.

An imposing steamer trunk, probably belonging to Handsome Harry Benson, dominated the room. The trunk stood three feet tall in unblemished leather with polished brass fittings, McBride's finest theatrical model freshly minted as a julep on race day. Jemmy ignored it—or tried to—as she searched the room and the wardrobe. The other Tom Loker's trunk with its dozens of hotel and train stickers looked well used in comparison.

She opened and sniffed every jar and bottle on the dressing table—bay rum, greasepaint, dry coffee grounds for that unshaved look. Nothing bespoke murder.

She examined everything except Harry's trunk at least twice. She retraced her actions from Thursday night—still nothing. Should she leave, or give the new trunk a quick check?

The big steamer chest could tell her nothing about the night of Sproat's death. It was a new arrival to the clutter in the dressing room. At length, curiosity won out over common sense.

As she tugged the steamer sections apart, noise in the hall set her heart thumping. She stumbled to turn off the electricity. Perhaps no one had noticed the light and would walk on by. But just in case, she dived into the trunk and pulled it shut.

The reek of tobacco-smoked clothes and horse sweat curled in Jemmy's nose. Her corset jabbed the tender flesh under her bosom. She crouched in panic. A door squeaked. The click of a light switch announced she was no longer alone.

A woman's voice asked, "Why did you bring me here?"

Jemmy could barely breathe in her cramped prison.

A man's voice answered, "Privacy. What place do you know with more privacy than a theatre on a day without performances?"

"Privacy is not required for our business."

"No need to play the coquette. You must know how deeply I admire you."

"If you think to seduce me, you're more of a buffoon than I thought."

"Most ladies find me agreeable. Do you mean to hurt my feelings by calling me clownish?"

"What I think is of no matter. Just give me what I came for."

"Very well, if money is all you're after." Footfalls moved closer to Jemmy's hiding place. The trunk separated an inch or more.

Jemmy's head swam with terror. Her bad ear hissed like a thousand rattlesnakes. What reason could she possibly give for hiding in this man's trunk? And if he's the murderer . . .

"On second thought, the unlocked trunk made me remember. I removed the money yesterday." He crooned in soft tones, "Come with me to my rooms. That's where you can receive your proper reward."

"Be at Union Station tomorrow at three in the afternoon, you insufferable egoist. The sooner I leave St. Louis and you, the better."

Jemmy heard the light click off and the dressing-room door squeak shut. Still trembling, she extracted herself from the trunk. At last she could stand and let air into her starved lungs.

The man had to be Harry Benson. After all, the trunk he started to open was the new trunk she'd chosen as a hiding place.

She tried to recall any detail about the woman. Nothing came, saving one piece of information—some female planned to meet Harry at the train station on Tuesday at three in the afternoon. Well, Jemmy would be there, too. She moved to turn on the lights and finish the job of examining Harry's trunk.

Singing in the hall sent her scurrying to hide again. " 'I love you as I never lov'd before, since first I met you on the village green.' "

This time she felt her way past the trunk to the wardrobe. Her ribs wouldn't stand another stint in a two foot by two foot by three foot wood and leather coffin.

Before she'd even closed the door, she knew the folly of her choice. The person who entered singing would leave the new steamer trunk alone. This mellow baritone belonged to the other Tom Loker.

" 'Come to me, e'er my dream of love is o'er. I love you as I lov'd you—when you were sweet, when you were swe-ee-eet sixteen.' " He ended the song with a lovely trill on the word *sweet.*

How long will I be trapped this time? At least I can stand up in this cupboard. It smells better, too. Jicky perfume. Why would a man's clothes smell of a lady's scent?

Jemmy tried to calm herself by thinking about Jicky. She had no doubts about the scent. A one-ounce bottle of the fragrance that made Guerlain the premiere perfume maker in Paris took place of honor on Mother's dressing table. Mother cherished that precious thing, that little cut-glass bottle, that remnant of luxury from the time of McBustle prosperity. It reminded her of the days when Father was alive and Bricktop was a family home instead of a boardinghouse.

No one was allowed to use the scent except on the rarest occasion. Just three months earlier, Jemmy had been granted a few drops for her handkerchief on what should have been the grandest occasion of her life—the evening of her debut into St. Louis society at the Oracle Ball. She'd worn the sweet and heady scent to dance with the handsomest man in the state.

After a few moments, Jemmy felt brave enough to ease the door open and peer through the crack. Tom Loker-Simon Legree hummed while leaning back in a chair with feet crossed on a stack of newspapers. He thumbed through The St. Louis *Illuminator.* Jemmy understood why—her play review. Her mind raced to remember what she'd said about him. Nothing popped into her head. She'd devoted most of her words to the other Tom Loker. But she'd added a line praising the real actor, too.

Loker-Legree read aloud: "Handsome Harry Benson's face and physique live up to his reputation. For the benefit of the theatre-going public, I advise him to perform in the ring, not on stage.

"If the two Tom Lokers were horses, the real actor would be Kentucky Derby winner Aristides to Mr. Benson's rag-picker's nag."

Loker-Legree's feet hit the floor with a double clomp. He fetched a pair of scissors from his case and began clipping the notice. She shifted her weight a fraction. Just enough to topple something hard on her head. Her hat absorbed the blow, but the noise brought Loker scrambling to the wardrobe.

Jemmy had to think fast. She squelched the hissing in her bad ear with a stroke of self-confidence. Sassy Patterson's example taught her how to play this scene.

When he flung open the door, she tumbled forward into his arms. "Oh, Mr. Loker, I'm so glad you found me. Another two minutes of looking at you through a teeny crack in the door, and I would positively swoon with excitement."

The scowl left his face as he helped her out of the cabinet. "Miss McBustle, what a surprise to find you in my clothes closet."

Jemmy rushed headlong into her best imitation of Sassy Patterson. "I can't imagine why you'd be surprised. Many young girls must be entranced to see you onstage. I'd be surprised if a few of them didn't seek out your dressing room—perhaps to find a souvenir. Confess it now. I'm right, am I not?"

"Girls have, on occasion, threatened to tear the very clothes from my back."

"I knew it. Who could resist?"

"But you're the first I've caught skulking around my dressing room."

"Skulking? A harsh word, but perhaps an apt one." Jemmy lowered her chin in what she hoped was a demure posture. "You caught me touching things you touched. And, yes, I was looking for a souvenir—something uniquely yours—yet something small I could keep close to my heart."

"Did you find something suitable to steal?"

"Don't call it stealing, I beg you. Call it borrowing a little token to cherish."

"Did you find your 'token'?"

She pursed her lips in a Patterson pout. "No, I found nothing. You came in too soon."

"Allow me to choose something."

Jemmy batted her eyelashes. "I'd revere it. 'If the two Tom Lokers were horses, the real actor would be Kentucky Derby winner Aristides to Mr. Benson's rag picker's nag.' I'd adore any belonging of the real Kentucky Derby winner—figuratively speaking, of course."

"I'll gladly provide a token with one condition. You must allow me to present the keepsake in more fitting surroundings. Might I have the pleasure of your company at dinner this evening?"

"Your invitation takes my breath away. I wouldn't be able to eat a single crumb sitting across the table from you. Although I ache to accept, I must decline. My mother expects me home for dinner. Also, she doesn't allow me to see men in the evening unchaperoned."

"Very wise, your mother. I see she allows you out unchaperoned in the daytime. Perhaps lunch tomorrow?"

Jemmy mulled over this chance opportunity to pump Loker during luncheon. She came close to telling him she herself had written those flattering lines in his *Illuminator* clipping. She stopped herself barely in time. *The last thing I need is for Loker to know I'm Ann O'Nimity the newspaper reporter. What can I do about that hideous name Suetonius Hamm foisted upon me with pure trickery.* "Perhaps I can slip away and meet you."

Loker-Legree walked her toward the door and opened it. "It's settled then. The Lindell Hotel at one tomorrow. I'll wait in the lobby for the charming young lady who memorized my review."

"I dare not meet you at your hotel. Appearances, you know. Perhaps at Union Station."

"The Terminal Restaurant at one?"

Jemmy pressed a gloved hand on her lips then his face. "I'll not be able to sleep until then."

"Nor I, Miss McBustle. *Adieu.*"

Thank heavens in a handbag. At least I didn't pan him in my review.

She took a last look around the room. One item stood out. The thing that had hit her on the head lay on the floor. Half in and half out of the wardrobe coiled a black snakeskin whip.

Where did that come from? Why didn't I find it when I rummaged through the wardrobe earlier? Jemmy tromped down the hall. She clambered up the stairs fuming at her ineptitude as a snoop.

Her performance as a siren pleased her no better. *What a spectacle I made of myself. None of the lies I've ever told made me feel quite so disgusted with Jemima Gormlaith McBustle as pretending to be smitten by that arrogant actor. So what if he is handsome as Apollo? I suppose I should be thanking Sassy for showing me how to be the second biggest flirt between Chicago and Kansas City.*

She had straightened her spine and composed herself when she saw Pops, the doorman, sitting on his stool. She slipped by him with head turned. A whiff of whiskey gave her hope the man was soused. Perhaps he wouldn't recognize her.

Her time in the theatre hadn't revealed much, but it did give cause for thought. *Why were Handsome Harry and some unknown female crossing words? Who owns the blacksnake whip that hit me on the head? Will my lunch date with . . . ? Heavens in a handbag. I have a luncheon engagement with a man, but I don't even know his real name.*

Trolley rides took her home to more trouble. Mother McB. now had two daughters sick in the maid's room behind the kitchen.

The flu bug had bitten twelve-year-old Minerva. Even though Nervy was the youngest of the four McBustle sisters, she was also the cleverest. She seemed never to be without a scientific experiment. She'd tried everything from an archeological dig in the backyard to making bug poison. She wrote voluminous notes on how long each type of garden pest lived after she doused it with her concoctions.

Mother had her hands full just convincing the girl to stay in a darkened chamber with the curtains closed like a proper sickroom. Nervy insisted on experimenting with methods to reduce her fever by placing ice packs on various parts of her anatomy. She recorded the results at fifteen-minute intervals. Conclusion: ice packs worked best in armpit and groin, but that resulted in chills and so was not the ideal therapy. At length, she opted for Mother McB.'s original treatment—soothing cloths for the forehead.

Nervy then tackled various patent medicines. So as not to expose anyone else to her germs, she fashioned a mask from cheesecloth before she traipsed upstairs in her flannel nightie. She knocked on the doors of all boarders and promised them a factual report on their ague remedies if they would allow her to test their favorites.

She rounded up a half-dozen bottles and jars. Glowing with enthusiasm, she devoted a page in her scientific journal to each. The brown bottles bore august names: Clark Stanley's Snake

Oil Liniment, Dr. Kilmer's Swamp Root, Smith's Glyco-Heroin, Metcalf's Coca Wine, Horsford's Acid Phosphate, Ayers Sarsaparilla.

She tried them all on herself. None brought down her fever; but after a few tablespoons of some nostrums, she slept for a good ten hours. She praised the sleep, but not the headache she had the next morning.

Mother returned the bottles to her tenants with apologies—after she'd chastised her youngest daughter. "Don't you realize those potions are nothing more than opiates in liquor? You didn't fall asleep. You passed out in an alcoholic stupor. You must promise me never again to take patent medicine without my permission."

"My findings on the elixirs are inconclusive, but I can endorse two other remedies from your own medicine chest, Richardson's Croup and Pneumonia Cure Salve and Doctor Lambert's Listerine Antiseptic, made right here in St. Louis. The salve on my chest helped me breathe, and the Listerine freshened my mouth. I didn't swallow, so it could not have caused my headache even if it does contain alcohol."

Having two sisters on the disabled list meant more work for the healthy two. Jemmy had hoped to write an article on the beginning of flu season but gave up the idea when sleep overtook her while she sat at her desk. The sound of her pencil hitting the wood surface woke her just in time to keep her head from banging on the hard walnut. She gave in to exhaustion and slipped into her flannel nightgown.

The sound of sleet against glass drew her to the window. Sheets of stinging ice sliced down St. Ange Street. Winter arrived before Thanksgiving.

Jemmy shivered as she pulled all the extra quilts from the cedar chest. The pungent smell reminded her of cutting boughs to decorate the parlor room mantel at Christmas. She spread the quilts over the other sleepers on their cots. Since Bricktop had become a paying establishment, she'd lost her lovely bedroom on the second floor. Now she shared the unheated ballroom on the third with her three sisters, as well as Gerta the cook and Dora the new maid.

Sleet drummed harder against the windows. *This bad weather is too early. We're in for a long winter.*

The last thought running through her head as she slid into bed was, "Maybe Frank James knows who murdered Quisenberry Sproat because he did it himself."

CHAPTER ELEVEN

Tuesday, November 22, 1898

Tuesday morning arrived at the end of a blizzard. Seven inches of new powder covered the ground. Falling snow dulled sound and sight. Tree branches dipped with white weight in the dim dawn.

Jemmy took less than a minute to appreciate the beauty as she waded off toward the trolley stop. Snow spilled into her galoshes, and the smell of wet wool from her cape drove all pleasant thoughts from her mind. She barely noticed that for a few hours at least, St. Louis skies sifted down white ice instead of black soot.

Jemmy's morning at the *Illuminator* began with Hal glaring down at her while she tried to write her influenza article.

"Where were you all day yesterday?"

"Take pity on me, Hal. Two of my sisters are sick with the flu. I have a full-time job here and another full-time job at home."

"That doesn't even begin to answer my question."

"I did what I'm paid to do. I gathered news—interviewed the coroner's assistant and Frank James."

"Kindly explain why you refused to take me with you."

"I had an appointment and no time to wait for you." The true facts didn't come to light. When she sneaked away from the *Illuminator,* she'd had no appointment. She eluded Hal on purpose.

"You could have left me a note telling me where to meet you."

"I am remiss on that score. I have no excuse—only that I was so rushed, I didn't think to write. Besides, what would you have photographed if you'd come along?"

"A picture of a famous outlaw is always worth something. If Hamm didn't want it, I could peddle it to the *Police Gazette.*"

"Then you must go to the jail with your equipment. I think the Jameses will welcome you. They're eager for good publicity. I warn you, though. Mrs. James keeps a strict appointment book, so you'll probably have to wait."

"And where will you be while I'm waiting to photograph Frank James—for the second time in less than a week?"

"Don't worry in the least. I'll be interviewing doctors about influenza. You know. Handy hints for keeping the ague away."

"Promise you'll let me know if you need pictures for anything else in the Sproat case."

"I'm not even thinking about that today." She waved him off and pretended to concentrate on her typewriting machine—a clacking beast she had yet to master.

"If I have to tie a rope around your waist to keep you from running off without me, I'll do it. Don't forget I'm your bodyguard. Truth is, I get paid for keeping you out of trouble. Taking pictures is just my sideline." Hal stomped off.

Jemmy hogged the news desk telephone for a full seventeen minutes while she called the big St. Louis hospitals. At each, she collected numbers of flu victims for the week before. She also gathered suggestions for treating those laid low—and for avoiding contagion.

By the end of the hour, she'd handed in her article and was off to poke around some more into the curious case of Quisenberry Sproat.

Her first stop was Autley Flinchpaugh's sports desk. "Mr.

Flinchpaugh, have you learned anything further about Mr. Sproat?"

"I'd be delighted to discuss Sproat over lunch."

"I would be equally delighted with your invitation if I didn't already have a luncheon engagement."

"I regret I am unable to speak with you now. I have an article to prepare on the Yale versus Harvard football game. I hate trying to write bouncy reports when I have nothing but dull telegraphed statistics."

Flinchpaugh pounded a single fist once on his desk to express his irritation. "Harvard and Yale! Why should a St. Louis newspaper print story after story on Harvard and Yale? Why won't Hamm send me to Columbia, Missouri? Answer me that!

"Never mind. I know the reason well enough. Since the Mizzou Tiger scandal in '96, local interest in the team has waned. What could you expect? The Board of Curators fired a reckless but great coach and suspended the players—and they were excellent football men, too. A veritable brick wall—magnificent.

"What was the coach thinking? Going all the way to Texas for a match was bad enough. But then traipsing another thousand miles for matches across Mexico—a foreign country—and all the way to Mexico City. How perfectly idiotic! No wonder the administration punished the team.

"Before the great fiasco, St. Louisans gobbled up articles about the Missouri University football team. They liked Mizzou better than our own St. Louis University team. The Tigers are miles away in Columbia. Still, many St. Louisans followed their successes with religious devotion. And I was on hand to see their home games in person. Now, Mr. Hamm keeps a tight rein on travel expenses—at least for everyone but you. You, apparently, can travel to Sedalia and stay for a solid week."

Such a tirade from Flinchpaugh took Jemmy by surprise. Still, she found the words to defend herself. "The trip cost the

108

Illuminator very little—less than six dollars for round trips on the train. We stayed with family friends and had no charge for room and board."

Flinchpaugh mumbled, "I'm sorry. I didn't mean to sound resentful. I just hate what that chowderheaded Mexican trip has done to the Tigers."

When Flinchpaugh softened, Jemmy ventured another plea. "Is there no small tidbit you can offer on the Sproat case?"

"Perhaps one thing. Q.B. asked Miss Isabel Patterson to be Mrs. Quisenberry Sproat. I apologize for my outburst. You're very kind to listen. I hope I haven't lost your good will."

"Don't give it a second thought. I often feel like letting all my frustrations roll right off my tongue. It helps to free the mind."

As she slogged through snow to the trolley stop, Jemmy wondered why Sassy had never mentioned the marriage proposal. Perhaps the pretty girl had so many offers, she couldn't be bothered or didn't remember.

Did some jealous suitor cross words and whips with Sproat? Almost before she knew it, Jemmy found herself at the home of the siren herself, Isabel Patterson.

A maid too young to have finished the eighth grade answered the bell. She had not earned top grades in housemaid schooling either. She uttered not a single word of greeting, just stood silent as a bell without a clapper. She filled the doorway while twisting the corner of her starched white apron. Jemmy presented her card. "Would you be so kind as to tell Miss Patterson I'm waiting?"

The girl gave a little snort. "Reckon you'll be a half-day older for that wait. Missy Patterson don't get up till 'bout three in the afternoon. Better come back then." The girl shut the door in the untimely visitor's face.

Before Jemmy could descend the snow-covered stairs to the sidewalk, the door re-opened. In pink silk wrapper with long, dark curls gently swaying over her shoulders, Isabel's mother appeared. Looking the perfect picture of an older version of her daughter, she stood shivering on the threshold. According to an old saying, a woman turns into her mother. If it's true, any boy would be reassured by seeing Mrs. Patterson.

She flung her arms open to Jemmy, "Why, Miss McBustle . . . Jemima isn't it? Please come in. My maid is so young and foolish. How could she leave you on the wrong side of a closed door in the midst of the first big snowfall of the season? I'll give her a good bit of my mind later. Right now, do come in out of the cold."

Mrs. Patterson took Jemmy's arm and escorted her into the hall as if they were the oldest and best of friends. "I just finished my morning correspondence. Please come into the conservatory and join me in a cup of cocoa to take the chill off your rosy cheeks."

Jemmy found no space in Mrs. Patterson's chatter for injecting a single word.

"I am delighted you've come. What a pleasure to sit across the table from a pretty girl. Sassy never deigns to make an appearance until well past noon."

She seated Jemmy under a date palm tree at a glass-topped table with filigreed wrought-iron legs. Mrs. P. stood back to assess her caller. "How wise you are to heighten your beauty by wearing clothes so plain and severe."

Was that a compliment? In her tailored suit of gray wool serge with a stiff-starched white blouse, Jemmy thought herself the very picture of a serious newswoman. Before she could cull through Mrs. Patterson's meaning, the lady was scraping her wrought-iron chair across the slate floor. She beamed at Jemmy.

The young maid hustled into the conservatory with a tray bearing gold-rimmed china cups and a pot covered by a tea cozy decorated with blue cornflowers.

"You silly girl. I asked for chocolate, not tea."

The girl mumbled, "Cook say we ain't got no cocoa."

Mrs. Patterson waved her out. "In true pioneer spirit we shall have to make do. Milk and sugar, Miss McBustle?"

Jemmy murmured, "Yes, please."

"I know you want to speak with Isabel, but perhaps you can delay for a bit. I'm simply starved for female companionship. Would you prefer marmalade or strawberry jam on your scone? You won't believe how light these scones are."

Without waiting for an answer, Mrs. P. splashed a dollop of marmalade on a plate and passed it to Jemmy.

"We've returned to St. Louis recently, so I'm hopelessly out of touch. Do tell me all the latest gossip about the twenty families. I've heard the Rough Rider himself, Mr. Theodore Roosevelt, is coming to personally visit men wounded in the war with Spain over Cuba. Is that true? And is the Imperial Club the most exclusive in town? I heard they turned away Mayor Ziegenhein himself. German—that must have been why."

"I'm afraid I know very little about the highest echelons of the St. Louis upper crust. My family belong to the Oracle Society, not the Veiled Prophet. Indeed, I'm not privy to inside knowledge about the people in the Oracle circle either. I've attended just one youth meeting since my coming out in August."

"Still, you must have learned something worth repeating. You debuted at the Oracle Ball, did you not?"

"I've learned this: it's not easy for a girl whose mother runs a boardinghouse to attend events that require a change of costume for so many activities—boating, ice skating, bicycling, and a new gown for every dance."

"I thought your aunt and uncle, the Erwin McBustles, might take a greater interest in your welfare."

"Oh, they do. Don't mistake my meaning. My Auntie Dee would supply me with anything I requested. But I have much to do at home. Just now my chores are doubled because I have two sisters ill with influenza."

Mrs. Patterson's bright-eyed rapture at listening to Jemmy evolved into a bored yawn. "Perhaps you ought to be home attending to them instead of traipsing out on such an unfavorable day. My daughter won't voluntarily come downstairs until mid-afternoon. You may go up and try to wake her if you like."

"Thank you, Mrs. Patterson, and thank you for the tea. It was quite perfect for conquering the chill of this freezing morning."

Mrs. Patterson rang a little bell, and the young maid appeared quickly—so quickly, she must have been eavesdropping. "Show Miss McBustle to Isabel's room; then come back to me. I wish to speak with you. Goodbye, Miss McBustle. Pleased to see you again."

"The pleasure was mine, and I thank you for your graciousness and your hospitality." Mrs. Patterson had already returned to her morning correspondence.

On the way upstairs, Jemmy tried to pry a little information from the maid. "Have you been working for the Pattersons long?"

"Long enough."

"Long enough to . . . ?"

"Long enough to know."

"Long enough to know what?"

"Long enough to know not to tell nobody nothin'."

The girl rapped gently on Isabel's door and said in a voice no louder than a dog pant, "A female here to see you, Miss Patterson."

As Jemmy expected, no sound came from Sassy's bedroom. The girl opened the door and motioned Jemmy inside. "She got a knob to turn on the light right by the door."

Jemmy felt for the switch in vain. As her eyes became accustomed to the dim light, she decided to open the draperies. On the way across the room, she tripped over discarded shoes and nearly fell when her feet tangled in some cast away bit of clothing.

At length she managed to pull the drapes aside. Sunlight fell on Sassy's glossy hair and rose-petal skin. The goddess Venus played favorites. The girl looked celestially beautiful even in sleep.

Gray daylight failed to waken her. Jemmy tried subtle throat-clearings to no effect. Next she tried shuffling a chair, then knocked it over with a crash. Sassy did not move a single finger. Jemmy wondered whether the body on the bed was still alive.

"Sassy, it's Jemmy McBustle. Please wake up. I need to speak with you. Sassy, do you hear me?" Even that got no response.

Jemmy strode to the bed and shook Sassy's arm. "Please wake up. Everyone has been telling me to come back this afternoon, but I cannot. I have an important appointment. Please wake up. I promise not to keep you long."

"Go away. I need my beauty sleep."

"I've never seen a girl less in need of beauty sleep."

"Was that a compliment? I can't tell so early in the morning."

"Yes, it was most definitely a compliment. When I awake, my hair is sticking out in all directions and my eyelids are red. Your hair spreads over the pillow in pretty curls, and your eyes aren't puffy at all."

Sassy struggled to rise, reconsidered, and tumbled back into her pillow. "I regret I am unable to rise."

"Please humor me for a few minutes."

"If you must ask me something, go ahead."

"Did you become engaged to Quisenberry Sproat?" A sweet snore like the purring of a kitten told Jemmy her question was not penetrating into Sassy's brain. "One question and I'll bother you no more."

"Haven't you gone yet?"

"Sassy, please. Did Quisenberry Sproat ask you to marry him?"

"What?"

Jemmy shook Sassy's shoulders until the girl sat bolt upright in bed. "Stop mauling me. What is so important it won't wait until I'm awake?"

"I have to know whether you were engaged to Quisenberry Sproat."

"He asked me, yes."

"Did you accept?"

"Yes and no."

"A girl can't answer a proposal 'Yes and no.' "

"I can."

"Perhaps you can tell me this. Did Sproat think you would marry him?"

"I'm not a mind reader."

"Please, Sassy. I don't understand."

"Jemmy, I have at least a half-dozen marriage proposals to consider on any given day. The only way to keep so many on offer is not to accept any."

"Isn't that dishonest?"

"Not at all. I do plan to marry some day. I keep hope alive with each man. Take my advice. Don't agree to marry anyone. I recommend being noncommittal. I can think of no better way to draw attention and gifts. Come to think of it, I do believe I live every girl's dream."

"Don't any of your suitors tire of playing your games?"

"I suppose *amour* is a bit of a game. Perhaps I'll marry one of the men I'm seeing now—perhaps the most persistent . . . or the most handsome . . . or the richest."

"What I really want to know is whether any of your other suitors might have slain Sproat. Could one be jealous enough to kill—or desperate enough to eliminate his competition?"

With a faraway look in her eye, Sassy brushed an index finger slowly along her cheek. "What a charming thought. A man so deeply in love as to kill for me."

Jemmy scowled. "You'd be happy to cause a man to commit murder, wouldn't you?"

"Hmmmm."

"Which of your suitors might do such a thing?"

"Really, Jemmy. You'd hardly expect me to know. I don't take any of them seriously."

"Please. Might I have the names of the current batch?"

"I'm seeing only four just now. Dr. Wangermeier, whom you know, Tony von Phul, Harry Benson, John Folck, Peter Ploog, and your cousin Duncan."

"That's six."

Sassy giggled as she rang the bell pull. "I must ask Father to sue Mary Institute. I've never learned my numbers."

"Thank you. I apologize for interrupting your beauty sleep. I'll go."

"But now that I'm awake, you must stay and chat."

"Really, I ought to leave. I am to blame for disturbing you."

"I won't hear of your going."

Sassy could talk a bull into giving milk. She talked Jemmy into staying for breakfast of something brand new called Purina Wheat from Ralston—"Where purity is paramount." Jemmy thought it odd—like hominy grits with sugar on top. Sassy talked and talked—without telling Jemmy anything of significance.

Fortified with three breakfasts, Jemmy should have been ready for anything. She wasn't.

The young maid escorted her to the door. From time to time the girl dabbed at a fresh cut on her face. When Jemmy stared at it, she said, "Tripped on the stair carpet, if you must know."

Jemmy thought it more likely to be the imprint of a diamond ring applied with the back of Mrs. Patterson's hand.

When the maid opened the door for Jemmy to leave, both girls were startled to see a man on the steps brushing snow from his coat. Tony von Phul tipped his hat. "Miss McBustle, pleased to see you again." He dumped his greatcoat, walking stick, scarf, gloves, and hat in the maid's arms without another word. Whistling, he breezed past the pair and headed straight for the conservatory.

Jemmy had to think fast if she wanted to stay and snoop. She launched herself into a phony coughing fit—an acting job worthy of the divine Sarah Bernhardt herself. *"Hacgh, hacgh, hacgh."*

The maid pounded her on the back with Tony's walking stick—a little too hard for comfort.

Jemmy took to wheezing in what she hoped resembled an attack of asthma. The maid dropped von Phul's appurtenances on the hall-tree seat. (Well, the hat stayed there. Everything else hit the floor.)

She led Jemmy to a chair and plunked her down. "You just stay here. I'll be back with a glass of water before you can say 'Jack Sprat.' "

The charade worked better than Jemmy could have hoped. As soon as the maid was out of sight, she raced back to spy on Tony and Mrs. P.

Even with a bad ear she could hear them arguing in the conservatory.

Tony said, "You can't keep me from seeing your daughter. If necessary I'll tell her the truth."

"I thought you cared about me. How foolish I must seem."

"I do care about you. There's no reason why we shouldn't go on as we have been."

"You fill me with disgust. Trying to seduce mother and

daughter at the same time."

" 'Trying?' Is that really the correct word?"

The maid's footsteps in the hall stopped Jemmy's snooping. She raced back to the chair and covered her mouth with her hanky.

"A sip of water to soothe your throat, and you'll be all better."

Jemmy drank the water. "Thank you. You've been most kind."

"Glad to help. I have an uncle who wheezes like that. Some kind of disease I can't say proper. Starts with an *A* I think. Coughing fits make him feel poorly for hours—sometimes days. You just rest yourself as long as you want. I have chores to do, but even the missus wouldn't push a croup sufferer out of doors after such a bout as you had on such a day as today."

When the sound of the girl's steps faded, Jemmy raced back to the conservatory door. No sound at all. What had happened? Was one of the two unconscious on the floor?

Jemmy ventured a peek—then closed the door as her face reddened.

CHAPTER TWELVE

November 22, 1898

She'd seen just a glimpse, but that was enough. It didn't take a genius to know what was going on. A woman with her eyes closed and her back snug up against a man did not want to be rescued. Her pink silk wrapper puddled around the lady's feet as her hands stretched upward to caress Tony's head. Jemmy would not soon forget the image of Tony von Phul's hands on Mrs. P.'s breasts. Clearly, no argument had erupted in the conservatory.

Jemmy mulled over the scene with Tony von Phul and Mrs. P. as she slipped out of the Patterson house. She shook her head to banish the sight. It stuck like mud on a shoe.

A chill wind and blowing snow forced her to set the vision aside while she looked at her notes. She recognized every name on Sassy's list of beaus except one—John Folck. *Why didn't I ask who this Folck fellow is? When will I think to ask the right questions before it's too late?*

She clicked her tongue at her lack of news reporter savvy.

Maybe Duncan would know the fellow. At any rate, it couldn't hurt to see Cousin Duncan. Jemmy's cousin was wild and unpredictable as a housefly in a bottle of smelling salts. But could Duncan be a murderer?

While in Cuba with American forces during the Spanish-American War, he did nothing but herd horses on and off the ship. At least that's what he told the family. Of course, he'd said those words in some heat, so Jemmy wasn't sure he actually meant them.

Two streetcar rides took her to Compton Heights and the grand home of warehouse owner Mr. Erwin McBustle. Unlike the barely housebroken maid at the Patterson home, the maid at the McBustle door knew how to treat guests. She smiled and bobbed her head, then helped Jemmy with her coat. "Please come in, Miss Jemima. I'll tell your aunt you're here."

Until that very moment, Jemmy had been so intent on her own designs she'd clean forgot that Aunt Delilah reigned over this little realm with iron fist in dyed-to-match kid gloves. There was simply no way to avoid visiting with her for at least an hour. And that would be before she could ask whether Duncan was even on the premises.

Auntie Dee burst forth from the drawing room with whirlwind energy. "My dear Jemima, just the person I want to see. How did you know?"

She linked her arm through Jemmy's and walked her toward the drawing room door. Over her shoulder she tossed orders to the maid. "Tea and some of those little spice cakes with the butter cream frosting." She turned to Jemmy. "Unless you'd rather have hot chocolate."

"Yes, cocoa would make a nice change."

"Tell cook we'll have hot chocolate and cream cakes. Now come in and let me show you what I've been doing."

The pair entered Auntie Dee's personal haven—her drawing room—Jemmy's favorite room in the entire world. She warmed her hands at an old-fashioned open fireplace. Most homes had closed in their drafty fireplaces with iron cheaters that burned coal. The result was cheaper, safer, less sooty, and infinitely warmer.

But Auntie Dee refused to let mere common sense ruin the cheery nook where she spent her mornings writing letters, giving orders, and making plans. A merry fire—a cozy wood fire—danced under a fireplace mantel of pale-pink marble.

The room took its character from that fireplace. Sky-blue velvet drapes framed three grand windows. White furniture with gilded curlicues and lion-paw legs graced the pink Aubusson carpet. Firelight glinted off blue fretwork painted on white porcelain tiles framing the fireplace.

With an index finger, Jemmy traced the blue lines on one of the tiles—girls in pointed caps skating on canals.

Auntie Dee chuckled. "How many times have I seen you as a little girl touch those tiles with a faraway look in your eyes—dreaming of storybook places and exotic people? And such questions: 'Auntie Dee, what's it like to wear wooden shoes? Those windmills look like houses. Do people live in them?' " Auntie Dee led Jemmy to a dainty lady's desk and held up a handsome brochure from the Cunard line.

Jemmy was far from hungry, but she couldn't resist nibbling a spice cake. She breathed in the fragrance of hot chocolate as she warmed her hands on the cup. "Your dreams are about to come true. Next spring, we set off on a great adventure—a grand tour of Europe. Who knows? You may find a prince charming to whisk you away to his palace."

How many times had Jemmy told Auntie Dee she longed to see the wonders of the world in person? Her wishes were about to come true, but too late. During her eighteenth year, the last thing she wanted to do was leave St. Louis. She'd staked her job at the *Illuminator*—her one chance for independence—on success as a journalist.

Once again that old quandary tugged her in two directions. *What do I really crave: a life of leisure as a "true woman" in a man's world, or the exhilarating chance to choose my own path in life?*

But what a temptation Auntie Dee offered! A grand tour of

Europe—what could be more captivating? How Jemmy had envied the rich girls at Mary Institute as they chatted away about gondolas on the canals of Venice and young lovers kissing on the banks of the Seine. Every one of them expected to make a grand tour—everyone except Jemmy, the pauper girl whose mother ran a boardinghouse.

Auntie Dee gushed about the upcoming trip. "I wish I could telephone my sister Tilly, but a letter will have to do. She's chaperoning a young girl on her way to join her father in New York City. The girl has been living with her grandmother here in St. Louis and attending Mary Institute. Her mother died in the oddest way. Seems she fell asleep under a sweet gum tree, and a black widow spider crawled in her ear."

"Spider venom must be a painful way to die."

"Oh, no, the spider didn't kill her. The spider was found in her ear—dead. The coroner couldn't find a bite mark, though."

"Then what killed her?"

"From various evidence, the coroner concluded that a strange series of events led to the woman's death. Waking up with a creepy-crawly in her ear set her off in a tizzy. She hopped up and started banging her ear with her hand. Sadly she lost her balance and hit her head on the sweet gum tree and knocked herself out."

"And that's what killed her?"

"No. I find it hard to believe, but the judge at the coroner's inquest swears this is what happened: The woman fell nose first into a little puddle of water held in a girdled root of the sweet gum tree and drowned. Drowned in less than a cup of water."

"How strange."

"There's a moral in that story, which we all must remember."

"What's that, Auntie Dee?"

"No matter what the crisis, stay calm. Panic imperils one's very life."

"An amazing story."

"Left her poor little daughter half an orphan. After the mother died, the father moved to New York. Needed a change of scene, I suppose. And we all know the girl's grandmother was better equipped to rear the child. But the girl fell in with bad company and became quite impossible to deal with.

"At length the grandmother despaired of being the girl's guardian. Called her the wild child of Borneo. Though, in fact, I'm quite certain the girl had never been to Borneo. I must confess I don't even know where Borneo is—nor does the grandmother, I'll warrant you that.

"Even my sister Tilly could not succeed in curbing the girl's recklessness. Why, the child began pulling out her own hair. The very idea. Bald girls attract few suitors. That you can believe.

"The upshot is the grandmother consulted Tilly, who suggested the girl be sent to her father. So, naturally, my dear sister was chosen to accompany her. You must agree no one in the entire United States can equal Turaluralura Snodderly when it comes to perfection in a chaperone.

"Well, a girl needs the influence of a father with a strong hand. Your Uncle Erwin and I are pleased to provide you with that familial care and concern. And we have arrived at the perfect solution to your mother's problem. Are you not delighted at the prospect of seeing the world next spring?"

Jemmy's mind raced from one bad idea to the next. She had to stop this nonsense, but nothing came—not even a lie. She offered a feeble nod.

"Too overcome with joy for words. Oh, my sweet niece. Won't we have the loveliest time?" In a fit of euphoria, Auntie Dee embraced Jemmy, then hustled her to the settee. For the next two hours Auntie described the places they would visit and the pleasures of a sea cruise on a fine steamship.

"How wonderful to return to those splendid cities and

romantic countries! My own tour was marred by civil disturbances in some places, but now I hear all is calm on the continent. You needn't worry about revolutions and such. At last I will be able to enjoy Paris with the leisurely stay I always desired. We had to leave abruptly, you know, or we would have been caught in the Siege of Paris.

"That insane Napoleon the Third! Losing the Franco-Prussian War, which he himself started. Ah well, we shall make up for it all on this magnificent trip."

Yes, Jemmy longed to go on the grand tour. But leaving for six months or longer would cost her the reporter's job at the *Illuminator*—and Hal's, too. *What am I to do?*

Over lunch of celery root soup and chopped-chicken-livers-mixed-with-mayonnaise sandwiches, she thought of one even more compelling reason not to go. Auntie Dee and Duncan would be exciting traveling companions. However, her own roommate would be the world's strictest chaperone.

Miss Turaluralura Snodderly, called "Aunt Tilly Lilly" behind her back, would insist on punctilious propriety. With her around, Jemmy would spend more time changing clothes and sitting still than she would enjoying the sights.

Jemmy knew what to expect from personal experience. Aunt Tilly Lilly had been prevailed upon to oversee Jemmy on a trip to Sedalia to interview members of Buffalo Bill's Wild West and Congress of Rough Riders of the World. Jemmy spent a good deal of time sneaking away or inventing excuses for sneaking away.

Subterfuge in Sedalia had been easy. Aunt Tilly Lilly had been preoccupied with tidying up the errant Koock household and reining in the unruly Koock husband and children. Besides, the Sedalia trip was only for one week.

A six-month trip with herself as the only wayward puppy under the thumb of the Caligula of chaperones sent chills through Jemmy's frame.

"Are you cold, my dear? I'll send Katy for a shawl."

"Don't bother, Auntie. I'm not cold. Someone walked over my grave, that's all."

"I suppose you're wondering why I invited that peculiar little fellow to escort you to the play, since he has no more property than a scarecrow. I do apologize. Dr. Wangermeier took pity on the poor man. I can see why. He must be so starved for companionship and entertainment, he'd gladly go to the opening of a pickle jar."

As she speared a sweet gherkin with an ornate pickle fork, Jemmy asked, "Isn't Cousin Duncan joining us for lunch?"

"No, my dear. These days he's off early in the morning doing heaven knows what. He rarely returns until past midnight. I scarcely see him at all since he returned from the war. Tell no one, but that's the main reason I want to go on this tour. Perhaps if he gets away for a time, he'll gain perspective and come home to his rightful place and join your uncle in the business he'll one day inherit."

Jemmy left the pickle on her plate untouched and tried to lean back in her chair. She couldn't—not without pain. Her midsection felt like a knockwurst about to burst its casing. Her corset squeezed her middle until she could barely breathe. *That's what comes from eating three breakfasts and a lunch—not to mention hot chocolate and cream cakes.*

Jemmy's head shot up. She was expected for another lunch at one o'clock. With an inward moan, she rose. "Auntie Dee, I hope you can forgive me for rushing away in the middle of your lovely lunch. I was so enjoying our plans, I nearly forgot I have an appointment at one. Please excuse me."

"Of course, my dear. You must attend to your employment for the time being. You wouldn't want to leave any job with a stain for unreliability upon your reputation. The end of the year is quite soon enough to resign your post. We'd still have ample time to organize our wardrobes."

"Thank you for being so understanding." Jemmy knew she should offer some word of caution. She had no intention of touring Europe with Auntie Dee, but she could not bring herself to offer the slightest hint. After all, Auntie Dee had entered upon a crusade to save Jemmy from herself. *No wonder she spent so much time looking at my head. In all likelihood, she was examining it for spots where I'd yanked the hair out by the roots like the wild child of Borneo.*

A vision of herself with a dozen silver-dollar-sized bald spots in her auburn hair made Jemmy roll her eyes. *Thank heavens in a handbag. My luncheon date with Tom Loker means I can put off for now telling her I'm not going to Europe. I am such a coward.*

Jemmy slinked away with Auntie Dee still sipping coffee in the dining room.

CHAPTER THIRTEEN

November 22, 1898

Three streetcar rides later Jemmy climbed the steps under the limestone clock tower of mammoth Union Station. Less than five years old, the enormous and elegantly grand St. Louis railroad depot boasted luxury service as its standard. Four hundred passenger trains arrived and departed every day at the world's largest rail terminal. Union Station was just one more reason city boosters called St. Louis "the next greatest city in America."

At the door of the Terminal Restaurant, Jemmy started to ask for the table of—Then she remembered. She forgot to look up his real name on her theatre program. Luck smiled on her. Tom Loker had been watching and was even now bounding across the restaurant to claim his luncheon guest.

"Miss McBustle, I'm delighted to see you."

"I apologize for being late. My whole morning has been a rush to catch up with myself."

"It's the prerogative of a lovely coquette to keep a man waiting."

"I assure you, I'm not a coquette, nor would I keep a man waiting had I a choice."

"I meant no offense. Please don't be cross with me. I'm looking forward to a pleasant meal in your company."

Their table sat in a cozy corner under a painting of a Missouri-Kansas-Texas passenger train. Ladies' heads turned in their direction as they wended their way across the restaurant. Not until then did Jemmy realize the women were gawking at her escort. And why not? He was eye-poppingly handsome.

That day he wore a brown pinstripe suit with a tan silk foulard tie. From his watch fob dangled a golden comedy-tragedy mask. An electric light in a sconce overhead brought out the golden highlights in his warm, brown eyes. His dark-blond hair refused to be corralled by pomade. It swooped in waves that ended in soft curls at forehead and neckline. Tom Loker (whose name she still did not remember) was the living definition of "matinee idol."

"How wise you are, Miss McBustle, in your choice of apparel. The plain cut of your attire is the perfect choice to show your comely features to best advantage."

Realizing how much she was envied by every female in the place should have made Jemmy bask in her triumph—or at least feel a little smug. Instead, the attention made her edgy as a mouse with his tail in a trap. *What if Handsome Harry and the mystery woman should turn up? Harry would surely notice Legree-Loker and come over to chat with the man who shares his dressing room.*

At least she could do one thing—finagle a way to get Tom Loker's back to the room while she had an open view to scout out newcomers. Naturally, Loker-Legree had taken the wall seat so he could spot Jemmy when she arrived.

"I know it's an imposition, but would you mind if I took the chair by the wall? The ladies seem so intent upon watching you I fear for their digestion—and mine. I think they'll be less inclined to stare if you turn your back to them."

He replied with a dazzling smile and a nod to the server. The reorganization meant extra trouble for the waitress. She had to rearrange the china and silver. Tom Loker didn't seem upset by Jemmy's quirks—merely amused. The smile playing around his mouth made him even more winsome.

"Do you flatter all your gentlemen friends so charmingly?"

"I assure you, I never flatter gentlemen. I wouldn't know how." Her obvious sincerity flattered him still more. He became even more attentive—and she became more alarmed.

Jemmy's nervousness created chaos before she even sat down. As she pulled off her gloves, one stuck until she tugged harder. The glove popped off with a snick and smacked her water goblet.

Sloshing water, the glass stood on the very brink of crashing over on its side. Fortunately, Tom was just as quick with his hands as he was with his compliments. He steadied the glass with his right hand and seated Jemmy with his left at the same time. His manual and mental dexterity seemed effortless—as though he expected to juggle stemware and ladies at every meal.

He motioned to the waitress and said, "The water mussed your sleeve, Miss McBustle."

"Please don't bother. After wading through a half a foot of snow, I'm used to a little damp."

The waitress laid a folded napkin over the wet spot on the tablecloth and offered a second to Jemmy.

As she dabbed at her sleeve, Jemmy's elbow caught the tines of a fork and popped it into an airborne cartwheel. With a graceful swoop, Loker-Legree caught the wayward utensil by the handle before it hit the floor and returned it to its proper place without even looking at the fickle fork.

"That's twice you've rescued me from myself in as many minutes."

"Rescuing you is both pleasure and honor, Miss McBustle. May I say how gratified I am you came to our engagement, despite inclement weather."

For the rest of the meal Jemmy managed to keep up her end of the conversation even though her mind was elsewhere. Her absent-mindedness revealed itself in physical ways. Her menu brushed the half-full water glass. It would have flopped over yet again if Tom had not saved it from flooding the table a second time.

Jemmy seemed to be all angles and elbows. When the waitress brought the potato soup, Jemmy's fist shot out as if drawn to it by magnets. Before her hand could reach the tray, Tom caught Jemmy's wrist and lowered it to the table while the waitress swayed her tray until the soup stopped splashing.

Jemmy tried to make a joke of her bumbling manners. "Clever of you to order cream soup. Not a drop spilled." When she tipped her plate of roast chicken, it would surely have landed in her lap if his hand had not shot forward to hold it down.

"You must think me clumsier than a camel on ice skates."

"I find you quite beguiling, Miss McBustle. If I may say so, everything you do surprises and delights me."

"Even my inability to successfully negotiate a spoonful of soup or a sip of water?"

"I believe your current difficulties are nothing more than the product of excitement. Since I consider myself the reason for the excitement, how could I be anything but disarmed and enchanted?"

Jemmy didn't know what to say to that, so she took another mouthful of chicken and found herself in considerable discomfort.

"Is something wrong, Miss McBustle?"

"I find myself unable to eat this lovely luncheon. My stomach seems to have soured." In fact, Jemmy was feeling the effects of three breakfasts, two lunches and morning cocoa with cream cakes. Her excess of food strained so against her corset that she could barely breathe. Indeed, she was sliding into a faint when the unthinkable happened. Her corset blew up.

Well, it didn't exactly blow up; it blew out. A lace must have broken. Jemmy could breathe again. But at what cost? That corset had kept her waist a good four inches smaller than her actual waist size—the wasp-waist size her seamstress used to fit her wardrobe. She could feel her flesh pushing against the seams of her blouse. It would only be a matter of time before the seams burst. Her jacket would follow suit. If Jemmy didn't make speedy repairs, she'd soon look like a pillow shredded by cats.

"Please excuse me. I must attend to my—Oh." Jemmy bent forward as one seam gave way with a loud *rrrrippppp*.

Tom was on his feet pulling out her chair, supporting her by the arm and extricating her foot from the edge of the tablecloth before it yanked the entire meal off the table.

"No, you mustn't come with me. Perhaps if you'd get the waitress . . ."

"I quite understand." He handed Jemmy over to the waitress with the words, "Return to me as soon as you've . . . as soon as you're feeling better."

The server escorted Jemmy to the ladies' lounge and turned her over to the attendant, a roly-poly gnome of a woman in black dress and white pinafore. She had ruddy cheeks and a nose to match. In red velvet she would have looked the perfect Mrs. Santa Claus.

The jolly woman kept up a steady stream of comforting talk as she helped Jemmy out of her jacket and blouse. "Don't think a thing about it, dearie. Young ladies in over-tight corsets are two-a-penny. At least three come to me for help every day."

The pudgy dame draped a Turkish towel around Jemmy's shoulders. "Here's the problem, dearie." She helped Jemmy unhook her corset enough to slide the laces in the back around to Jemmy's front.

"I don't have spare laces, so you'll need to make repairs on the ones you have." She deftly undid the bows and loosened all the lacings. "There now. Try threading the torn ends through the eyelets. Then tie a good knot, and hope it will hold until you can replace the laces. Meantime, I'll see what I can do with this seam."

The woman put on her glasses and sat on a stool with her sewing basket on her lap. "Ah. You're in luck. The material held. A few stitches, and the garment will be right as rain on a train."

In moments, she had finished the blouse and was ready to return it to Jemmy—after one small adjustment. As the little woman loosened Jemmy's newly knotted laces, she said, "I'll not ask you to pull in your breath. You'd do well to let your middle be a bit broader. Avoid embarrassment in public. Much healthier, too. I know a gal about your age fractured a rib. The broken end stabbed right through her lung. Two days later the poor child died—died from over-tight laces."

As the little woman helped Jemmy into her blouse, she said, "There now. The blouse is a little snug, but the material is strong. I think it will hold even with a slack corset."

To show her gratitude Jemmy tipped the lady a dime, even though a nickel would have been enough. "Wait, dearie." The woman pinned a sprig of yellow button mums to Jemmy's lapel. "Just the thing to pretty up your jacket—and keep folks eyes away from the waist, which is a bit crowded in appearance."

Jemmy walked out of the lounge and stopped dead in her tracks. *Who should be walking toward the grand lobby but Handsome Harry Benson?* All thoughts of Loker-Legree and her second lunch forgotten, she followed Harry, unnoticed, in the crowd of people moving to and fro.

He stopped under the glowing globes of a light stand and lit a cigarette. From time to time he looked at his pocket watch. Jemmy retrieved a discarded newspaper from a wire waste paper basket and hid behind it. A nasty interruption halted her alternate reading and peering over her paper at Handsome Harry.

"Just so. If it isn't my old classmate Jemima McBustle.

Perhaps I should call you 'Ann O'Nimity.' What are you doing here at Union Station?"

"Pervia, I hardly recognized you under your veil."

At Mary Institute, Pervia Benigas was one of the most snobbish rich girls—not one of Jemmy's favorites.

Jemmy always thought the girl was jealous of Jemmy's looks, because Pervia was not overly attractive. She was too tall—at least five feet, ten inches—and much too haughty, with her close-set eyes and prissy bow mouth. Jemmy thought Pervia should stick a policeman's whistle between those lips. Her long arms would look perfect directing traffic at the corner of Washington Avenue and Sixth Street.

"Are you off for another of your great adventures as a newspaperwoman?" She said the word *great* as though she wanted to scrape the word off her tongue with a trowel.

A clever lie flew from Jemmy's mouth. "No. I've been sent to meet the train. My Aunt Tilly was supposed to be here earlier this afternoon, but she failed to arrive. She's returning from New York. Perhaps she missed her connection. I thought I'd wait for the next train."

"I've always had such fun telling people I know the famous Ann O'Nimity, though I must admit, I can never keep a straight face when I say the name. With such a wealth of wonderful pseudonyms, why did you choose that one?"

Jemmy stiffened. "My editor thought it artful and attention getting."

"Just so. I suppose it is that. It certainly makes for a few minutes of fun at the dinner table."

Jemmy tried not to sound snide. "I do hope you are leaving St. Louis. Please tell me the particulars. I'll write it up for the society page."

"No, not today. I have important business to attend before I could possibly leave town."

"Perhaps you should be seeing to it, then."

"Just so. I hope your aunt comes in on the next train."

"If she doesn't appear today, perhaps she'll arrive tomorrow."

"Goodbye, Miss Ann O'Nimity. Pleased to see you again."

"Likewise, I'm sure. Goodbye, Miss Beni-gassss."

Pervia buttoned the frog closures on her fur cloak and sallied out the main entrance.

Jemmy wondered why Pervia was at the station. Did she see someone off? Had she come to meet someone who didn't show? *Perhaps she made up that excuse on the spot like I did? Heavens in a handbag! I didn't even think to ask her why she was in Union Station.*

Still annoyed by her lack of reporter intuition, Jemmy moved behind a light standard so as to better hide from Handsome Harry.

At half past three, he took slow steps toward the main entrance with a scowl on his face. Jemmy followed him out into the snow and up Market Street. Apparently, the mystery lady had failed to appear. When he boarded an eastbound streetcar, Jemmy returned to the station.

Back at the Terminal Restaurant, she found herself locked out. A sign announced the restaurant would re-open at five p.m. Loker-Legree was nowhere in sight.

CHAPTER FOURTEEN

November 22, 1898
Some journalist I am. I never even found out Tom's real name. After the shameful way I've treated him, he'll probably never speak to me again.

Her thoughts bounced back and forth between regret over one Loker-Legree and curiosity about the other. *I wonder why Harry's mystery woman didn't appear—and who she is.*

In their dressing room at the Palace Theatre, Handsome Harry and the other Tom Loker will both curse the cruelty of women.

A few minutes before four o'clock in the afternoon, Jemmy stepped off the Chouteau trolley and waded toward St. Ange. Still wrapped in thought, she heard a familiar voice. A man called out, "Jemima McBustle, come with us. We're going sledding."

The voice came from one of Jemmy's rejected beaus, Peter Ploog. Jemmy rounded on him with choice words on her lips. "Peter Ploog, I'm a serious newspaperwoman. I have no time for childish—"

Just then another voice chimed in, "Don't be a luddy-dud, Jemmy. We're going to the big mound." That musical lilt belonged to none other than Sassy Patterson.

Soon a chorus of shouts came from the sleigh. "We have sleds and dishpans. It will be great fun."

"Come on, Jemmy, before we lose the light."

"We'll have a jolly time."

"Get in the sleigh, Jemima. Stop dawdling."

"Don't make me kidnap you."

Some eight or nine people of Jemmy's acquaintance hollered from the sleigh, urging her to join them.

That very day Sassy had named Peter Ploog as one of her suitors. *I may not have a better time to observe just how deep Peter's devotion might go. Peter is a rounder and a cad, but is he capable of murdering Quisenberry Sproat?*

A tall fellow in a tweed overcoat whisked Sassy and another girl out of the sleigh. He unceremoniously plunked the girl—Jemmy's sister Randy—atop the pile of people in the back seat. His stratagem became clear when he boosted Jemmy up to sit next to Peter Ploog, the driver. He then lifted Sassy aboard as he slid under her. *How very neatly he managed to have me sit beside Peter and to fill his own lap with Sassy.*

Jemmy was not surprised at how deftly he managed to please himself at Peter's expense. The man in tweed was her clever cousin, Duncan McBustle.

At that moment, Sassy looked more beautiful than ever in a cranberry wool cape lined with arctic fox. The hood framed her pretty face, while the cold brought out the roses in her cheeks.

Peter's face turned redder than Sassy's roses, somewhere in the vicinity of red-hot poker points. He muttered under his breath, "If he keeps up such shenanigans, I may have to kill your cousin. Would the family miss him?"

"Indeed they would. My Auntie Dee and Uncle Erwin would never rest until they put a rope 'round your neck. At very least, they would make sure you stayed tucked up in the Jefferson City penitentiary until you died of old age."

"Would you come to visit?"

"No."

"Would Sassy?"

"I doubt she'd have time. So many parties . . . so many male acquaintances."

He sighed. "I bet you'd testify against me at my trial."

"Naturally. Duncan is family."

"Guess I'll have to find another way."

Peter smacked his reins on the rumps of two well-matched bays, and the sleigh lurched forward in a jangle of bells. The group in back tittered and chatted away in festive tones, but Peter said not another word on the way to the big mound. He glanced at Duncan and Sassy every time one of them giggled. The motion put Jemmy in mind of a turnstile at the fair.

Every time his head jerked toward Duncan and Sassy, Peter's jaw muscles twitched with the effort of keeping his mouth shut. His lips drew a fine pink line across his face as he urged the horses into their fastest trot.

Jemmy felt sorry for him. That surprised her. She'd once had a crush on him, but that was before she'd seen him in his true element—drunk in his unmentionables.

From that time on, she'd expected to feel nothing but contempt for him. She'd shown him only a nose in the air and the back of her hat ever since. She'd caught him nearly naked in scandalous circumstances at a shady establishment. And yet, Ploog pretended to be the perfect suitor for Mrs. McBustle's daughter. *Flirting with me at Sunday school, no less!*

Peter Ploog presented a false face to the world. Perhaps he did have a homicidal as well as an unsavory nature. At that moment, he glowered at Duncan with a murderous eye.

The big mound was one of the few left standing. Even so, locals called St. Louis "Mound City" from time to time. The area along the Mississippi had once been home to dozens of heaps of earth piled up by prosperous American aboriginals two thousand years earlier. Most had been leveled to make way for warehouses and street beds. No one had ever discovered why the Indians built them or what the hills signified, but they made for dandy sledding.

Jemmy set herself to take special notice of the trip. An article called "Sledding on the Big Mound" might take a little tarnish off her reputation at the *Illuminator*. Of course, nothing was likely to endear her to Editor-in-Chief Suetonius Hamm.

Many considered the best sledding place in St. Louis to be the big hill in Forest Park. It had one drawback, though. Too vigorous a ride could shoot a sled out onto a frozen pond—or into its icy water.

Jemmy preferred the Big Mound. One side had a gentle slope for easy climbing. Several parties had already worn a ladder in the snow while dragging their sleds. The top was the ideal place to launch out in a dishpan or on a sled with a pleasant companion.

Peter had to tie the horses to a fence and so was last up the hill. Ploog's party trudged up the track behind Duncan, who pulled a sled with one hand and Sassy with the other. When Jemmy reached the top, all she could see of the pair was the back of a tweed coat behind bits of red cloak as they flew down the hill.

Jemmy had no time to enjoy the vista. Peter slapped down his sled and hustled her on it. Before she'd found her balance, he leaped on board, and they were careening down the hillside.

They didn't get far. Jemmy tried to gain her balance by grabbing whatever her fingers could find. Her hand fell upon one end of the steering bar. As she pulled hard to right herself, the sled veered sharply to the left, heeled over, tumbled the pair, and they went rolling down the hillside.

At the bottom of the mound, Jemmy and Peter dusted globs of snow from their clothes. From the top of the hill, a chorus of laughs, whistles, and applause mocked the mishap. When Peter raised his hand—probably to make an obscene gesture, Jemmy grabbed it and vigorously dusted gouts of snow from his sleeve.

On the way back up the snow ladder, Peter hissed, "Why on earth did you make us crash?"

"Why on earth didn't you give me time to get settled on the sled? I was half on and half off."

"So now it's my fault, I suppose."

"That's what you suppose, and that's what I suppose."

"It made me look stupid."

"You made you look stupid."

"I'd like to take you over my knee and spank you for making us crash."

"Then you would really look stupid."

"How so?"

"Cousin Duncan would put you over his knee. I think he'd quite enjoy defending my honor. And you know he's capable of manhandling you."

"Are you calling me less of a man than Duncan?"

"What I'm saying is that he is taller, heavier, and has the training of a soldier. How do you think you would fare?"

"I guess I'll leave the spanking for another day. But I'll thank you to stay off my sled."

"Although I'd rather go down the hill in a tin bucket, I think we'd best stick together for at least a run or two."

"Why are you saying something so pea-brained?"

"You heard them jeer and clap when we fell. If we don't at least pretend to take the spill as part of the fun, they'll tease us until even the very old and very decrepit cows come home."

"I suppose you're right."

"And this time, don't push off until I tell you I'm ready."

Peter and Jemmy's arrival at the top met with more clapping and whistling. Jemmy dropped a curtsy and Peter followed her lead by making a sweeping bow with his cap. That put an end to the jibes. Peter made a great show of locating a swath of fresh snow. He helped Jemmy onto the sled with all the decorum and ceremony his first attempt lacked.

As they breezed down the hill, Jemmy thought this giddy slide would be exhilarating fun—if someone other than Peter Ploog were sitting snug against her shoulders. *Oh, well, even a murder suspect can be useful as a back warmer.*

After a second successful run and climb to the top, Peter called over his shoulder to Jemmy. "Find a different sled." He sprinted to Sassy's side. She was, for the moment, unattended.

Duncan was retying a frayed knot on one side of his sled's steering bar. Good thing his back was turned. He didn't notice Peter stealing Sassy away and lifting her onto his sled. The pair glided lightly over the edge.

With a quizzical look on his face, Duncan said, "Ploog better watch himself. Shooting dice with the devil can be hard on the pocketbook and the knees."

Jemmy hoped her response struck Duncan as playful. "I had no idea my cousin was a devil. What will Auntie Dee and Uncle Erwin say when I tell them their son is Satan himself?"

"I'm not the devil, cuz. Devils wear red—or didn't you know?" He nodded toward Peter and Sassy, who were lingering at the bottom.

"So, Sassy's the devil. I wonder where she keeps those devil dice."

Duncan burst out laughing. "I'm sure you'll figure out where all ladies keep their devil dice when you're married—if not sooner."

Jemmy didn't quite know what to make of that.

Duncan held out his hand. "Come on, cuz. Fly down the hill with me."

As they zoomed down the hill, Jemmy noticed they weren't taking a straight line. Duncan veered the sled to the left. He engineered a direct path toward Peter and Sassy.

"Stop steering toward them. Duncan . . . Duncan! You're going to run them over. Stop!"

At what seemed the last possible moment, Duncan pulled the sled rope hard to the right. They missed Peter but managed to cover his shoes with snow.

"Sorry, Old Dewdrop. Didn't mean to freeze your feet." Duncan's lopsided grin denied his words of apology.

"Tell lies often, Old Dewdrop?" Peter sounded more disgusted than angry at the insult.

"Why, Dewdrop, you surely aren't accusing me of trying to run you down."

"Of course not. If you deliberately tried to assault me with your sled, you'd have to answer to the police. But I suppose a man of your character is used to answering to the authorities."

Duncan's grin mutated into a scowl. Jemmy half expected him to hit Peter and start a bout of fisticuffs then and there. But the grin returned. "At least I'm fully dressed on such occasions. Too bad you can't say the same."

Peter frowned and took a step forward. Duncan braced himself. The pair looked for all the world as if they were about to exchange blows. But then Peter ducked down to grab a handful of snow. He flung it in Duncan's face.

Duncan grabbed a fistful of snow while simultaneously grabbing Peter's arm. Duncan spun the smaller man around and crammed his handful of snow down Peter's collar.

Duncan raised his foot as if to give Ploog a swift kick in the keister. He must have thought better of it. His next move was to pick Ploog up under the armpits, swing him in a circle, and plop him down in a snowdrift.

When Peter saw himself stuffed into a pile of ammunition, he did the only logical thing—lobbed a snowball at the enemy. He missed Duncan. He hit Jemmy.

Duncan grabbed Jemmy and ducked behind a pile of snow. Duncan and Peter began hurling snowballs at each other. At first, each waited for the other to pop a head up over their snow forts.

Not a single one hit the target. Efforts on both sides were too little, too late. Both sides lobbed snowballs without hitting their targets until Jemmy caught Peter unawares. She splatted him a good one right in the face.

He yelled, "I'll get you for that."

Duncan tugged at Jemmy's skirt. "Get down, Jemmy. Make snowballs as fast as you can." The snowball fight was leading up to its big climax.

Big climax was right. By now, the whole Ploog sledding party—including several people they didn't even know—had chosen up sides. The players massed hundreds of snowballs. Both armies poised in readiness.

Duncan waved his white handkerchief.

Ploog called out, "Surrendering without a fight?"

"Joke while you can, Old Dewdrop."

"Why did you run up the white flag?"

"Protocol. Generals are supposed to meet beforehand to define the rules of engagement. Come out to the center to parlay."

"Truce until we return to the trenches?"

"Exactly. Armies on both sides must not exchange fire until commanders return to their forts."

The pair walked to the center to weigh important considerations. Duncan began with, "We must speak loud enough for all to hear."

"Agreed."

"Duration?"

"Five minutes, or until all ammunition is spent."

"In the event of real casualties?"

"All hostilities cease until the wounded are attended."

"Illegal actions?"

"Snow down the back. Rubbing someone's face in it. Pushing someone into the snow."

"Might we say this? No personal contact—snowballs only."

"And no ice balls."

"Anything else?"

Peter leaned forward to speak into Duncan's ear. Duncan laughed. "I can't tell them that."

Peter laughed, too. "I can't think of any other rules."

The pair solemnly shook hands. Duncan said, "If we do meet again, why, we shall smile; if not, why, then, this parting was well made."

"If we do meet again, we'll smile indeed; if not, 'tis true this parting was well made."

Jemmy clucked her tongue. "What play-acting drivel. Butchering Shakespeare at a snowball fight."

With a military salute and a regimental about face, Duncan rejoined his team behind the snow pile.

Jemmy shook her head. "Misquoting *Julius Caesar.* I'm disappointed."

"My recitation was quite perfect. Ploog was the one who dropped a line. Cassius is supposed to say—"

Jemmy and Duncan had no more time to debate the matter. The battle royal had begun.

It started with a lob that dropped neatly onto Duncan's hat. "I'll have to teach Ploog some respect. He insulted my hat. I'll have you know this is a genuine Rough Rider hat—handed to me by the Assistant Secretary of the Navy himself. Teddy Roosevelt gave me this hat."

"Calm down, Duncan. You need a plan."

"And I suppose you have a plan."

"I do." Jemmy ignored the fact that her plans practically never ended the way she meant them to.

"Are you going to tell me, or should I wait until we're buried in snow."

"Find a way to distract them while Randy and I sneak around and catch them from behind. When they turn toward us, make a mad charge and pelt them down."

"A flanking maneuver. You're a good soldier." Duncan gave Jemmy a battlefield promotion. "Lt. Duncan McBustle hereby names you, Jemima Gormlaith Snodderly McBustle, sergeant of the Snowball Irregulars."

Jemmy saluted. "Sir, thank you, sir. I'll try to be worthy of your confidence."

"Carry on, soldier."

Jemmy whispered the plan to Randy while Duncan passed the word to the troops.

Jemmy and her sister kept low as they dodged behind bushes on the way to the enemy rear. Still-abundant crabapple and forsythia leaves gave them good cover. Green and brown peeked out in contrast to the white of the unseasonably early snow.

Jemmy felt the cold bite into her lungs. The crisp air smelled of cedar instead of horse manure, its usual scent. Excitement made her head light.

For a change, Jemmy's plan worked the way it was supposed to. When they got in range, she and Randy started hurling snowballs at the enemy's undefended backs. When the Ploog platoon turned to counter, Duncan's division charged over their snow pile fort and pelted the enemy at a blistering pace.

Caught in a crossfire, the Ploog people did their best but finally gave up all resistance in the face of overwhelming forces.

Duncan's side won. Ploog surrendered. "You win, McBustle. To the winner go the spoils. What do you demand of us?"

With his usual magnanimity, Duncan said, "My demands are few. Prisoners of war: come with me to Baxter's for coffee—my treat." He produced a flask from his coat pocket. "I even have a

143

little something to take the chill off."

After a good five minutes spent whisking snow from coats and trousers, the group trouped back to Peter's sleigh.

As the fellows were tying sleds on the back shelf of the sleigh, Sassy Patterson put a damper on the gaiety. "Take me home, Peter."

"What? Now? Everyone is looking forward to warming up at Baxter's."

"I'm not. I'm chilled. Not to mention wet through and through. I must look a sight."

"With your hair in ringlets and the glow in your cheeks, you make Venus look a positive hag."

"I don't listen to flattery when my ears are freezing." Sassy's lips curved in a pretty pout. "Take me home, Pittypat-Peter."

Peter announced to the group, "Miss Patterson is feeling poorly. We'll have to take her home right away."

The festive party ended on a note of gloom.

Reaching her own home brought Jemmy still more woe.

CHAPTER FIFTEEN

November 22, 1898

"Goodbye, traitors. Just wait until our next snowball fight. I promise to get even." Peter laughed as he said it, but Jemmy heard a hard edge behind the banter. The sleigh jolted off through the slush on Chouteau Avenue.

"Better bring the Rough Riders," Randy hollered after them. "Wasn't that great fun? I love the snow."

"It's Tuesday afternoon. Why weren't you at your piano lesson?"

"Pure luck. I happened to be walking down Chouteau. Peter stopped and—Oh, damn."

"Mind your tongue. Mother would have a hissy fit if she heard you cuss."

"I left my music on the sleigh."

"I'm sure Peter will bring it by when he finds it."

"Then Mother will know I skipped my lesson to go sledding."

"She's sure to find out anyway. You know I won't lie to her—not to save you, anyhow."

"But you're no tattletale. You wouldn't speak of it at all, would you?" A note of pleading crept into Randy's voice.

"Heavens in a handbag. Even our hair is wet. She'll know we've been up to something."

Randy moaned and hiked her skirt to climb over a snow drift. At sixteen, she was two years younger than Jemmy. Randy was a born flirt, with springy, coppery curls. Two hours of frolicking in the snow made her locks of hair stick out from her green, wool sock cap in stringy clumps. The tresses formed lazy *S* shapes that looked like fat, red worms escaping from an oversized green apple.

Little sis stomped the snow off her feet on the welcome mat. "I'll probably have to clean the coal stoves for the next month, even though we just hired a maid to do the heavy work."

All thoughts of punishment vanished when they opened the front door at Bricktop. The hired domestic staff of the boardinghouse—all two of them—were in uproar.

Dora, the new maid, clomped down the hall at a dead run to meet them. "Miss Jemma, I'm glad you're here."

Jemmy had met Dora when she went undercover as a maid at Doctor Lyman's Sanitarium for the Care of Ladies Afflicted with Nervous Mental Disorders. Dora was a sturdy fireplug of a girl with a pimply face and hands made coarse and purply from lye soap and scrub water. When the sanitarium closed, Dora was thrown out of work. Luckily, that was about the same time Mother could afford to hire more help.

"Lower your voice. Do you want all the boarders to hear our business?"

Dora whispered, "I can't make head nor tail of what old krauthead wants."

She pointed toward the kitchen. Gerta the cook stood in the doorway holding a rolling pin. "See there. Makes like to beat me up with a rolling pin."

"Miss Jemmy, goot you here." Gerta pointed to Dora with the rolling pin. "I tell maid do tis, do tat, but she no do vat I say."

"Mother told you a thousand times: Dora doesn't understand German. You must speak to her in English."

"Ven I vork, I tink in Deutsche—can't make English so fast."

"Then you must slow down. Dora is a good worker. It's not her fault she can't understand you when you speak German."

Gerta muttered and waved the rolling pin as she turned back into the kitchen.

"Why isn't Mother out here to settle this hash?"

Dora crossed her arms. "You'd best see for yourself and not let the grass grow, doncha know. She's in the room behind the kitchen."

The thought sent a prickle of shock down Jemmy's back. "Are Merry and Nervy worse?"

"It's your mama that's worse."

"Don't tell me Mother is sick, too."

"No doubt about it. Your mama come down with the flu bug."

Jemmy tried to get her mind around this sorry business while she took off her coat and galoshes. With Thanksgiving just two days away, Mother had the flu. *Thank heavens in a handbag, the house has two strong and healthy workers—cook and maid—to keep the place going. Why can't the pair of them get along?*

Jemmy stuck a few pins in her damp hair and marched through the kitchen toward her interview with Mother.

She had walked as far as the maid's bedroom doorway when Mother called out, "Don't come in, Jemima. The air must be full of contagion."

"I'm sorry to hear you're ailing. Is there anything you want Randy and me to do?"

"Help Gerta prepare for Thursday. What will become of us if we're all down sick? You know the boarders may bring guests for Thanksgiving dinner. We're hard pressed to have everything ready when all of us are healthy."

"How many are coming?"

Nervy chimed in, "Six boarders with one guest each. That's twelve. Plus, we let Mrs. Hendershot have two more because she pays the most." Mrs. Hendershot was the Bricktop's best boarder. She paid a premium to occupy the finest room in the house, the front room with big windows overlooking St. Ange Street. She was brave and faithful, too. She remained when Grandma McBustle went on her shooting spree. All Mrs. H. asked was to be moved to a back room—one less likely to be riddled with bullets.

Jemmy raised her eyebrows. "I've never known Mrs. Hendershot to invite one person, let alone three."

Nervy chimed in. "She says her nephew from Brussels, Belgium, is coming with his wife and daughter."

"I was beginning to think her nephew didn't exist. She never gets mail from him. Did he cable?"

"I don't think so. Was Western Union here, Mother?"

"We've never had a telegram delivered for her so far as I know."

"Do you want Randy and me to play hostess?"

"No. Randy can eat with Gerta and Dora. You yourself must sit at the head, Jemmy. Plan on fifteen at the dining table. You'll have to bring in the extra leaves and use two tablecloths. I hate to put everything on your shoulders, Jemima dear."

"Gerta and Dora are very capable, so don't worry."

"God works in mysterious ways. Perhaps he's using this trial to guide you to your future."

"What do you mean?"

"I shan't be able to carve. You must step in."

"You want me to preside at Thanksgiving dinner and to carve the turkey?"

"Naturally. I'm sure you will present yourself as gracious lady of the house. It will be good training for the day when you manage your own household. You'll enjoy playing 'Mother,' won't you?"

Jemmy could think of few things she would like less—maybe getting her foot caught in a bear trap or falling off an elephant.

"Yes, Mother," she said.

That evening Bricktop erupted in a flurry of activity. After dinner, Gerta set to work chopping pumpkins and cooking down the flesh for pies. Randy collected the scarves and doilies that protected furniture from greasy heads. She soaked them in soda crystals, then scrubbed them on a washboard. The smell of Carnauba wax permeated the downstairs as Dora buffed the wooden floors.

Jemmy tackled the chimneys of the gas lamps. By the time she scrubbed the lampblack off her knuckles, they looked almost as purple as Dora's. She slathered her poor raw hands with bacon grease and stuck them in an old pair of mittens.

Exhausted, but confident everything would turn out well, except carving the turkey—and keeping her job at the *Illuminator*—Jemmy fell into bed.

In what seemed seconds later, she woke, dressed, and stumbled down to the kitchen. Dora and Gerta were already at cross purposes. Dora said, "I don't know what you're on about. I don't know nothin' 'bout fixin' flowers. I don't even know what an Eee-pern is."

"Hush up—both of you. The last thing sick people need is for you two to interrupt their wholesome sleep with your fussing."

"Miss Jemma, Gerta says she knows what flowers to buy at Soulard Market. She buys the same kinds every year, and your mama makes them into a fancy centerpiece. Well and good for your mama, but she wants me to fix them flowers nice. I can't. I cannot do it."

"How do you know until you try?"

"I have tried. I saw that Matron Pernelle do up flowers at the sanitarium. I picked me some wild flowers and had a go. Those stems had nary a petal left after me wrestlin' with 'em. Not a pretty sight, doncha know."

Jemmy adopted what she hoped was an authoritative voice.

"Dora, after you finish polishing the good silver, I want you to take the rugs out and beat them. Don't trouble yourself over flowers."

Dora shot a defiant look in the cook's direction. Gerta fisted a hand on one hip while she stirred oatmeal.

Jemmy said, "Gerta. Don't buy flowers. Buy well-shaped fruit. We'll leave the epergne off the table and use a mound of fruit in the crystal punch bowl instead. That will be pretty, and it won't take long to arrange. I'll fashion it myself.

"Now you both have important jobs to do. Please try to keep out of each other's hair. And, Gerta, slow down when you talk to Dora, and don't speak in Deutsche."

Jemmy left without breakfast—and without seeing that her orders were followed.

On the way to the *Illuminator*, she composed her sledding article in her mind.

Even with the multitude of mistakes her fingers made while typing her article, she finished in less than an hour. Most of the staff had not arrived. She eluded Miss Turnipseed and Editor Hamm—an added bonus. Leaving before Hal made an appearance had been the main reason she'd set off as early as the streetcars started rolling.

She promised herself to be nice to Hal when next she saw him. Perhaps she'd ask Sassy to pose for him. That would surely make up for her own bad treatment of partner and bodyguard.

She considered returning to Auntie Dee's to ask Duncan about John Folck. *Heavens in a handbag. I spent two hours with Duncan and never even thought to mention Folck a single time. Heavens in a handbag. I spent the same two hours with Sassy Patterson herself—with never a single thought about getting the story I need to keep my job.*

By the time she'd placed her sledding article on Miss Turnipseed's desk, she decided to wake up Sassy for the second day in a row.

She breathed relief along with coal-sooty air when she boarded the Washington Street trolley. The rest of the day was hers. She promised herself, "Today I discover who killed Quisenberry Sproat."

At the Patterson house, the untutored maid let her in. "I reckon you know Miss Isabel is still in bed, and I reckon you know how to get to her room."

Mrs. Patterson failed to fly out of the conservatory with arms open in welcome. Jemmy wondered idly whether Tony von Phul would make an appearance—or whether he already had—and . . . She shook her head to erase yesterday's shocking picture of Tony and Mrs. P. from her mind.

This morning Jemmy had better luck in finding the light switch in Sassy's darkened room. As usual, Sassy looked like Sleeping Beauty, with her dark curls gently framing her radiant face. She looked so lovely, Jemmy felt an overwhelming urge to smack her in the nose with a mud pie.

Since no mud pie came to hand, she settled for shaking Sassy's arm a little more roughly than was strictly necessary.

Sassy opened one eye. "Are you here again, or am I having a nightmare?"

"I'm real enough."

"Go away."

"I will. But first you must tell me something."

"Please go away. Come to the Mary Institute Thanksgiving recital tomorrow afternoon. We can talk then."

"You have to tell me now."

Sassy rolled to the middle of the bed and pulled the covers over her head.

Jemmy yanked the covers down. "I won't let you go back to sleep until you tell me what I want to know."

151

Sassy snatched the covers up to her chin. Jemmy yanked them back down. This tug of war continued until Jemmy grabbed the covers and flopped them off the end of the bed.

"Jemmy, put my blankets back. I'm cold."

"Of course—just as soon as you tell me how to find John Folck."

"John Folck? What do you want with him?"

"Information."

"Information about what?" Sassy shivered and clutched a pair of pillows to her bosom.

"Information about a story I'm working on."

"What story?" Sassy sat up and threw the pillows aside.

"Never mind. Just tell me where he is."

"Barr's Department Store, if you must know." Sassy crawled toward the end of the bed to retrieve her bedclothes.

"Where in Barr's Department Store?"

"The shoe department. John Folck sells shoes."

"Thank you. I'm sorry I interrupted your sleep." Jemmy tossed the covers back over Sassy and headed for the door.

By now Sassy was well and truly awake. "Jemima McBustle. Don't think you can steal beaus from Isabel Patterson. Especially not John Folck. Frankly, Jemmy, you don't have the wherewithal."

Stung by the insult, Jemmy turned back in self-defense. "I have no romantic interest in your Mr. Folck. I have beaus of my own—beaus even you would envy."

Sassy arched an eyebrow. "And just who would these heart-throbs be?"

"Among others, the good-looking-and-then-some actor who plays Tom Loker in *Uncle Tom's Cabin.*"

"Oh, yes. Doesn't he also play Simon Legree?"

"He has to stick coffee grounds on his face to make himself ugly. Actors must make sacrifices."

"I'm glad you have a handsome beau. Perhaps Tony and I can find an entertainment for you and your new boyfriend." Sassy propped herself up on one elbow. "And, Jemmy, be careful. John Folck is not a man to trifle with."

Chapter Sixteen

Wednesday Morning, November 23, 1898

The temperature stood at a mere eighteen degrees. The air took on its usual smell of sulfur from burning coal. Clean, white snow had turned grimy gray. Jemmy took comfort in one thought. In the frigid air, snow couldn't melt to drag her skirts in icy water.

Before nine o'clock, Jemmy arrived downtown on the hunt for another of Sassy's beaus. She considered popping into a cafe for breakfast, but yesterday's bout of corset-busting changed her mind.

Jemmy arrived to a nearly empty Barr's Department Store. Few shoppers ventured out so early on such a raw, cold day.

Her spirits rose when she reached the shoe department. One man stood dusting the shoes on the display table. With supreme confidence that he was Sassy's John Folck, she marched up to him.

The bespectacled fellow tucked his feather duster under his arm and nodded his head in a little bow. "May I help you, miss?"

"This weather has revealed weakness in my shoe leather. I find myself in need of new boots."

"Yes, of course. I'll call upon our Miss Leimgruber to help you." He motioned to the floor walker, who disappeared through yard goods and notions.

Jemmy should have remembered. In a well-ordered place of

business, modest ladies would no more allow a strange man to fondle their feet than to fit her derriere for drawers. He gestured toward the ladies' shoe display. "In the meantime, perhaps you'd like to examine these. We always have the latest fashions. How fortunate we are to have both Brown and International Shoe manufactories right here in St. Louis."

Jemmy's mind raced to find the right approach. She had no more than two or three minutes to discover whether this man could be a murderer. "I believe we have an acquaintance in common. She praised you as the finest salesman in town."

"How pleased I am to hear such compliments. Might I inquire who gave me that glowing recommendation?"

"Miss Isabel Patterson."

"I wish I could claim friendship of the lovely Miss Patterson, but I fear you have me confused with another."

"You're not John Folck, then?"

"Regretfully, no. Mr. Folck seems to be late this morning. I customarily work in the haberdashery section. Ah, here's our Miss Leimgruber now." He made a stiff little bow and exited in the direction of menswear.

Miss Leimgruber reminded Jemmy of a cocker spaniel, all bouncy with light-brown curls and big brown eyes yearning to please.

"How may I be of assistance, Miss . . ."

"McBustle."

"It will be my pleasure to serve you, Miss McBustle. Have you chosen a style?"

"No, I . . ."

"With winter coming on early, I'll wager you want a fine storm boot. We have one with an eight-inch top made of heavy calf leather. A more waterproof boot you'll not find this side of rubber galoshes. And so easy to clean. Rub with a bit of flannel, then glaze with patent leather polish. These boots can take a lady to the trolley stop on a muddy street or the opera, with equal ease."

The salesgirl paused for a response.

Jemmy was too busy thinking about how to find the missing Mr. Folck to reply—or to sit down, either. She pretended to examine the display-table merchandise.

"If you'd care to sit, I could take measurement of your foot." The salesgirl pattered on. "Of course, I may be mistaken in your needs. Perhaps you want a dressy shoe. Just in yesterday, we have a lovely low cut—so flattering to the foot and so light. We call it the Gibson Tie. It's exactly what a Gibson girl would wear. If I may say so, your face would grace a Gibson girl poster better than many of Mr. Gibson's models."

Jemmy still didn't reply, just kept inspecting shoes and holding them up to the light as if they were jewels. She tried to think of something to ask the salesgirl about John Folck. Nothing came to mind.

Meanwhile, Miss Leimgruber continued her sales pitch. "I see you like the Blucher style. The detailing on the patent leather upper is exquisite. And note the charming Cuban heel. Exciting, isn't it? Our little war with Spain has given us new elegance in shoe fashion."

In hopes of stalling long enough to see at least a glimpse of John Folck, Jemmy scrutinized every shoe in the entire display. The salesgirl had opened her mouth to launch into another peppy spiel when Jemmy said, "I'm terribly sorry to have wasted your time. I must fly to an important appointment, but I shall return. I am in great need of shoes that can weather the weather."

The girl called after her, "Yes, the Storm Queen boot. So reasonable, too. Just one dollar and thirty-eight cents. I'll remember, Miss McBustle."

Jemmy beat a hasty exit and found herself once again at loose ends. She resigned herself to the inevitable. She'd have to go back to the office and face Hal.

A short walk took her to the *Illuminator*. She climbed the stairs to the third floor and took a deep breath to brace herself for what was to come—an onslaught of cross words from her bodyguard-photographer-partner Hal Dwyer.

She didn't have long to wait. By the time she reached her ancient pine desk with its splintery legs, Hal towered over her.

"I can't believe you were here this morning and left again without so much as a by-your-leave to me again. Where were you?"

"Getting a story."

"When Hamm came in, I had to fake cleaning my lenses—which I always keep spotless. It was a close call, I tell you. If he catches me shirking, I do believe he'll fire me on the spot."

"I suppose your little ruse means you're still an employee of the *Illuminator*."

"Not much longer, unless I bring in some photogs for the art department to sketch."

"Aren't you glad I've been out working on a story? A story that will be much improved by the addition of your meager talents behind a camera."

Hal ignored the insult. "It's about time. I'll get my equipment."

"Don't be in such a hurry. I have to make some notes first."

"Could you at least tell me the subject so I can choose the right lenses?"

"Shoes."

"Shoes?"

"Yes, shoes. I'm going to write a feature article on shoes for one of our advertising clients."

He went away mumbling, "Shoes! Next she'll want photogs of slugs on the sidewalk. I'll need special lenses for that."

157

After writing a draft for the shoe piece, Jemmy made certain John Folck would be present at her next visit to Barr's Department Store. She telephoned and asked for him.

After several moments, a deep voice said, "Yes, this is John Folck. You wished to speak with me?"

"This is Ann O'Nimity from the St. Louis *Illuminator*. I'm planning a story on winter footwear. Since Barr's is a client and nearby, your shoe department seemed the perfect place to research the topic."

"Yes, I'm sure Mr. Barr will be very pleased."

"I'd like to bring my photographer over straightaway, if that would be convenient."

"Yes, I'm looking forward to meeting you."

Jemmy hung up the receiver wondering why she hadn't thought to telephone before her first trip. She muttered, "Wonderful invention, the telephone."

Hal already had his coat on. "Wonderful for the people who can afford it."

Hal annoyed Jemmy with his hints that the McBustles had money. "Yes, Bricktop has a telephone—strictly for business purposes. My sisters and I are forbidden to use it except in emergencies."

"I'm sure you must keep the wires humming. With you, everything is an emergency—except helping me keep my job."

"Grumble, grumble, grumble. If you don't watch out, you'll open your mouth to say sweet nothings to your lady friend and nothing will come out but 'grumble, grumble, grumble.' "

"If that does happen, you won't be around to see. I'd never let a lady friend of mine within ten feet of your snobbish nose."

"Do pardon me for saying such a silly thing. You couldn't grumble, grumble, grumble to a sweetheart. You don't have one."

"So now you're saying I can't get a sweetheart, right?"

"No. I said you don't have a sweetheart at the moment. You don't. Do you?"

"No." Hal stuck out his chin. "But I could if I wanted one."

"I thought every normal young man wanted a sweetheart. Is something wrong with you?"

Hal furrowed his brow. "No. I want a lady friend, but I can't afford one—not when a sundae at Baxter's costs a whole nickel. Who knows how long my job here will last, when you won't even tell me where you are, much less show me anything good to photograph?"

And so the pair bickered like old marrieds until they arrived at Barr's shoe department.

Four Barr representatives lined up in a row like soldiers ready for military inspection. Mr. Barr himself stood first in line.

He shook hands with Hal, then took Jemmy's hand in both of his. "Miss O'Nimity. How delighted I am with this additional attention from the *Illuminator*. Please bear my gratitude to Mrs. Willmore. I have been considering larger advertisements for either the *Post-Dispatch* or the *Illuminator*. Your extra concern for Barr's Department Store will make my choice much easier. I'm looking forward to your article."

Mr. Barr motioned for the floor walker to take over. "Please excuse me. I promise you full cooperation from our staff."

Hands clasped together, the floor walker tilted his head. "I'm remiss not to have welcomed you better on your earlier visit. I hope you'll accept my apology."

"None needed, I'm sure."

"How gracious of you to say so. May I introduce the members of our shoe department staff? Miss Leimgruber you've already met."

"And a most excellent saleslady she is." Brown spaniel curls bouncing, Miss Leimgruber blushed and rocked up on her toes with excitement. Jemmy thought the girl would run in circles if free to follow her instincts.

"Miss Leimgruber inspired my desire to write this article. Your saleslady is a true fountain of information. And, of course, an article on winter footwear for men and for women would be most timely while people recover from Monday's blizzard."

Jemmy turned to Hal. "Mr. Dwyer, would you please set up your camera near the chairs. I'd like you to take a picture while Miss Leimgruber fits me for a new pair of winter boots."

The floor walker suggested, "Perhaps you'll also want to interview our Mr. Folck, our head clerk in men's shoes."

"Yes, delighted to meet you, Mr. Folck."

John Folck was not at all what Jemmy expected. So far as Jemmy knew, Sassy's beaus were respectable and rich like Doctor Wangermeier, or young and rich like Peter Ploog or Cousin Duncan. Tony von Phul probably had money—and other talents as well, considering his effect on Mrs. Patterson. Quisenberry Sproat had good prospects. He was famous and seemed to know how to turn his fame into hard cash.

Homely John Folck and comely Sassy Patterson—Jemmy couldn't envision the pair as a couple. He appeared to have nothing at all to recommend him. He sold shoes in a department store, something no rich man would do. As for looks, Folck would be more likely to turn stomachs than heads.

He was tall and thin with oversized hands and feet. His nose ended in a ruddy bulb. His hair hung in dank clumps, and his Adam's apple bobbed up and down when he talked. His enormous shoes of polished brown leather seemed out of proportion to his lanky frame.

Something wild and compelling flitted about his eyes. Jemmy couldn't identify it, but she'd seen the same narrow look come over a cat as it gathered its sinews to pounce upon a bird with a broken wing.

"Do you have questions for me, Miss O'Nimity, or should I

call you 'Miss McBustle'?"

"Either will do. The idea for a feature about shoes came to me while I was here earlier this morning. Otherwise, I would have called myself by my pen name."

"Which would you want me to use?"

"Please call me Miss McBustle, or Jemima if you prefer. After all, we enjoy the same circle of friends."

"Do we, indeed?"

"Yes, Isabel Patterson is a dear friend."

Folck's eyes darted left and right in his frozen face. He murmured, "You must have me confused with someone else. I am acquainted with no one by the name of Isabel Patterson."

"My mistake. I do apologize."

"Yes, think nothing of it."

Jemmy went through the motions of taking notes and asking questions for the next half hour. All the while she puzzled over Folck's words. Why would anyone lie about knowing Sassy? Meeting Miss Patterson would puff up the ordinary man and make him float off telling the world he'd met the goddess of love and beauty. Yet John Folck, a man Sassy herself counted as a beau, denied he knew her at all.

Miss Leimgruber was all agog at the opportunity to have her picture in the newspaper. She seemed quite taken with the photographer as well. Hal scouted camera placements and taught the salesgirl how to pose. "If you'll look directly into the lens, I'll be able to show your pretty face to best advantage."

Jemmy snickered at such brazen flattery.

Hal stood at the back of his camera and ducked halfway under its black cloth. Hidden from all but Jemmy, he stuck out his tongue at her.

When time came to photograph the shoe fitting, he went all out to impress. He fussed for a time, then declared, "I must be close to the floor. I must put my camera on the floor. Leaving it on its tripod creates an impossible angle for a proper shot of the shoe fitting."

Hal had drawn a crowd by the time he'd finished his preparations. He looked like the victim of medieval torture as he sprawled on his belly under a black cloth.

Jemmy could barely stifle a chuckle. A wooden box seemed a fitting head for her blockheaded partner.

With Folck, the floor walker, and more than a dozen others watching, Miss Leimgruber deftly removed Jemmy's boot and inserted her foot into a wooden contraption to measure it.

The salesgirl made notations on a pad, then disappeared through dark-green velvet portieres into the storeroom. In short order, she returned with three pairs of boots—two that laced and one with straps and buttons.

Jemmy had to borrow thirteen cents from Hal to make up the one dollar and thirty-eight cents for the Storm Queen boots. She had spent a week's worth of lunch and trolley money, but the venture paid off more handsomely than she could have imagined. For the rest of the day, she caught fleeting glimpses of a head ducking inside an alleyway—a dark shadow flattening against a wall when she looked back.

John Folck was following her.

CHAPTER SEVENTEEN

Wednesday Morning, November 23, 1898

Suetonius Hamm's bald-headed self met them at the door with a gruff, "My office. Now."

Hal hustled to park his camera equipment and ran to catch up to Jemmy. Hamm stood in the open office door with the knob in his hand. Hal flattened himself to slide in without touching Hamm's protruding belly.

Hamm shut the door and tromped round to plop behind his desk. "What's this I hear about shoes?" His lower lip drew up in a pout that made him look even more like an English bull terrier.

Thoughts raced through Jemmy's head. *I've gone and done it now. Hamm is going to fire both of us.*

Hamm smacked his desk with a copy of the *Illuminator*. "Well? Say something. McBustle, who told you to butter up one of our advertisers?"

All of a sudden, Jemmy's wool cape seemed to grow twenty pounds heavier. Perspiration trickled down from her hat and made her forehead itch. An overwhelming desire to cast it aside flooded her brain. She didn't dare move, not even to take off her smothering gloves.

Some stunt reporter I am. Getting myself fired—and Hal, too—because I'm always after the big story instead of sticking to my assignments. "It was all my fault, Mr. Hamm. It was my idea. Please don't blame Hal."

"Blame? Who said anything about blame?"

163

Hal and Jemmy traded sidelong glances at this unforeseen development. *Is Hamm going to fire us or not?*

Jemmy ventured, "I don't quite understand."

"What's there to understand? Mr. Barr called Mrs. Willmore and doubled the size of his adverts. Mrs. Willmore invited me to her office to congratulate me on my good business sense.

"I felt a ruddy fool, I can tell you. Had no idea what she was talking about." He pointed at Jemmy with his rolled-up *Illuminator*. "Next time you let me know before you charge off on some wild-haired plan. If advertisers are involved, you let me know."

"Does that mean you're happy because we did something right?"

Hamm snorted. "As Virgil says, '*Felix qui potuit rerum cognoscere causas.* Happy the man who could search out the causes of things.' "

"So Mrs. Willmore liked the idea of my feature story on winter shoes?"

Jemmy felt Hal's elbow nudge her arm. "And the picture? Does she approve of using a photograph, too—even with the added expense?"

"Mr. Barr said photography clinched the deal."

Reluctance written all over his face, Hamm opened his cigar humidor—the humidor reserved for handing out honors to reporters who landed big stories. He delivered one each to Jemmy and to Hal. "Back to work with you two, and, next time, ask permission."

Jemmy had previously earned two of Hamm's cigars. Of course, she had to open the humidor herself and appropriate them as her just and proper reward. This was the first time Hamm actually handed her a cigar. So what if he only gave her the cigar because Jemmy made Mrs. Willmore happy?

No longer overheated, Jemmy walked calmly into the pressroom and held her trophy cigar aloft. She motioned for

Hal to follow suit.

The pair stood for a minute, basking in their collective triumph. Jemmy noted reactions across the room. Some nodded and smiled. Miss Turnipseed stuck her nose in her typewriter. Amadee Boudinier clapped his hands slowly in snide approval. He sauntered over to ask, "What did you two do to deserve Hamm's precious claro cigars? Didn't steal a crime beat story from me, did you?"

Boudinier had grounds for being jealous and territorial. Jemmy trod on his toes every time she encroached on his police beat. Of late, such offenses kept him sore-toed more often than not. Still, the true source of his resentment came from personal secrets Jemmy knew about him—secrets he didn't care to have revealed.

From time to time, Jemmy made use of her knowledge to secure Boudinier's cooperation. She always felt ashamed to take advantage but rationalized the guilt away. Her future was at stake. If she didn't get the goods, story-wise, she'd lose her job. Getting fired would ruin her only hope of running her own life. When a little pressure would secure Boudinier's help on something important, a teensy bit of blackmail could make him knuckle under.

Hal rocked up and down on his toes, something recently learned from Miss Leimgruber. "Pleased an advertiser. The fellow was so grateful, he doubled the size of his adverts. Likes my photogs."

"Are you two showing a little business savvy? Amazing!"

Hal stuck his chin in the air. "People don't call me 'Flash' for nothing."

"People don't call you 'Flash' at all."

"Maybe not, but I keep asking them to."

Boudinier shook Hal's hand while he looked at Jemmy. "I'm impressed. I thought you two were all about big-time news

165

stories. Imagine Miss Ann O'Nimity coming up with her own idea instead of filching stories from a veteran reporter's wastebasket."

Jemmy ignored the insult as she shed her cape. "I've been working here for nearly a year. You shouldn't be surprised I've become a professional journalist."

"In that case, I salute you." He made such an absurdly deep bow that his arm brushed the floor.

Jemmy had been trawling for a juicy murder story when she fell into the lap of the god of commerce. She had no idea writing a feature on an advert customer would warrant kudos from the boss. *I doubt Boudinier would be joking if he knew the truth.*

Smug with undeserved satisfaction, she strolled to her desk. *Maybe I am beginning to think like a newspaperwoman—at least in my subconscious mind.* She tucked the notion away to enjoy.

She concentrated on writing a piece to please Mr. Barr and Mrs. Willmore and Editor Hamm. *Forget pleasing Hamm. There is no pleasing Suetonius Hamm.*

An idea struck when she saw Hal return from tending his photographic plates. She motioned him to her desk and tucked her own prize cigar in his pocket.

Hal smiled. "You're sweet to give me your Lorillard. I forgive you."

Jemmy scowled. "It's not for you."

"Uh-oh, here we go again."

"Nothing bad. A little gift for your uncle—you know the one."

"A bribe, you mean."

"No, of course not. A little token of good will for the smartest detective on the police force, nothing more."

"What do you want this time?"

"Find out all you can about the Sproat investigation. And be sure to find out what evidence the police have against Frank James."

"You're hoping he did it. That's right, isn't it?"

"Hoping he's guilty? No. If he should turn out to be guilty, I'm hoping to get the real story—and get it first."

"I'll do my best."

"While you're at it, see what you can dig up on the actor who plays Tom Loker and Simon Legree at the Crystal Palace Theatre."

"What's his real name?"

"I keep forgetting to look it up in the program."

"How about your review notes?"

"Not there, more's the pity."

"You don't expect my uncle to tell me anything without a name, do you?"

"It couldn't hurt to try."

Hal looked at Jemmy as though she'd just slobbered on his collar. He turned to leave.

"One more name—John Folck. There's something shifty about him. And Hal, take your camera. I think your uncle might be more talkative if you were taking his picture. What's he done lately that's newsworthy?"

"Shot a squirrel in the attic that was keeping him up nights."

"That's not precisely what I had in mind, but it may have to do. I'll think of some way to make it sound heroic."

After Hal left, Jemmy meandered over to the sports desk. "Mr. Flinchpaugh, I have a favor to ask."

He didn't look up. "What favor would that be?"

"Come with me to the Northside Turner Hall. I have to speak to Handsome Harry Benson."

He tapped his pencil on his desk. "My dear girl, you know the place is for men only. What's the point?"

"The boxers must stop training to eat. Perhaps they might be having lunch at their favorite restaurant when we just happen by."

Flinchpaugh hunkered down even lower. "When a boxer is in hard training, his manager has special food brought in. I doubt they'll leave the hall at midday."

"Is Benson scheduled to fight soon? What about his job in *Uncle Tom's Cabin?*"

"Some people have more than one job."

"But he's a big-name fighter all the way from Chicago. If he were on a sports card locally, surely I would have read about it in your column."

Flinchpaugh pushed back his chair with a sigh. "He's fighting Friday night. It's the kind of fight no one advertises in the papers."

"An illegal fight? The kind that breaks noses and knocks out teeth? The kind that could turn Handsome Harry into Quasimodo?"

Flinchpaugh nodded.

"Why would he? Does he need money badly enough to risk turning Handsome Harry into Horrifying Harry?"

Flinchpaugh shrugged. "Maybe he thinks he's too good to get hurt. Maybe he likes the danger or the pain."

"Then I simply must speak to him now. It can't wait until after his fight. Who knows if he'll even be able to talk afterwards? And tomorrow is a holiday. I must see him now, today. It's most urgent."

"I don't suppose you're going to tell me why your need is so desperate."

"I regret that I cannot. It's of a delicate nature."

Flinchpaugh scrunched his eyes and gave his head a quick shake. Jemmy imagined he was thinking unsavory thoughts about Handsome Harry and Jemima McBustle. *Well, let him. If that will gain his help, let him think I'm a fallen woman. Time enough later to set him straight.*

Flinchpaugh walked Jemmy to the cloakroom. From time to time, he sneaked a peek at her midsection. Jemmy sailed down the stairs in front of him, head held high as if she dared him to ask the big question.

At the Northside Turner Hall, he parked her outside the rear door while he went in. Seconds later Handsome Harry came out bundled in a raccoon coat with a towel loosely draped around his head. Red flannel underwear sprouted up from the soft black leather of his boxing boots.

He jogged in place. Each exhalation of air curled upward in gusts of fog. He smelled of sweat and Watkins liniment.

"Autley said a beautiful young girl had news for me. He was right about the beautiful part. How may I help you?"

"Tell me about the woman."

"What woman?"

"The woman who was supposed to meet you at Union Station yesterday."

Harry stopped jogging in place and leaned over with his hands on his hips. "Women don't desert Harry Benson. Whoever told you a story like that is a liar."

"No one told me. I saw for myself."

Harry's eyes bored into Jemmy's, but she stared back every bit as fiercely. He said, "Stay out of things that don't concern you. And if you've been following me, stop right now."

"I'll stop when you tell me what I want to know."

"Bossy females get hurt when they don't mind their own business."

"Are you threatening me? I'll have you up on charges. You'd have to miss your big fight."

When he raised his arm as if to hit her, Flinchpaugh stepped between them and gently walked Harry backwards. "Wouldn't do to hit Miss McBustle. Think of your reputation with the ladies."

"Then make her forget about seeing me at the station."

Jemmy stood on tiptoe to make herself bigger. "I won't forget. I'll find out somehow, so you may as well tell me and make your life easier."

"Maybe you should tell her what she wants to know. She hangs on like a bulldog once she's got her teeth into something."

Harry backed Flinchpaugh up a step or two. "She damn well better keep her teeth out of me."

"No need for foul language. Why not tell her whom you expected to meet? Can it be as harmful as what Miss McBustle might do with her typewriter and a three-inch column in the *Illuminator*?"

Harry might not have been the sharpest needle in the sewing basket, but he finally saw common sense. "All right. All right. Do you promise to leave me alone?"

Jemmy put a hand over her heart. "I swear."

"I was supposed to meet Pervia Benigas."

"I owe you many thanks for helping me. You're very kind."

Jemmy could feel Harry Benson staring after her as she walked away on Flinchpaugh's arm.

"I've never seen Benson so wrought up outside the ring. You'd best be more careful."

"Yes, I'm sure you're right."

"Do you know this Pervia person?"

"Yes, she was a classmate of mine at Mary Institute."

"What does her failure to meet him signify?"

"I wish I knew."

"Would you tell me if you did?"

"I can't say. Not until I—" Jemmy broke off in mid-sentence. She was too deep in thought to hear Flinchpaugh's next word.

Pervia must have jilted Benson because she stumbled across me. I wonder why my old classmate didn't want me to see her meet Harry.

CHAPTER EIGHTEEN

Wednesday Afternoon, November 23, 1898

"You haven't heard a single word, have you?" Autley Flinch-paugh muttered into Jemmy's good ear, but it didn't penetrate her brain until he raised his voice.

"I'm sorry. I've been trying to understand why my old classmate jilted Harry just because she saw me at the station."

"People often take extraordinary steps to avoid members of the press, especially people with secrets."

"Yes, of course." Her stomach growled like a drunken katydid singing "The Star Spangled Banner." She put her hand over her middle to quiet the rumbling.

He chuckled. "On the other side of Hyde Park is a cafe that serves a tasty chicken pot pie. Let me treat you to lunch."

"I admit to being hungry. Still, I must refuse your kind offer. I have an engagement elsewhere." That wasn't strictly true. Jemmy had no advance agreement to meet with Pervia. But the thought of getting answers from the snooty Miss Benigas made Jemmy's heart beat faster. A talk with her might break through this welter of confusion that had Jemmy stumped.

A trolley ride and a brisk walk later, Jemmy stood on the doorstep of the Benigas mansion on Lucas Place. The house-keeper answered the door with a pleasant "Good morning." She was dressed in dark-blue fustian. Her well-cushioned shoulders extended forward and around her sunken bosom like an upholstered wing chair. "Miss McBustle. So nice to see you again."

"I hope Pervia is ready for our luncheon date. I'm famished."

"Please come in. Miss Pervia is in the music room."

The housekeeper's ample rump bumped up and down as she led Jemmy to the piano. Pervia's deft fingers filled the whole downstairs with echoes from a Chopin etude.

When Jemmy entered the music room, Pervia stopped in mid-measure.

Jemmy flattered, "How wonderfully you play. You should be on the concert stage."

"I am. I'm performing in Cincinnati on Saturday."

Jemmy gushed on in hopes the housekeeper would leave. "I waited for you in the hotel lobby until people started to stare. It's not like you to miss a luncheon appointment. I came to see if you're ailing and forgot to send word you weren't coming."

Pervia played along with Jemmy's ruse. "I get so wrapped up in my music that I scarcely can remember where I live. I must apologize. I fear we've already eaten lunch, but I can have something prepared for you." She motioned to the housekeeper.

"No, please. Don't trouble. I have another commitment and cannot stay." The housekeeper bobbed her head and left.

Pervia scooted to the edge of the piano bench. "We had no luncheon date, as you very well know. Why did you come here?"

"You never did spend much time on small talk, did you?"

"I have to practice. Please get to the point."

"Harry Benson told me you jilted him at the train station yesterday. I want to know why."

"Oh, I see. Harry's little girlfriend is jealous of big bad Pervia."

"I'm not Benson's girlfriend, nor am I jealous. Why did you jilt him?"

"If you're not his girlfriend, why do you care whom Harry

meets or doesn't meet?"

"I know that Harry is fighting bare knuckles on Friday. Before then I have to find out why you jilted him. It's because you didn't want me to see the two of you together, isn't it? Don't try to deny it. Benson himself told me he was waiting for you."

Pervia slammed the keyboard lid on the grand piano with a *thwock*. She seemed genuinely surprised as she slipped off the bench. "Since you know so much, tell me where this fight is to be held?"

"I don't know."

Pervia rose to her full height. Her hot breath bored down on Jemmy's forehead. "You seem to know rather a lot. Surely you know something as important as where an illegal fight is to be held."

"I don't, but I can find out. I might be persuaded to share that information if you tell me why you jilted Harry at Union Station."

"The truth is, I don't travel in circles with persons who engage in pugilism. Mr. Benson is the only boxer I know."

"But you seem quite interested in this fight." Jemmy stuck out her chin and leaned forward until her nose hit a veritable wall of Pervia's perfume. Even if the scent of the woman's Jicky made her feel so lightheaded she couldn't say a sensible word, Jemmy was not about to back down.

Pervia must have thought she'd won. "I find blood sport quite barbaric as a rule, but you must have noticed how attractive Mr. Benson is."

"Is he your beau?"

Pervia threw back her head and laughed. "Asking questions like that could get you into trouble."

"Well, is he?"

Pervia eased back onto the piano bench and said nothing for half a minute or more. "Very well. *Quid pro quo.* Something for something. When you tell me where the fight is to take place, I'll tell you why I failed to meet Mr. Benson and what our connection might be."

Convincing Pervia had been too easy. Jemmy took a deep breath and tried to think of something else to say, something else to ask. Nothing came.

"We can trade information at the matinee at Mary Institute tomorrow. If you have no other business with me, I'll show you to the door."

Jemmy did think of something else to ask, but not until after Pervia left her on the front porch. *Is Pervia just another one of Handsome Harry Benson's female admirers? Or is there something sinister between them?*

Jemmy's stomach rumbled loudly enough to draw notice from a passerby.

A nice little diner on Fourteenth Street served breakfast all day long. Jemmy's mouth watered with the thought of hotcakes slathered in butter and maple syrup. She walked halfway there before she remembered she had not a penny in her reticule. Worse still, Autley Flinchpaugh was no longer around to pay for her trolley rides. She'd have to pick her way across icy sidewalks all the way back to the *Illuminator.*

By the time she reached the office, she was well-nigh frozen. Her hunger had disappeared, though not the stomach rumbles. Miss Turnipseed's head bobbed up from her typewriter. "Please do something about your digestive system. It sounds like a tom cat in a trash can."

"I haven't eaten anything today. Maybe some water will quiet my insides." At the drinking fountain, she filled paper cone after paper cone, but the rumbling only ratcheted up from baritone to soprano.

At length, Miss Turnipseed sacrificed her own afternoon pick-me-up. Every day at four o'clock exactly, she ate a shiny, red apple. "Thank you, Miss Turnip—I mean, Miss Buckley. You can't imagine how grateful I am."

Jemmy set the apple down on her desk while she breathed on her fingers to warm them.

Before her hands felt properly thawed, Hal bounded in from the darkroom. "Here's the picture you wanted. Pretty darn good—excuse the language—pretty good. If I do say so myself."

Hal handed her a picture of his uncle holding a dead squirrel by the tail. "What do you think? Will this make a good subject for a line drawing by the art boys?"

"Cut the picture so it's just his head and enough chest to show his badge."

"But the squirrel is the best part."

Jemmy feigned a shocked look. "But that's a squirrel with rabies—perhaps. Can't have our hero holding up a possibly rabid squirrel—not even a dead possibly rabid squirrel."

Hal offered a resigned, "Oh, I see—a little journalistic license."

As he turned, Jemmy caught him by the sleeve. "What did you find out?"

"Which do you want first—the good, the bad, or the indifferent?"

"This is no time for games. Just tell me."

"You have to choose."

Nobody, not even sister Randy, could exasperate Jemmy so quickly as Hal. "Any one will do."

"No, no. Pick your poison."

Jemmy heaved a shuddering sigh. "All right, all right. Let's hear 'indifferent.' "

"That would be Frank James." Hal paused for effect.

"Heavens in a handbag. What about Frank James?"

"Nothing. No change. He's still in jail and still accused of killing Quisenberry Sproat."

Jemmy stomped her foot in frustration. "What did you find out about the investigation? What about Loker-Legree and John Folck?"

"Which will it be—good or bad?"

"I don't care."

With palms up, Hal hunched his shoulders in a silent question. Jemmy shuddered again. "Oh, all right. Tell me the 'good.' "

"Tom Loker is not a crook."

"What's his real name?"

"Don't be a ninny. All I had to go on was an alias."

"Then how do you know the actor who plays Tom Loker is not a crook?"

"My uncle never heard of any crook with the alias of 'Tom Loker.' If my uncle never heard of him, he can't be a crook."

" 'Tom Loker' isn't a fake name. It's a role in a play. Not the same thing at all."

Hal shrugged off her criticism. "Are you ready for the bad?"

"Please."

"My uncle had plenty to say about John Folck. He's a small-time thief who's often been arrested but never convicted. He sometimes works as muscle man for Amos Medley."

"Harry Benson's manager?"

"The same. Does that mean anything?"

"I wish I knew." Jemmy shook her head at the image of Folck as an enforcer. "Folck is tall and skinny. Not my idea of a muscle man."

"A man looks plenty muscular with a whip in one hand and a pistol in the other."

"Has Folck been known to use those weapons?"

"Suspected—but the victims won't talk. Too scared, I guess."

Miss Turnipseed snatched her gift apple from Jemmy's desk. "I see you're not really hungry after all." She sank her teeth into the apple as she walked away.

Jemmy's hollow stomach ached, and her bad ear buzzed until she felt giddy. She braced herself on Hal's arm. "Thanks, Hal. You've given me lots to think about."

"Say, are you all right?"

"Just a little lightheaded. I haven't eaten all day."

"I wish I had another nickel to give you, but you already took my last cent."

"I'll be all right. Come stand by my typewriter to give me the particulars on the squirrel story while I write it."

An hour later Hal was off delivering story and cropped picture to Hamm. Jemmy covered her typewriter and made ready to go home. She very nearly collapsed when she tried to stand. In a flash Autley Flinchpaugh was at her side.

"Miss McBustle, are you all right?"

"Just a little dizzy. I haven't eaten today."

"You must take better care of yourself, especially now."

Jemmy was too woozy to grasp his meaning. "It's my own fault. I spent my lunch money on new boots."

He fished two nickels from his pocket. "Here. Buy a pretzel, then take the trolley home. You need food and rest."

"Thank you, Mr. Flinchpaugh. I'll pay you back tomorrow."

"I'll just get my coat to see you to the trolley stop."

"Don't trouble yourself. Hal will be back soon. But there is something you can do for me."

"And that would be?"

"Tell me where the bare-knuckles fight is to be."

"Why would you take interest in a knock-down-drag-out?"

"A friend wants to know."

"That fight is not for a person in a delicate state."

"But truly, the information is not for me."

When Flinchpaugh said no more, Jemmy became desperate enough for a small ruse. She pretended to swoon in his direction. He caught her and seated her back in her chair. "I'll be back with a pretzel in a moment."

"No, please. Just tell me where the fight will be held. I can't go home until I know."

"Promise me you don't plan to see the match."

"I promise."

"Uhrig's Cave."

"Thank you, Mr. Flinchpaugh. You are a godsend."

Flinchpaugh helped her into her coat. "Please let me escort you to the trolley stop. I'd be mortified if you fainted on the way."

"No, you must stay and finish your work. I'll be fine as soon as I have something to eat."

Just outside the door of the *Illuminator*, she gave a nickel to a little Negro pretzel girl of eight or nine. "Thankee kindly, Miss Newspaper Lady." *How sad to see so many children freezing on the streets when they ought to be in school.*

Before she could take a bite, another little Negro girl held out an apple. This poor waif wore a threadbare coat and no stockings on her skinny legs. Jemmy parted with her remaining nickel and her father's muffler. When she wrapped it around the girl's neck, the girl said, "I never had nothin' so nice and warm. Thankee, thankee."

When the girl grabbed her hand and kissed it, Jemmy nearly broke out in tears. *What will Mother say when she finds I've lost Father's muffler, the second scarf I've lost in less than a week?*

Once again, she had not a single cent in her reticule. She'd have to walk home, but at least she had both pretzel and apple to eat. The food and the long walk—her second of the day—lifted her spirits and bolstered her energy.

Racing up the steps to Bricktop, Jemmy arrived breathless and chilled to the bone but jubilant. At last she could thaw her aching fingers and warm her stomach with a hot drink. She could all but taste Gerta's steaming apple cider with cinnamon.

179

Alas, it was not to be. When Jemmy entered the hall, Randy came flying out of the kitchen with crushing news. Jemmy's long day was about to get much longer, her burdens much heavier.

CHAPTER NINETEEN

Wednesday Evening, November 23, 1898

Randy's face flushed crimson through her freckles. "What will we do now? Mother and Gerta are both down with the flu. What are we going to do?"

"Give me a minute to warm up, will you? I had to walk home from the office. I can't feel my feet."

Jemmy pulled off her gloves and held her hands over the black metal of the coal adapter in the dining-room fireplace. She tried to sound cheerful. "I see you've set the table for supper. Well done. Is the food ready?"

"I suppose so. Early this morning, Gerta put on a big pot of beans with ham hocks."

"Did she bake bread before . . . ?"

"Yes, I guess we're lucky she didn't feel poorly until this afternoon."

"What about dessert?"

"Apple Betty with cream. And you're wasting your time trying to warm up. The coal stove is cold."

"Get Dora in here. Why hasn't she tended the fires?"

"Gone."

"Gone where?"

Randy thrust her head forward with mouth ajar. She looked for all the world like an organ-grinder's monkey waiting for a coin to drop in her cup.

"Just gone. Mother sent her to the market for fresh oysters

because the batch Gerta brought home went bad. She never came back."

"It's not like Dora to shirk, but we can't worry about that now. We have to bring up coal and get these fires going. The boarders would kick up a royal fuss if they had to eat beans in their overcoats and mufflers."

A few trips down cellar and a few pounds of coal soot later, the fires were stoked—even the one in the sickroom. "Let's clean up and get supper on. We're a half hour late already. I'm surprised old Mrs. Hendershot isn't—"

A high voice with a slight quaver asked, "Might we expect sustenance soon? Unless my timepiece has stopped, suppertime was shed-yoold for an hour ago." The reedy voice pronounced *scheduled* without a *K*.

"Mrs. Hendershot, so good to see you with a hearty appetite. I was just about to ring the gong."

With only two of them to represent the family, Randy and Jemmy ate ham and beans with the guests. Most seemed well pleased with the savory combination Gerta had concocted, but Mrs. Hendershot was less than impressed.

"Might I assume this repast is a deprivation to give us proper appetite for tomorrow's feasting?"

"You've been to Thanksgiving dinners here at Bricktop, Mrs. Hendershot. I think you will be well pleased. Gerta's pumpkin pies are heavenly."

"Quite so, but Gerta doesn't seem to be about. I hear no sounds of activity from the kitchen."

"I imagine Gerta went to market for some forgotten delicacy to put the crowning touches on tomorrow's dinner."

"Surely the markets have closed by now."

"I can't imagine what's keeping her."

"And what of the other girl, Dora? Where is she?"

"I remember now, Gerta went to look for Dora because she

hadn't returned from the market."

Before Mrs. Hendershot could poke another hole in Jemmy's dike of lies, Jemmy said, "I'm so glad your nephew and his family will be with us tomorrow—all the way from Brussels, Belgium. You must be excited."

"Indeed. Though I'm not certain he will arrive in time to join us. Trains are so unreliable these days."

Trains coming and going at Union Station were a marvel of promptness and efficiency—and scheduled to the minute. With a twinge of sadness, Jemmy understood Mrs. Hendershot's little subterfuge. Thanksgiving Day would fail to produce Mrs. H.'s mythical nephew from Belgium.

And so the supper proceeded without further mishap. As the sisters washed dishes and cleaned the kitchen, Randy asked, "How do you think we can manage a big feast tomorrow—not to mention breakfast and supper?"

"We'll keep breakfast simple. I checked the pantry. Gerta made cinnamon bread. We'll toast that and offer soft-boiled eggs. We'll use two jars of Gerta's canned peaches as a special treat. Supper will be cold turkey sandwiches."

Randy chuckled and shook her head. "Since when have you become a magician?"

"What do you mean?"

"We don't have a turkey."

"How can we not have a turkey? Mother ordered one weeks ago."

"You just looked in the larder. Did you see a turkey?"

A horrible thought made Jemmy's head swim. Could the turkey Mother ordered be a living fowl? Since mother opened Bricktop as a boardinghouse, Jemmy had plucked chickens more often than she'd care to admit. To date, she'd never had to actually slaughter one. The idea knotted in the pit of her stomach.

She trotted out the back door with Randy calling after.

"Where are you going?"

Half expecting to see a crated turkey in the backyard, Jemmy peered through the gloom. She sighed with relief to discover neither crate nor living bird.

She shuffled back into the house with one sobering thought. How could she and Randy present a Thanksgiving feast without a turkey?

Randy looked expectant. "Well, what are we going to do?"

"One of us will have to go to Soulard Market in the morning and buy a turkey—or a leg of lamb or fine rump roast. Who said we must have turkey anyway?"

Just then the front doorbell rang. On the porch stood an ambulance driver who tipped his cap. "I believe this young lady is in your employment."

By his side stood Dora, wet and muddy as a ragdoll dropped in a puddle—with her right arm in a sling.

"What happened to you, Dora?" Jemmy called back over her shoulder, "Randy, put the kettle on. Come on in. Some hot tea will warm you right up. Throw that muddy cloak on the porch." Despite the cold, the wool had a distinct stench of horse manure. "We'll see to it later."

The ambulance driver cleared his throat. In her agitated state, Jemmy needed a few seconds to realize what he wanted. "I thank you for bringing Dora home. What is the charge?"

"Eighty cents, ma'am."

Outraged by such heartless extortion of money from poor women who had no recourse but to pay, Jemmy left the man standing out in the cold. "Stay right there." She stomped to Mother's room and returned with Mother's coin purse. She counted out each coin carefully as she pressed it into his palm.

When the man had gone, she helped Dora to the kitchen and out of her muddy socks and shoes. Dora's swollen fingers hung like pink sausages over the edge of her sling. With those useless appendages, she couldn't so much as unbutton her shirtwaist.

At length, Dora sat in her unmentionables with a shawl around her shoulders and her feet in a dishpan of warm water. She put a cup of tea to her lips but burst into tears before she could drink a single drop.

"There, there, Dora. Tell us what happened to your arm."

Dora blotted her eyes with her good hand. "Beer wagon ran me over."

Randy laughed out loud. "Don't be silly, Dora. A beer truck weighs thousands of pounds—not to mention thousands more pounds of draft horses. If a beer wagon ran you over, you'd be dead."

Dora burst into another round of tears.

"Randy, look what you did. You made her cry. Be quiet and listen, will you?"

Dora wiped her nose on a dishtowel and began her tale. "Like I already said, a beer wagon ran me over. The oysters spoiled, so I was on me way to Soulard Market to buy more and to buy pretty fruit just like you told me. Well, I crossed a street and lost me shoe in the mud. I was diggin' around to find it when what should I see but a pair of giant horses not three feet away bearing straight for me. So there I was a-standing on one foot about to be run down and kilt for sure." She burst into another round of tears.

Eyes big as dinner plates, Randy let out an impatient, "What happened then?"

"I hunkered down in the mud and got run over by a beer wagon."

"And all the damage done was a broken arm?" Randy sounded amazed.

"I was that lucky, doncha know. I stayed right in the middle of horse hooves and wagon wheels. I never thought I'd be grateful for mud, but I do believe mud saved me life this day."

"So how did you break your arm?"

"That's the strange part, doncha know. After the beer wagon passed over me, I got up and thought I was fine. The wagon driver stopped and came back to see was I all right. He wanted to know was there anything he could do and said he was mighty sorry, but he was looking at his delivery sheet and didn't see me standing there in front until it was too late.

"What am I doing standing in the street, he wants to know. I told him I lost me shoe, and he pokes around in the mud until he finds it. He wanted to give me a lift home. I said I had to buy some things at the market. He said he'd like to wait but he had important deliveries to make. So he apologized again, and then he left."

"You still didn't tell about the arm."

"Well, that's the funny thing. I didn't know it was broke. I went to put some fancy oranges in me sack. It's a good thing I brought flour sacks along. The wagon wheels ran right over my basket and smashed it to smithereens, doncha know."

Randy let out a screech of exasperation. "Dora, what happened to your arm?"

"I'm getting 'round to that. When I tried to pick up an orange, a great ache came on me arm. I saw me hand was all red and swolled up. Well, I knew right away that arm was busted. The lady running the stall sent her boy to find a policeman. He took me across Broadway to a doctor's office where they set me arm and wrapped it up to keep it in place. They even called the ambulance, though it didn't come for the longest time. So that's how I got home. If I'da known the man would make you pay eighty cents, I'da walked."

Randy sounded weary from asking. "But you still haven't told us how you broke your arm."

"That doctor charged me a dollar to set my arm. Took every cent the beer wagon man gave me. I still have the grocery money though. It's in the pocket of me skirt." She made a clumsy attempt to stand. "I'll give you the money, then put the skirt in some water to soak the mud out."

Jemmy shoved her gently back into the chair. "I'll do it. You stay put."

Randy stood with her hands on her hips. "For the last time. Dora, how did you break your arm?"

"That's the thing, doncha know. I have no idea how come me good right arm got broke."

Randy shook her head. "Why couldn't you say that in the first place?"

"I didn't know I didn't know. Doncha know. I had to work through the whole story to find out."

After helping Dora divest herself of mud, the trio climbed up two flights of stairs and slept the sleep of the vast, overworked masses.

Jemmy's first thought when she arose well before dawn on Thursday was not one of thanksgiving. She yanked on working clothes and rousted Dora and Randy before she sprinted downstairs. She stood in the doorway of the room behind the kitchen and called from the door. "Mother, we have no turkey. What should we do?"

"Don't worry, Jemima dear. I insisted the turkey be brought this morning. I wanted it to be fresh. The poulterer will be here in good time—by five o'clock at the latest. He promised."

"I'm sorry to have bothered you. Please go back to sleep."

Had Jemmy waited two minutes longer, she would not have needed to wake Mother. A firm knock on the back door sent Jemmy to find Mother's purse.

The poulterer tipped his cap as he pocketed the money. "Finest turkey in the state, home grown in Jefferson County and fresh as a just-laid egg." The man waved his arm in the direction of a crate. A huge bird with brown-red feathers stuck his head through the slats.

"Just look at the color on them wattles—red and manly. That's the kind of bird we grow in Jefferson County. I'll just tie up them legs and put him here on the porch so you have no trouble catching him."

The man made short work of tying the beast's legs. With another tip of his hat, he picked up his crate and was off down the alley.

A sudden panic hit Jemmy. She ran to the alley and called after him, "Aren't you going to kill him for us?"

She barely heard his reply as he drove away. "I've lots of deliveries to make. I'm sure you'll manage."

Jemmy walked slowly into the kitchen to face Randy and Dora. The three walked to the back porch in silence as if they were marching to the gallows. Randy set a coal-oil lamp on the ice box and turned up the wick.

Jemmy had observed the demise of chickens, but she'd never had to kill one. Gerta had always been a most efficient executioner. She would wring their necks. Jemmy had often seen her grab hold of the head in her powerful hands and twirl until the headless body flew off to flop in the grass of the backyard.

This turkey weighed twenty pounds or more. She doubted even Gerta's work-hardened muscles could twirl that heavy body. In a hushed voice, she asked, "What's the best way?"

Dora said, "My grandmother just stepped on the bird's neck and pulled the body right off."

Jemmy brightened. "Perfect. Go ahead, Dora. Do it."

"Me right arm is broke, doncha know. Got no strength to speak of in my left. You'll have to do it."

Randy piped in, "Why don't we chop off its head with a hatchet? Stay right here. I'll get one from the carriage house."

In seconds she was back—not with a dainty hatchet, but with a full-sized ax. "I couldn't find a hatchet, but we can use this."

"Just how do you think this ax will get the job done?"

"You hold the turkey's head, and I'll chop it off."

"Not me, Randy. I'm not risking my fingers to your aim with an ax you can barely lift. Look how little the bird's neck is."

"Then I'll hold the head, and you use the ax. Go ahead. I'm not afraid."

"No. I'd rather eat bread and water for Thanksgiving than risk maiming my sister for life."

At that, the big tom turkey added his own two cents. He flapped his wings and tried to stand upright on his tied-together legs as if to say, "Well, if you three can't put on a better execution than this, I'll just take my business elsewhere."

He had very nearly managed to right himself when Randy's stubborn streak took over. She commanded, "Dora, go stand on the concrete step by the cellar door. Jemmy, bring the lamp. Dora's going to stand on the head. You and I will each grab a drumstick and pull."

When all three were ready, Randy spoke to the big tom. "I appreciate your patience with us this morning. I want you to know that we've never had a more handsome bird for Thanksgiving. Goodbye, Mr. Turkey."

Randy stretched his neck out by his red wattles so Dora could get a good foothold on the head. "Yank as hard as you can Jemmy—then throw him toward the fence. We don't want blood on our skirts if we can help it."

The first attempt was a total disaster. Dora's foot slipped off the head. Randy and Jemmy chucked the tom a good fifteen feet in the air. It banged against the wooden fence. Clearly annoyed by another bout of incompetence, the bird squawked and gobbled in protest.

"What happened, Dora?"

"I'm plum off balance without me right arm. I need something to brace meself, but the house is too far away."

Randy trotted back to the carriage house and returned with a long-handled spade. "Will this do?"

Dora got a grip on the spade and nodded. Once again Randy pulled out the bird's head for Dora to step on. When Dora nodded that she was ready, Randy and Jemmy each bent down to grab a leg.

"On three. One—two—three." Randy and Jemmy heaved with all their might, but old tom's head stayed firmly affixed to his body. It was Dora who hit the ground. The act of pulling at the bird's body knocked her clean off her feet.

This time the bird didn't bother to flop. He only made a feeble gobble as if to resign himself to being abused indefinitely.

They stood Dora up and brushed her off. Randy said, "Maybe we should use the ax after all."

This time it was Jemmy who took control. "No, Randy's plan is a good one. We simply have to make it work. If it takes all morning, we shall succeed."

Jemmy drove the spade into the ground to make a solid brace for Dora. Once again Dora planted a foot on the turkey's head while the girls pulled at the body. This time they kept right on pulling until the bird separated into two parts. Of course, the poor bruised body was too exhausted to flop for long.

Not until the bird came to rest by the fence did Jemmy notice the morning chill or the blood on her skirt.

CHAPTER TWENTY

Thursday Morning, Thanksgiving Day, November 24, 1898
Randy brought a dishpan and a kettle of boiling water to loosen the turkey's feathers. Plucking them out and singeing off pinfeathers over an open flame took the better part of a half hour.

To Jemmy's surprise, Randy volunteered for the smelly job of gutting the turkey and cleaning the edible innards. "I appreciate your willingness to take on such an ugly job. You've been a real trouper this morning."

"I've always been curious about what's on the inside of animals and people. Besides, I let big tom down, and I'm trying to make it up to him."

Jemmy didn't know what to make of that, but she was glad to let Randy deal with the bird's insides. She rinsed the body in salt water while Dora lit the oven. She tied the legs together with string while Dora brushed butter over the bird. At last it was ready for the roasting pan. Jemmy wanted nothing quite so much as a nice nap, but getting the bird in the oven was just the first chapter in what promised to be a long, long day.

Randy, Jemmy, and one-handed Dora brought a new standard of teamwork to breakfast at Bricktop. They fed the boarders and the sickroom patients. Already tired, they could sit down to enjoy their own cinnamon toast and canned peaches.

Jemmy stopped in mid-mouthful. The realization hit her. The turkey had already been in the oven for more than an hour. It was just seven thirty in the morning—yet it felt more like eight thirty at night. Jemmy marveled at how easily Gerta turned out three meals a day, every day except Sunday. With twelve or more people at every sitting, Gerta dished up more than two hundred meals a week.

The rest of the morning flew by with preparations—chopping celery and onions and cubing stale bread for dressing, peeling sweet potatoes, grinding cranberries and oranges for relish. The feast came together in fine fashion. Jemmy crossed her fingers the boarders didn't miss Gerta's knack for seasoning.

At last, the potatoes were mashed, the giblet gravy thickened, and the heavy cream for the pumpkin pie whipped. Randy dipped a finger in the potatoes and crowed, "Better than Gerta's."

"Let's hope the boarders agree." Jemmy blew kisses to her sister and hustled upstairs to change into her Sunday-go-to-meeting dress.

All spruced up, she stopped outside the parlor to smooth her hair and listen to the voices. She peeked in to see boarders sipping hot mulled cider and chatting with their guests—all except Mrs. Hendershot, who sat alone in the corner.

Jemmy picked up the gong mallet and was just about to call everyone to dinner when the doorbell rang. All the other boarders' guests had arrived. *Who could be at the door?*

Standing on the porch in his Sunday best was none other than Jemmy's own photographer-bodyguard Hal Dwyer. "Sorry to interrupt your holiday, but I thought tomorrow might be too late." He handed her a packet wrapped in brown paper and turned to walk away.

A thunderbolt of an idea slammed into Jemmy's head. "Wait, Hal. Don't go. You could do something wonderful for a sad and lonely woman."

Hal turned back and blinked twice. "I didn't know you had

begun to take a romantic interest in me."

"Not me, you fool." Jemmy slid out onto the porch and closed the door gently. "You could bring such joy to a lonely old woman. She insists that her nephew is coming from Belgium. But there's no nephew. She has no one. If you could pretend for just a little while, it would do her no end of good."

"I'd like to help out, but—"

"Please, please. Have dinner with us. Everything is ready. I've never known a time when you would turn down food—turkey, pumpkin pie with whipped cream, all the trimmings. Just for an hour, pretty please."

"I'd do it, Jemmy, but I'm not alone." He waved at the girl with bouncy, light brown-colored curls on his yellow-green tandem bicycle. Miss Lucine Leimgruber waved back.

"Wonderful! Mrs. Hendershot's nephew is married."

"Hold on, Jemmy. We're supposed to be at Lucy's aunt's home by two."

"Not a problem. You'll be out of here in good time."

He took her arm and muttered between partly closed lips, "I wanted a little time alone with Lucy."

"Shame on you. Miss Leimgruber is a nice girl."

"To talk, just to talk."

"You have days and weeks and months and years to talk with Lucy. You only have now to be a godsend to a sad, sad lady."

Hal sighed. "I give. But only if you can talk Miss Lucine into it."

Jemmy rushed down the steps and embraced Lucy. "Miss Leimgruber, I'm thrilled to see you here because I know you are a Good Samaritan. I see it in your eyes. You could never deny aid to a poor soul in distress. Tell me you'll help. I beg you."

"Well, if you put it like that, how can I refuse?"

"Perfect. As I was telling Hal, Mrs. Hendershot has told everyone her nephew and his wife from Belgium are coming for dinner, but there is no nephew. How generous you two would be to play those parts—just through dinner—just for an hour. You'd bring more happiness than you could ever know to a sweet, sad old lady."

"We'll do it." Lucy leaned the bicycle against a lamppost. "Tell us all you can about Belgium."

Lucy beamed. Jemmy beamed. Hal rolled his eyes.

Jemmy crooked her arms through Hal's and Lucy's and guided them into the house. On the way she told them what little she knew about Mrs. Hendershot's imaginary nephew.

As the trio stood in the parlor doorway, she announced, "Ladies and gentlemen, let me introduce Mrs. Hendershot's guests, her nephew from Brussels, Mr. Harold Hendershot, and his lovely wife, Lucine."

Under her breath, Lucy asked, "Which one is she?"

Jemmy put an arm around her waist and steered her to the old lady.

Lucy kissed Mrs. Hendershot on both cheeks and emoted, "Nana Hendershot, I'm so pleased to meet you."

Hal kissed the old lady, too, but he drew his lips away as fast as if she'd been a wet bar of lye soap. Jemmy couldn't hear what he said, but it must have pleased Mrs. Hendershot. The old lady stood on tiptoe and took Hal's face in both hands. She planted a big, wet kiss smack on Hal's lips.

Purple streaks raced up his ears like red berry juice up poke stems in summer. Jemmy could see he longed to wipe the slobbers off his face but didn't dare. Mrs. Hendershot hugged them both as a gusher spouted from her eyes. Her emotion swept across the room until every eye—even Jemmy's—shed at least a few tears.

Lucy fetched her hanky and dabbed at her eyes. She gave Hal a look of warning. He got the message and fetched up his own handkerchief and offered it to Mrs. Hendershot—without even wiping a stray tear from his own face.

Lucy gave Hal another "look" until he put his arms around Mrs. Hendershot. She wept silently into his shoulder. This show of familial tenderness seemed to please Lucy, Mrs. Hendershot, and everyone in the room except Hal. All the same, he gamely put on a smile while Mrs. Hendershot soaked his lapels.

Jemmy excused herself to bang the dinner gong. With more than a little pride, she slid open the dining-room pocket doors to reveal the festive table with its unusual centerpiece of turkey tail feathers. She escorted the newly minted Hendershot family to one side with Mrs. H. between Hal and Lucy.

While Jemmy said grace, she surprised herself with the emotion she felt. She truly meant each word. The struggle of bringing dinner to the table had given her a brand new view of what it means to give thanks.

Jemmy presided over the feast. She carved the turkey not into elegant, thin slices, but odd-shaped chunks. Still, she managed to carve the bird without cutting herself—or anyone else. Randy and Dora waited table and served turkey soup and toast to the flu sufferers in the back room.

The food might not have had Gerta's deft touch with seasonings, but it was palatable enough to receive a good bit of praise. Mrs. Hendershot declared she preferred dressing without oysters. In short, the dinner was a resounding success, thanks to the multitude of setbacks the girls overcame in preparing it.

All through dinner, Lucy chatted away to Mrs. H. When anyone spoke to Hal, he stuffed a fresh forkful of food into his mouth.

By the time each bite of pumpkin pie had found its way into an already overstuffed stomach, Jemmy had to stifle a yawn. A nap would be a fine thing, but piles of dirty dishes needed washing, and leftovers needed tending.

What's more, Hal had cast a pleading look in her direction

on three separate occasions. At length Jemmy took the hint. "Ladies and gentlemen, I am more gratified than I can say to have you join me on this day of giving thanks. I would be overjoyed to linger, but I have duties to attend. Please stay at table as long as you wish. I'll bring out fresh coffee and seconds on pie for those who still have room. I'd be happy to serve it to you in the parlor if you would find that room more comfortable."

Hal jumped up from the table faster than a jack-in-the-box. Jemmy thought he would bolt straight out the front door if he could pry Lucy away from Mrs. H.

Jemmy's admiration for Lucy rose higher by the minute. She helped Mrs. Hendershot stand and walked arm in arm with her into the hall. The celebration of new-found relations concluded with at least a half-dozen tearful hugs. As she walked out the door, Lucy promised the couple would visit as often as they might before they had to return to Belgium. Jemmy patted Mrs. H.'s hand and walked her back to the dining room.

By then most of the company had risen. Some meandered off to the parlor to play chess or backgammon. Mrs. Hendershot suggested a whist game and found three like-minded souls. Jemmy's little deception had worked wonders on the old lady's attitude.

Jemmy couldn't help feeling proud. *I'll have to think of something nice to do for Hal.*

Jemmy started on chores while Dora and Randy ate. Not until after the last dish was dried did she remember the brown paper packet Hal had brought.

One look at the contents cleared Jemmy's head. All weariness evaporated. She had less than an hour to get ready and locate some means of transportation. With a little luck, Jemmy would soon be in the right place to find answers. *Handsome Harry Benson, Pervia Benigas, John Folck, Sassy Patterson—get ready.*

Jemima McBustle is going to find out what you know about the death of Quisenberry Sproat.

She sashayed to the kitchen, where Dora was rubbing her arm through its sling. Randy sat with head down on the kitchen table. "Put on a nice frock, Randy. You wouldn't want to miss the program at Mary Institute."

"Why would I want to go to Mary I on a day when I don't have to?"

"You know full well the girls will gossip about you behind your back."

"Let them. I've given them plenty of ammunition. The day I arrived, they were already looking down their noses at the poor girl whose mother takes in boarders."

"But today is special—the Thanksgiving matinee program."

Randy shot Jemmy a glare that could set paper on fire.

"Auntie Dee says you'll get an excellent education, excellent social contacts, and that public school won't turn you into a proper lady. Mary Institute can and will." Randy sat with her jaw set like a pug dog of Chinese porcelain. "Get up and get ready to go. You get demerits for not attending."

"Don't you think I know? I'm hoping to get so many, they boot me out of that miserable place. I'd much rather go to public school."

"Nonetheless, you and I are going."

"Be sensible. We'd never get there in time if we walk."

Jemmy had to chuckle at Randy's demand to be sensible. Being sensible to Randy meant eating dessert first because a tornado might strike during the meal. "I'm calling on a friend to take us."

"Who?"

"Someone I'd rather not even speak to, but someone who lives nearby, someone I think I can persuade to provide transportation."

As Jemmy picked up the telephone, guilt clawed up her spine. She looked behind her to see if Mother might be glaring at her. Mother would surely leave her sickbed to keep her daughter from making a forbidden personal call.

A tinny voice said in a lilt, "Number please."

Jemmy answered as loudly as she dared, "I'm sorry I don't know the number. I'm trying to call the Ploog residence on Albion Place. I wish to speak to Mr. Peter Ploog."

Mr. Bell's invention worked. A Ploog maid said she'd fetch Mr. Peter.

"Hello, Peter. This is Jemima McBustle."

"You sure are full of surprises, Jemmy."

"I know it's an imposition, but I'd be forever in your debt if you would escort my sister and me to the Thanksgiving matinee at Mary Institute."

"You mean today? Right now?"

"Yes, I know my asking is downright rude, especially on such terribly short notice. Ordinarily, I would have made arrangements in advance. We've had such turmoil here I didn't believe we could manage an amusement. But Miranda has been begging. You know she will earn demerits if she doesn't attend."

"I'd love to help, but my family expects—"

Jemmy cut him off. "I believe Sassy Patterson will be there."

"I'll be at your house in fifteen minutes."

On the way across town in Peter's phaeton, he asked, "Are you sure Sassy will be there?"

"No one can ever be sure about Sassy, but she said she'd see me there. That was on Tuesday, I think."

He answered by flicking the buggy whip over his pacer's ear. The shiny black gelding accelerated from trot to canter.

At Mary I, ushers rushed the trio into the recital hall. They had to sit at the back because the matinee had already begun. Pervia Benigas's fingers flew across the keys in some extraordinarily showy and impossibly difficult piano piece by Franz Liszt.

Turning pages for the pianist was none other than the homely shoe salesman for Barr's Department Store. In fact, John Folck wasn't turning pages. He was standing at the piano not turning pages. Pervia knew the piece by heart.

While Pervia took her bows, Folck left the stage. When he seated himself next to Sassy, Peter said, "Who the devil is that man next to Miss Patterson?" Jemmy shushed him with a finger to her lips.

A succession of fresh-faced schoolgirls entertained. First came a dramatic scene from Shakespeare's *Troilus and Cressida*. Next on the bill was a tableau of the three fates, with Lachesis pointing her staff toward a globe to represent birth, Clotho spinning the thread of life, and Atropos with a sundial to remind us of the shortness of human existence. *Leave it to schoolmarms to make sure people couldn't have a good time without at least a little subtle preaching.*

Poem recitations, sentimental songs, and nostalgic letters from alumnae in faraway places led to the grand finale. In tribute to soldiers newly back from winning the war in Cuba, the audience stood to sing the "Battle Hymn of the Republic."

After that thrilling end to the matinee, performers and audience alike mingled in the hall over milk punch and lady fingers. Peter Ploog trotted off in Sassy's direction.

Jemmy pushed her way into the circle around Pervia. "I wanted to wish you good luck in Cincinnati and to say how deeply I admire your skill at the pianoforte. Might you have a few words for the *Illuminator*?"

"I suppose I should say what everyone expects, 'Practice makes perfect.' "

"But that's not what you want to say to me, is it?"

"No. I'd say this: a person who spends as much time practicing as I do should be quite sure her dedication is not misplaced."

"Could you explain what that means?"

"No. I'll leave it to you to figure out. Do you have news for me?"

"I'll tell you as soon as you satisfy my curiosity on a few matters." Jemmy burned to ask one question: why did Pervia deny knowing any fighters other than Harry Benson? This place was far too public to ask. She'd have to maneuver Pervia away from her admirers.

The item in brown paper Hal had thought important enough to bring to Jemmy's house on Thanksgiving Day was a picture—a photograph of Quisenberry Sproat seated in a chair. Pervia Benigas stood behind him with her hand on his shoulder. The pair posed like couples in many formal photographic portraits—formal wedding portraits.

CHAPTER TWENTY-ONE

Thursday Afternoon, Thanksgiving Day, November 24, 1898

"Miss Patterson doesn't want to hear anything you have to say." With everyone else at the reception, Jemmy turned to see the drama at the far end of the hall. John Folck had taken Peter's arm and was forcing him towards the door.

Peter called back to Sassy, "I could understand losing out to Duncan McBustle or Tony von Phul, but to a shoe salesman? I thought you had better sense and better taste."

At that, Folck swung Peter around and raised him off the floor with an uppercut to his jaw. Ploog hit the floor with a dull thump. With Randy close behind, Jemmy picked up her skirts and ran toward her fallen escort.

On the way, Jemmy handed her hanky to her sister. "Wet this, Randy."

Jemmy pushed her way through the girls and their families gawking down at Peter.

Blood trickled onto Peter's vest as he struggled to prop himself up on one elbow. He dabbed his handkerchief at his nose. "I'll have the law on you, Folck."

"Prissy rich boys should think twice before they insult grown men."

"Shoe salesmen should think twice before they insult their betters."

Folck raised a foot and seemed about to land a kick square on Peter's cockiness. An audible intake of breath swished through the crowd. In the hush, Folck changed course. He backed away from Peter and offered his arm to Miss Patterson.

Jemmy looked at Sassy, the cause of all the trouble. The lovely Miss P. had her hand over her mouth as if to hide her shock, but her twinkling eyes told a different story. With a sinking feeling in her midsection, Jemmy saw the truth. Sassy relished her role as bone for these two dogs to scrap over.

Sassy didn't speak to poor Peter. Instead, she clung to Folck's arm as he led her toward the exit.

Jemmy raised her voice over the murmurs of the crowd. "Please return to your refreshments. Mr. Ploog is fine. He just needs some air. The set-to is over."

Randy returned from the water fountain with the damp hanky. The girls bent down to help Peter sit up.

Peter managed a hoarse whisper. "Did you see what he did, the bully? I couldn't fight back. He held my right arm while he belted me a good one."

The girls each took an arm and pulled him to his feet. Jemmy said, "Let me wipe the blood off your face."

Peter stood with his arms at his side and his lips trembling like a five year old letting his mommy fix a boo-boo.

Jemmy cooed, "There, there. That John Folck is no gentleman."

"He didn't give me a chance to fight back."

"And a good thing that is, too. You can charge him with assault. Everyone here will bear witness that he struck the only blow."

"Don't talk such garbage. I'm not about to parade my feebleness in a court of law. After all, the damage isn't too bad, is it?"

"Not too bad. Let's take inventory. Bloody nose—not broken though . . . at least I don't think so, bloody vest, swollen jaw. All in all, about the amount of pain you'd have if you ran into a door."

Peter touched his puffy jaw and winced. "Let me take you home. Cold air will be good for the swelling."

On the way, Jemmy tried to make small talk. "Pervia played brilliantly, don't you think?"

Peter grunted.

"On the Liszt piece, I mean."

Peter grunted.

"Mother says Franz Liszt deliberately composed complicated music so no one else could play it."

Peter grunted.

Jemmy quit trying to make conversation.

Back at Bricktop, Randy and Dora made turkey sandwiches while Mother dictated her mayonnaise recipe to Jemmy. The boarders picked at their cold supper—all but Mrs. Hendershot, who had a splendid appetite. Mrs. H. even praised the sweet potatoes with maple syrup and pecans. She said they tasted better cold than hot.

After clearing the dishes, Jemmy felt ready to fall into bed despite the early hour, but this eventful day had still more incidents in store.

Hal was back, this time without Lucy Leimgruber—and with his camera strapped to his ugly, yellow-green bicycle built for two.

Jemmy made a feeble attempt at a joke. "I had no idea I had such a magnetic personality. You've come back to see me twice on your day off."

"Now you're playing the fool. My reason for coming is purely professional. I came to give you a ride."

"A ride to what?"

"Frank James has called a meeting of newspaper journalists for this evening. We'd better not miss it. He says he'll announce who killed Quisenberry Sproat."

"Pretty clever, that Frank James." Jemmy nodded knowingly.

"Tomorrow's papers will be short on news because not many journalists have been out digging up stories. Breaking news about the Sproat murder would rate the front page on every newspaper in town."

"Hurry up. And you'd better do your share of pedaling if you want to be there when he starts talking."

By the time Hal set up his camera outside the city jail, Frank James was walking out the door wearing manacles. An escort of two burly policemen bracketed the famous bank robber like the back wheels on a tricycle.

The three stopped on the top step. Frank raised his arms. "Do you see these chains? I won't be wearing them much longer."

The audience chatter stopped.

Frank talked for a good five minutes about his innocence and about the district attorney's lack of evidence against him. Jemmy was in the middle of a yawn when he sprang his humdinger surprise.

Frank took a white paper from his pocket and held it up in his shackled hands. "Sealed in this envelope is the name of the person who murdered Quisenberry Sproat. I am going to give it to Miss Jemima McBustle for safekeeping until after the police have arrested the true culprit." He motioned for Jemmy to come forward.

He handed her the letter and said loudly enough for all to hear, "Miss McBustle, I am relying upon your discretion. I know these reckless men of the press. They wouldn't hesitate to meddle in police business—and possibly come to harm or allow the killer to escape.

"However, a nice young lady with high moral standards would never open a forbidden letter—not even for the grandest news story since Hamlet killed Laertes and Laertes returned the favor. So I charge you not to break this seal until the police have arrested the real murderer. Then you may read the letter and reveal all."

To the crowd, he said, "I'll leave you with these words from the great poet and dramatist William Shakespeare in *Richard the Third*. It describes my situation perfectly. 'True hope is swift, and flies with swallow's wings; Kings it makes gods, and meaner creatures kings.' "

Murmurs of discontent rippled through the crowd. "Giving the killer's name to that upstart girl—what's Frank James thinking?"

"I suppose you think he should give it to you."

"And why shouldn't he give it to me?"

"He probably knows you'd read the letter."

"Well, so would you."

"Damned straight. That's why he gave it to her."

One fellow tried to snatch it from her hand. Jemmy stuck the folded letter down her bosom—much to the delight of the crowd.

Frank James chuckled. "See there. I entrusted my secret to the right person."

The disappointed crowd disbanded. "What a waste of time. I wish I'd stayed home in front of the fire."

"Have you got something better for the front page tomorrow?"

"No. Guess I'll write the story—not that it is much of a story."

Hal found the perfect angle to take a picture of Jemmy holding the letter by the *City of Saint Louis Jail* sign.

While he strapped his camera gear on the bicycle, he asked casually, "So, are you going to open it?"

"Don't you think I have the moral fiber to resist?"

"I think you're the most curious female I ever met. I bet wondering what's in that letter is just about driving you insane."

"I'd greatly appreciate it if you would drop the word 'insane'

205

from your vocabulary."

"Sorry, I forgot."

Jemmy had often warned Hal not to mention anything about madness or insanity. That same summer, she'd tried to copy Nelly Bly by going undercover in a local asylum. That plan nearly met disaster. It was not an experience she recalled with pleasure.

Hal prodded again. "I've heard steaming is the preferred method for snooping in mail. A little glue and no one can tell."

"I can't steam this one open."

"I bet you put the kettle on the minute you get home. I want to watch."

"I'll admit I'm tempted, but I'm not going to try anything underhanded."

"Come now. I know you."

"I don't dare open it. If you don't believe me, take a look." She shoved the letter toward him. The letter *J* rose from a quarter-sized seal of red wax. "You can see for yourself. Steaming won't work."

On the way to Bricktop, Jemmy tried not to smile as she planned what to say in her Friday article. She couldn't help feeling smug. Frank James had chosen her from among all journalists in St. Louis.

Did Mrs. James have a hand in the decision? Why did he pick me? A sly thought that he might be mocking her because she was female sneaked into her consciousness. She shoved it away. He had chosen her because she was more trustworthy than the others. Frank James probably didn't know how useful a little deceit could be in the newspaper business.

Of course, a little deceit might also come in handy in the outlaw business. She decided to stop asking herself questions and think about how to open the letter when the time came. Perhaps another ceremony on the steps of city jail would show the grand opening to its best advantage. A little drama makes even a humdrum news story come alive.

All of a sudden, the bicycle stopped. Hal put a foot to the street as the tandem heeled over. He barely kept it from hitting the bricks of Chouteau Avenue.

Jemmy half fell, half skittered off. Her skirts and petticoats saved her from serious injury, but she landed in an icy puddle that dragged at her hems.

Hal rescued the lantern and placed it on the street while he unfastened the straps on his satchel.

"What happened?"

Hal didn't answer right away. He was too busy checking his equipment.

"Did we run over broken glass?"

"Not to worry, the photog plates are fine."

"Leave it to you to rescue little bits of glass instead of your partner."

"You need rescuing about as much as an earthworm needs a derby hat."

"This little earthworm would like to know what happened."

"Hold up the lantern while I take a look." Jemmy picked up the lantern to reveal the sad facts. The front wheel was wrenched out of shape and the tire punctured.

"For one thing, the tire is flat. New tire, too. But a flat tire wouldn't stop the wheel from turning."

"Did you hit a rock?"

"Would you look here? The spokes are all bent around a metal rod."

"Where did that come from?"

"I can't imagine. I guess it was just sticking up from the street. Either that, or someone stuck it in the wheel on purpose." Hal laughed a little nervous giggle and took the lantern from

Jemmy. He turned in a full circle as he pointed the light into the gloom.

"Must have been the boogeyman."

Two sets of eyes searched the darkness for attackers as the pair walked the rest of the way to Bricktop. *Is Sproat's killer desperate to get his hands on Frank James's letter?* Jemmy shivered—and not just because her skirts were cold and soggy. She was glad she'd worn her sturdy new Storm Queen boots. They'd come in handy for walking home in the slush.

Jemmy felt a stab of fear and imagined the boogeyman leaping out from behind each tree and hedge. One thing was clear: she wouldn't have a moment's peace until Sproat's killer was tucked up in St. Louis city jail.

As they trudged along, Jemmy said, "Hal, do you think you might stay near me? As long as I have the sealed letter, I mean."

"I guess that's what I'm getting paid to do. I'll have to go home for a sidearm though."

CHAPTER TWENTY-TWO

Friday Morning, November 25, 1898

Jemmy dreaded meetings with her editor. Still, she marched straight up to Suetonius Hamm's office the minute she'd hung her coat on a cloakroom peg.

He answered her knock with, *"Vita brevis est."* Hamm had the annoying habit of tossing apt Latin phrases into every conversation.

Jemmy stopped in the doorway to translate each word, "Life— short—is."

"Well, don't just stand there wasting time."

"Mr. Hamm, please look at this." Jemmy handed him the iron rod that had wrecked the tire on Hal's tandem bicycle. "Do you know what it is?"

"Looks like a bar from an iron fence." He pushed his glasses to the top of his bald head and turned the rod over in his hands. "Why show it to me?"

"It ruined the front wheel on the bicycle you gave Harold Dwyer."

"Can't see that running over this bar would destroy the whole wheel."

"We found it inside the tire—caught in the spokes."

"Must have been sticking up."

"Why would it be sticking up through the bricks of Chouteau Avenue?"

Hamm heaved an exasperated sigh. "Well, why don't we ask it?"

He held the bar in a vertical position. "Hello, iron fence bar. Would you be so kind as to tell us why you were sticking up through the bricks on Chouteau Avenue?"

He cocked his head as if to listen to the bar's reply. He nodded and said, "There you have it, Miss McBustle. Heard it with your own ears if you listened closely. Knocked out of a fence and dragged through the snow by a sleigh until it stuck between street bricks. Mr. Dwyer with his unerring sense of irony—if you'll pardon the pun—found it. That's how this little iron bar came to wreak havoc on *Illuminator* property."

"So you don't think someone threw it at us?"

"Why would I think that?"

"Because of this." She held up Frank James's sealed letter.

With a quick dip of his head, Hamm plopped his eyeglasses on his nose. "Ah, yes, the letter naming Quisenberry Sproat's killer."

"Might the killer have thrown the rod at us to get the letter?"

"Not likely."

"Why not?"

"You're here this morning—with the letter. If the killer had been determined to get the envelope, wouldn't he have bashed the pair of you on your empty heads? Then he could dash away with the letter."

"I had it hidden."

Hamm chuckled. "I understand everyone at the jail saw where you secreted the missive."

Jemmy gasped. "Do you think a man would—"

"I imagine a desperate killer would do just about anything. You must admit your bosom—while marginally effective against gentlemen—is not comparable in security to the big safe at Boatmen's Bank."

All this talk of her bosom made Jemmy decidedly uncomfortable. "Nonetheless, Mr. Hamm, I want the world to know that I am not in possession of this letter."

"What do you propose?"

"You say the safest place is the vault at Boatmen's Bank. Let me lock away the letter. Hal can take a picture of me handing it over to the bank president. I've already written the story."

"Far too late for this morning's paper."

"You could put out an extra edition."

Hamm snorted. "Wishful thinking is a petty indulgence no true reporter would condone. *Ad praesens ova cras pullis sunt meliora ad quem ad quod.*"

"I'm afraid my Latin is not sufficient to—"

"Eggs today are better than chickens tomorrow."

"In that case, I offer you the best of both worlds. I always deliver eggs today. You must admit my stories sell papers."

Hamm dipped his head in an almost imperceptible nod of acknowledgement.

"I solemnly promise to also deliver chickens tomorrow."

"Please don't stretch the metaphor any further. It's about to snap like a cheap garter." No sooner did the words escape his mouth than Hamm apologized. "Pardon my lack of delicacy."

"I'd be pleased to drop the metaphor if you'll print banners for newsboys to hold up. The banners should say 'James Letter Safe in Boatmen's Bank.' I'd also like the same notice posted on the sandwich board out front."

Jemmy smiled sweetly. "And, don't forget, you specifically asked me to consult you if I wished to write a news story featuring an advertiser."

"All right. All right. Take Dwyer and get a picture at the bank. I'll call Boatmen's president and pave the way, but don't forget you have a regular assignment. I expect your articles on time. I won't tolerate your slipping by on your looks just because your whims and fancies please a few advertisers."

As Jemmy turned to leave, Hamm stopped her with a request. "Before you go, would you please fetch me one of those aspirin powders."

Jemmy poured a glass of water and brought him a paper packet from the top of his file cabinet. Hamm tossed the powder to the back of his throat and chased it with water. He shuddered at the sour taste. "*Yaacch.* Why on earth would Frank James give the name of the killer to you in a sealed envelope?"

"I've been wondering that myself."

Hamm pushed up his glasses and rubbed his temples. "I shall never understand why the newspaper gods continue to smile on you. Why can't they beam just a little ray on a real reporter from time to time?"

Hamm's words hurt. As if that weren't painful enough, another male ambushed her the minute she left the editor's office. Amadee Boudinier blocked her exit from the cloakroom. "If it isn't little miss know-it-all-before-anyone-else."

Jemmy could hold her tongue no longer. "Perhaps you should spend more time on the streets of the city and less time at your warm and comfortable desk. Maybe then Frank James would choose you to carry his mail."

Boudinier stuck his oversized nose in her face. His breath smelled like sour milk and green onions. "Don't forget I'm the ace crime reporter around here. I have more contacts and a better nose for news than anyone else at the *Illuminator.*"

"So that's why it's growing longer. Silly me. I thought the legend of Pinocchio was just a children's story."

"Watch out, little miss smarty mouth. Knowing too much can get a person in big trouble."

Somewhere deep in the recesses of her consciousness she realized one truth. Sparring with enemies could never come to anything good. Even so, she couldn't stop ranting. "I guess that's why my stories sell papers. You must never have noticed that big trouble means big stories."

Boudinier stomped off. "Stick to your assignments. I'd say covering the Hebrew fair would be about right."

Oddly enough, Boudinier had done Jemmy a favor. She'd forgotten she was slated to interview the president of the fair that morning. She mumbled to herself, "What's a girl to do? My newspaper job keeps interfering with my real newspaper job. How am I supposed to get to the bottom of an important murder story when I have to spend hours at flower shows and bazaars?"

She longed to re-visit the elixir lady to find out the names of her customers. Jemmy thought she'd even buy a potion if that was the only way to get the woman to talk. Her interview with Mabel Dewoskin would have to wait until she'd been to Boatmen's Bank and to the Jewish fair.

While Hamm telephoned Boatmen's president, Jemmy re-read the message on the outside of the envelope: "This envelope to remain sealed until Quisenberry Sproat's true killer is discovered, at which time it is to be opened by Miss Jemima McBustle IN PRIVATE." The last two words were capitalized and underlined.

Why does Frank James want me to be the one to open the letter, and why must I be alone? Jemmy had little time to ponder Frank James's methods. She and Hal had news to make and news to cover.

Hamm's telephone call to the bank brought excitement to the dignified hush of the bank's cold and substantial marble. Entrusting Frank James's letter to the vault pleased the Boatmen's Bank staff in a big way. The president struck a majestic pose as he accepted the envelope from Jemmy. After Hal's flash lit up the scene, the assembled tellers applauded. When the president emerged from the vault, he insisted Jemmy and Hal have tea with him in his office.

"Miss McBustle, what are your thoughts on the best way to handle the letter once the culprit who killed Mr. Sproat is brought to light?"

"I hope to return, follow the directions on the envelope, and then make a public announcement."

Hal nudged her with his elbow.

"Of course, Hal will come, too. He'll take a picture of the two of us with the opened letter."

"That's all well and good, but I really can't have my business disrupted again as it has been today. My clerks are all in a dither and getting very little work done."

"Don't you agree that free publicity is good for your business? Won't people remember that Frank James and trustworthy Jemima McBustle chose the big vault at Boatmen's as the safest place in St. Louis?"

"Yes. I hadn't thought of these events in those terms. Still, I hope you'll plan to come near the close of business hours."

All the way back to the *Illuminator*, Jemmy glowed with special awareness. By pure chance, she had stumbled onto a grand way to conjure up a story when news was slow. All she had to do was cook up a pretense to feature an advertiser in a news article.

Of course, her immediate problem was to scout out a story no one could advertise—at least not in newspapers. She needed to know more about the bare-knuckles fight. She had to find information to trade with Pervia Benigas. Without Pervia's help, she had no way of discovering why Harry Benson had been johnny-on-the-spot to replace Sproat after he was murdered.

While Hal was off developing his photographic plates, Jemmy had a few precious minutes. She stopped by Autley Flinch-paugh's sports desk. "Be a dear and tell me what time the bare-knuckles fight is to start."

He looked up in alarm. "Miss McBustle, you shouldn't know such brutality even exists—a young lady like yourself, and in such a delicate state."

Jemmy started to deny she was in any state except Missouri but thought better of it. She dabbed at the corner of her eye. "How can I make you understand, dear Mr. Flinchpaugh? This is my only chance to see him—you know, my young man."

"In my opinion you're better off without him."

She placed her hand over his. "My necessity is urgent. After tonight, I think he will go back to Chicago."

"What do you hope to achieve?"

"I must tell him something very personal. Perhaps I can persuade him to remain in St. Louis."

Autley sent a furtive glance around the room to see if anyone was watching. He slid his hand out from under Jemmy's and said, "Won't a letter do?"

"Some news must be given face to face."

"Well, then, I suppose you must go—and I suppose I must go with you. You'd need a shoulder to lean on if—Well, you need a true friend to help you face him."

"Bless you, Mr. Flinchpaugh. I'd be eternally in your debt."

"I'll collect you from your home at ten o'clock this evening. The fight is scheduled after usual business hours."

"Perhaps now you feel free to tell me when it starts."

"Well, I suppose I could tell you but only if you promise I will be allowed to accompany you. Do I have your word?"

Jemmy nodded solemnly.

"The fight is to begin at Uhrig's Cave at midnight tonight."

Jemmy shuddered. *A cave—why does it have to be a cave?*

She felt guilty at deceiving the sports reporter but not guilty enough to tell him the truth—not just yet.

When Hal appeared from the darkroom, he and Jemmy set off for the Coliseum to report on the last day of the Hebrew charity fair. The fair had been in full swing all week. Jemmy interviewed the president of the United Jewish Societies, Julius Lesser.

President Lesser reminded Jemmy of a bramble bush after the leaves have fallen in November—all crossed twigs and bristles. He sported a full beard spurting from his high, round collar. A little round cap perched atop the crown of his curly-haired head. Dark hair sprouted from every bit of skin peeking out from his three-piece suit. Most remarkable of all were his eyebrows. They looked like the pelt of a small, furry rodent.

Jemmy was well-nigh hypnotized by his eyebrows. With every syllable President Lesser spoke, they twitched like an animal caught in a trap.

"I'm more than happy to tell the *Illuminator* that the fair is exceeding all our expectations. We hoped to raise thirty thousand dollars to build a free school to teach poor children skills needed in industry. I now believe we'll raise forty thousand or more."

Mr. Lesser rubbed his hands together in his excitement. "You should have been here for the matinee on Tuesday. Six thousand people came to watch the acrobats from Japan. And the Monster Cake Walk—more than a hundred couples cutting monkey shines."

Jemmy had learned a little praise will often bring out the best in an interview subject. "The Coliseum has never looked better. Where did you find such glorious flowers to decorate every booth? I see red, white, and blue bunting in graceful swags everywhere I look."

Mr. Lesser chortled and grinned. "St. Louis can be proud of this grand place. We should thank the tornado of '96. Who would have thought St. Louis could construct a bigger and better one in just two years? It does show up well in the lights—eight hundred electric lights. When they were first turned on, I thought I'd go blind."

"How many booths do you have?"

"Thirty-five. Let's walk down Dewey Avenue to see a few."

"I see you named your streets after heroes of the Spanish-American War."

"Yes. It seemed natural to name our biggest thoroughfare after the admirable admiral. We are nothing if not patriotic. Your Mr. Dwyer missed a wonderful photograph. At the opening, one hundred and twenty-five school children of about the same height became a living flag with forty-five stars."

"What a novel idea. But I see you have many excellent ideas. Which are your most popular booths?"

"They're all splendid. We sell everything from furniture to candy. We're particularly proud of our orchestra booth." He nearly popped a vest button in his exuberance.

"The orchestra is in Milwaukee, but you can hear it over a telephone wire right here."

He bent to speak softly into her ear. "To tell the truth, I think pretty girls are our biggest draw. One of the most popular booths is manned—I suppose I should say 'girled'—by lovely young ladies from Mary Institute. They sell copies of the St. Louis *Post-Dispatch*."

Jemmy blinked.

"I'm sorry. I shouldn't have named your rival. No doubt you can't mention that other newspaper in your article."

"The *Post* is an evening paper, Mr. Lesser. Since The *Illuminator* is a morning publication, we're not in direct competition."

The three walked on in silence until Mr. Lesser stopped in front of the burlesque booth. "I'll take you inside, but you must promise not to reveal what you see here until after the fair closes tomorrow night—and no photographs, please."

Jemmy was intrigued. What would she find on the other side of those blue velvet drapes?

The booth displayed signs over items presented as if they

217

were genuine memorabilia in a museum. But those banners bore tongue-in-cheek descriptions. "Early home of Washington" was propped up in front of a cradle. "Assistant Editor" stood comic guard over a pair of scissors.

Hal hooted and pointed at a spoof on the army, "Mustered In and Mustered Out," behind a pair of mustard jars, one full and one empty.

They strolled on past the Tennyson Club, the Palmistry Booth, and the Beer Knelpe. Mr. Lesser treated them to lunch in the restaurant. "Be sure to try the knishes" were his parting words as he was called away to solve some crisis involving the Turkish tobacco booth.

After taking a few steps, he rushed back to hand free passes to the pair. "Be my guests tomorrow night for the grand finale. We're announcing the winner of the Most Popular Girl Contest, and we're closing with a confetti battle. You wouldn't want to miss that."

Jemmy wrote her Hebrew fair article between bites of savory chicken soup with tasty dumplings called matzo balls. Hal agreed the food was excellent. "I've never had a better sandwich than the spiced beef tongue."

Story finished and camera equipment secured, the pair headed for the exit nearest Washington Avenue.

A high voice called out, "Stop. Red hair man. Red hair woman. Stop, damn you. I say stop."

Chapter Twenty-Three

Friday Afternoon, November 25, 1898

As Jemmy and Hal were leaving the Jewish fair, a tiny member of the Japanese acrobats darted in front of them. Jemmy thought the girl could be no more than ten. She stood less than four feet high and couldn't have tipped the scales above seventy pounds carrying a cannonball.

"Stop, damn you! I say stop. Damn, damn rude not stop."

Hearing cuss words from that tiny female shocked the pair into following orders. Jemmy looked at Hal. His brow furrowed in surprise and disgust.

"Photo san. I show ass trick." She whipped off her sky-blue kimono embroidered with yellow butterflies and scarlet birds. In her pale tights and clinging silk jersey blouse, she looked like an enormous white grub worm.

"I make letter *M*. Watch, damn you. I make you shitface happy." The girl bent over backwards until her head formed the middle of a capital *M* inside her two legs.

"How you rike Kyoto Nakamura hijinks?"

Neither replied.

When she righted herself, no one could have called Kyoto's face happy—with or without obscene qualifiers. Hal had been so immobilized by the filth erupting from this nearly naked girl-child's mouth, he had not even set up his camera. The color in his pink ears deepened to red.

"Shitbrain, why you no take photo? I do double letter good."

She stood glowering with arms akimbo and hands on hips.

Jemmy said, "I didn't quite get your name. Could you please spell it for me?"

"I sperr name for newspaper bitch if shitbrain man take photo."

At Jemmy's nod, Hal unslung his equipment. With scarlet ears and pursed lips, he banged his tripod on the floor.

Jemmy opened her notebook and took down the spelling. "K-Y-O-T-O. May I please have your age for my article?"

"I twenty-six year."

Jemmy dropped her pencil. "You look much younger."

"No eat. Fat hog no can bend. No bend, no pisshead job."

Jemmy had never heard such cussing in her entire life—and from a grown woman. She'd had about enough of Miss Naka-mura's offensive speech. "I don't believe I can interview you any longer if you insist upon insulting my ears with curse words."

With praying hands, the girl gave a little bow. "My Engrrish bad. I hear in circus cuss words. Arr time cuss words. I beg forgive Kyoto."

Jemmy nodded. "Well, then, Kyoto, if I may call you 'Kyoto' in my article?"

Kyoto nodded.

Hal said, "Hey, isn't Kyoto the name of a city?"

Kyoto nodded. When she opened her mouth, she pronounced the words slowly. "Kyoto home, not true name. Nariko girr name. No can come here if girr. Make rike Chinaman have thing from pig ass on head. No—no, bad word." She put her hand over her mouth.

Hal said, "I think she means 'pigtail.' "

Kyoto cocked her head. "Kyoto get. Say 'tairrl' okay. Say 'ass' not okay. Kyoto know now."

"I see. You pretended to be a Chinese boy in order to get into this country?"

Kyoto nodded with enthusiasm. "You smart-tail missy."

"But why did you do that? I thought Chinese women were barred from coming here, but not Japanese."

"White men thick in head. No see with eyes. Think China woman, Japan woman—same."

Jemmy knew right well the feeling of being misunderstood. She considered herself a serious journalist; but other people, especially men, didn't. All too many of both sexes lumped her into the category of giggling schoolgirls with nothing on their minds but pretty clothes and cute boys.

"I'd like to use your real name if I might."

"Nariko. Means child work hard. But acrobat name Kyoto. You use prrease."

"Nariko is a lovely name, and clearly you are a hard worker. However, I will call you 'Kyoto' if you wish."

"Kyoto thank missy."

"Miss Kyoto, how long have you been in the United States?"

"Since I am fourteen year."

"Have you always been an acrobat with the Japanese company?"

"Kyoto acrobat even before come U.S. of A. First work circus."

"I've always found the circus thrilling. Are you sorry you left?"

"Not Kyoto. Circus have three ring. Too much. Must finish same time in three ring. Many show. Work too hard. Much better work for acrobat master. *Sensei* much worthy."

"Just now, you dislocated your shoulders. Doesn't that hurt?"

Kyoto shrugged. "When master first teach, hurt much. Now, not much."

"How old were you then?"

"Six, seven. Who know?"

"Didn't your parents stop him?"

221

"Parents trade Kyoto. Get two pig."

Jemmy's heart went out to this tiny woman who could twist her shoulders in and out of their joints but who'd never had a warm shoulder to lean on. "When did you go to school?"

"Not go. Have more better Engrrish if go."

"What do you think of the fair? You must have seen a great many. How does this one measure up?"

"Some bad. Some good."

"What parts were bad?"

"Monster cake walk bum."

"Why was it . . . ?" Jemmy couldn't bring herself to say "bum"—not in front of Hal.

"Cake walk no good dance. Good dance have two do same turn same time. Cakewalk man and woman not same turn. I show." Kyoto threw out her chest, stuck out her chin, and rolled back one shoulder. While holding the brim of an imaginary hat, she made high kicks right and left, then a high hop into a spin that ended in a jaunty stroll.

"Partner not dance same. See." Kyoto tucked her chin to her chest, pulled her shoulders in, and made the same movements. But this time, she kept her gestures tiny and refined. Instead of kicking three feet high, her feet rose just three inches.

Jemmy couldn't squelch her laughter over the comical show. "Well, ladies have been taught not to show their ankles, much less their legs."

"Bad dance. Bad singer, too. Kyoto not rrike."

"What do you like about the fair?"

"Most pretty. Fairy magic. And the rradies. Such fine dresses. Must have much dorrar."

"Yes, the ladies are wearing their most expensive finery."

"Kyoto work hard. Get fine Engrrish gown."

"Wouldn't you rather wear a kimono? The one you threw on the ground has beautiful embroidery."

Kyoto kicked at the sky-blue silk. "Kimono much bad. Must take tiny step. Engrrish gown free feet. Take big step. Much good. Much free."

Jemmy thought an American gown was about as free as a straitjacket, and she had personal knowledge of both. Of course, Kyoto weighed no more than a medium-sized wet dog. Surely she didn't wear a corset, so perhaps she did feel free.

"The Chinese garments I've seen look free—like pajamas."

"Chinese cheap. No buy American. Kyoto not cheap. Kyoto star. Kyoto buy American gown."

"Yes, I can see why you're a star acrobat. You entertain and amaze."

"I show good trick. Kyoto put tairr on own head. You watch." Kyoto tucked her head down and stood on her forearms. She curled her body backwards in a big letter *C*. Her ballet shoes touched her hair. She slipped her legs forward still more until her behind rested on her head.

Hal took a picture. Jemmy applauded. "That's the most astounding feat of flexibility I've ever seen."

Kyoto's feet found the floor. She gracefully finished a somersault to end up in a bow. "Kyoto thank."

Kyoto posed for one final picture, then bowed again. "You put Kyoto picture in paper. Make boss damn happy. 'Scuse bad word, prrease."

As Kyoto shrugged into her kimono and left with one more bow, Jemmy handed her article on the Jewish fair to Hal. "Take this to Hamm. He can run it with a picture of President Lesser."

"The pictures of Kyoto would be more interesting."

"I'll write a separate feature for Kyoto. Hamm can use her story later."

"If I go back to the *Illuminator*, what will you do?"

"I'm going to see someone about a story I've been working on."

"Then I have to go with you."

"I don't need you to watch over me. I'm paying a visit on an old classmate."

Hal perked up. "Are you going to see Miss Patterson?"

"Stop drooling. You'll ruin your photography plates. I'm not visiting Sassy Patterson. I'm paying a call on concert pianist Pervia Benigas. What she lacks in beauty, she makes up for in moodiness and talent."

"I'm supposed to go with you. Do I have to keep reminding you that I'm your bodyguard?"

"You'd be in the way. Honestly, how could Pervia and I have a private, personal conversation with you twiddling your thumbs in the hall?"

"Well then, if you promise not to get into trouble, I guess I should go back to the paper."

"If you don't go back now, you may miss the deadline."

Jemmy hadn't exactly lied to Hal. She did plan to visit Pervia Benigas—but not right away. A short streetcar ride whisked her to the hotel home of Mabel Dewoskin, the evil witch of elixirs.

To avoid the greasy desk clerk, Jemmy traipsed back to the alley behind the seedy establishment. What she saw there made her duck behind a trash barrel. Fortunately, the man turned the other way as he hoofed it toward the street.

Although she caught only a glimpse of his face, Jemmy knew for certain the man was John Folck of the big hands and feet. He even wore the same highly polished brown spectator shoes that seemed out of place on his loose-jointed frame. Sassy's shoe-clerk beau tucked a bottle of something in his pocket as he raced off.

Jemmy wondered whether Folck had been to see Mabel. The item he stuck in his pocket was the right size to be Mabel's cordial. Perhaps he bought paregoric for himself, or for Sassy. She filed the scene in the back of her memory.

The kitchen door opened to her touch. She eased into the dimly lit room with the intention of surprising Mabel. Instead, Mabel surprised her.

CHAPTER TWENTY-FOUR

Friday Afternoon, November 25, 1898
Jemmy tripped over an obstacle and had to fight to keep her balance. She would have sprawled on the kitchen floor if her hands hadn't found the top of the iron stove. Luckily the fire had burned out long ago.

When she looked down at the blockage on the floor, she froze.

Wearing a Snow Queen boot, very like her own, was a leg. The leg probably belonged to Mabel Dewoskin, though the fancy new boots and royal-blue wool skirt didn't seem at all Mabel-like.

The rest of a woman's body lay hidden under the stove. Cautiously, Jemmy pulled the cord on the electric light and bent down under the place where Mabel cooked her tonics. Shadows obscured the place between the curved feet of the huge iron stove. She still couldn't see the woman's face.

There was only one way to know for certain. Bad ear roaring with the blood pulsing through her temples, Jemmy grabbed the leg to pull the woman out from under the stove. One good tug did the trick. A key ring with a dozen or more keys rattled free of the woman's clenched fingers.

Jemmy recognized the mortal remains of Mabel's scraggly, gray, corn-shuck doll face—now mottled with purple.

Oddly enough, Mabel dressed better in death than she had in life. Her pale-mauve silk blouse and wool suit cut in the latest fashion bespoke an honest business woman. Her scraggly, gray

226

hair had been tamed into a sedate bun. She looked as though she knew she was about to die and wanted to leave this world looking her best.

Not until after she'd studied the body for several minutes did Jemmy remember one crucial fact—police didn't like people to meddle in crime scenes. Still, Jemmy wasn't sorry she'd dragged Mabel's corpse into the light.

Around the woman's neck a noose of thin wire cut into Mabel's flesh. Purple bruising bloomed around the wire. Apparently she'd been strangled. Clotting blood on her neck where she'd clawed at the wire revealed the violence of her death. One fingernail hung, torn and bloody, as testament to her desperate fight to breathe.

An overwhelming outhouse odor struck Jemmy's nostrils. Heaping humiliation on horror, Mabel had shat herself. Jemmy sat looking at the body for five minutes, then ten. Thoughts raced through her head so fast, she couldn't catch one to examine it.

Should she find a policeman? *If I tell the authorities, I'll have to stay here until they say I can leave. What would happen to my plan to see Pervia Benigas and find out what she knows?*

Should she sneak out? *What if someone sees me? I could be accused of killing this woman.*

Something rough and wet tickled her fingers. All on its own, her hand must have been stroking Mabel's ugly cat. She jerked back in shock and disgust to discover it licking her hand. The calico jumped away and hid under the stove. Then Jemmy's heart went out to the poor homely beast.

At least the cat had brought her back to reality and set her brain to functioning.

One thing became clear. She couldn't stay in the kitchen staring at Mabel Dewoskin's corpse. Any minute someone might walk in to find her standing over a dead woman. *How am I going to explain to Mother what her eldest daughter was doing in the kitchen of a paregoric maker—a dead paregoric maker?*

At length, Jemmy calmed her fluttering nerves enough to do what she had to do. She used Mabel's keys to unlock a cabinet door. She read the labels aloud, "Aconite, Adder venom, Arsenic. Belladonna. Poisons. The cabinet is filled with poisons."

She relocked the cabinet and dropped the keys before she marched out to the lobby. "I believe you have a telephone. Please summon the police. Mabel Dewoskin has been murdered."

The greasy-haired clerk raced back to the kitchen, then reappeared in the lobby.

His face paled, and his chest heaved. He collapsed in a chair with a *whomp* that sent dust particles floating in the air. He put his head in his hands while he moaned, "Bad for business, bad for business."

She had to make the telephone call herself. As she stood on tiptoe to speak into the wooden box, she became aware of movement under her skirt. An involuntary shriek sent her feet upward, but there was nothing to jump upon.

What emerged from her skirt was not a mouse, but Mabel's cat. It raced behind a big vase filled with umbrellas. She apologized for the outburst. "Your cat scared me."

"It ain't my cat."

"The hotel cat, I mean."

"The hotel has no cat."

"Was it Mabel's cat then?"

"Unlikely. We have a 'no pet' policy." He bestirred himself from his chair, grabbed the cat, and flung it out the front door. "I don't need no cat to take care of. My own responsibilities are quite enough for what I'm paid."

Before long a clanging police wagon arrived with several men, including the coroner. Dr. Wangermeier glared at Jemmy. He didn't so much as speak her name or make any sign he knew her—just walked straight back to the kitchen.

The desk clerk and several policemen accompanied him. One stayed in the lobby and took out his notebook to interview her. She recognized him from the Bertillon system lecture at police headquarters. He was the same young lieutenant who'd shown her the weapons case.

His first question was, "Did you kill Mabel Dewoskin?"

CHAPTER TWENTY-FIVE

Friday Afternoon, November 25, 1898

"Me? Kill Mabel Dewoskin? You have no right to accuse me!" Jemmy dug her nails into her palms to keep from screaming at the thought.

"Please don't be insulted. I'm not accusing, merely asking. It's a question I have to put to you." Lt. Sorley O'Rourke thumbed the pages of his notebook and poised his pencil.

"You don't really think I murdered her, do you? Would I have called the police? Would I still be hanging around this hotel to answer your outrageous questions?"

"I apologize, Miss McBustle. By thunder, the last thing I want to do is upset you. We can postpone our talk if you'd like."

Jemmy sighed. "Go on. Ask your questions. I have no desire to stay here one minute more than I have to."

He jotted answers to question after question. "When did you arrive?"

"About one o'clock."

"How did you enter the kitchen?"

"I came in through the alley."

"Why didn't you use the main entrance?"

"The last time I was here, the desk clerk wanted a bribe. I was trying to avoid him."

"What brought you to this hotel today?"

"I wanted to talk to Mabel Dewoskin."

"What about?"

"I wanted to get the names of her cordial clients."

"For what purpose?"

"I am a journalist. I was working on a news story."

"I understand the lady makes elixirs. Making cordials is not illegal—or proper news either. Why did you want the names?"

"I thought knowing Mabel's customers might help me find the killer of Quisenberry Sproat."

"What connection does Mabel Dewoskin have with Sproat?"

"I believe he was a customer, or that he bought paregoric for his mother. I saw one of Mabel's bottles at his home. That's why I came here in the first place." Jemmy conveniently forgot Mabel's letter demanding that Sproat pay up.

"Were you a friend of Sproat?"

"No. I never met him."

"Then why were you at his home?"

"I saw him die. I went backstage with the coroner. Frank James took us. When the police arrested Mr. James, I didn't think he could have killed Sproat. So, I started an investigation of my own."

"Why don't you believe Frank James is guilty?"

"For one thing, the timing was wrong. Sproat died early in the play. Frank James takes tickets out front. Sproat was backstage. I don't see how the two men could have been anywhere near each other. Besides, Mr. James was completely polite and helpful—just a man doing his job."

"You could be describing a cold-blooded killer."

"My feminine intuition tells me otherwise."

"By thunder, meddling in police affairs could be dangerous."

"Not to mention frustrating. I seem to be going around in circles."

"Can you shed any light on Sproat's death?"

"No. I don't believe I've discovered anything important."

"Not even by reading Frank James's letter?"

"The letter is in the vault at Boatmen's Bank—unread."

The lieutenant shut his notebook. "I hope you're being truthful. Police don't take kindly to amateur sleuths. By thunder, you could be placing yourself in a killer's gun sights." He rose to leave—after writing down her address.

"I might have one more bit of information."

"What's that?"

"The name of the person I saw leaving down the alley behind the hotel just before I found Mabel's body."

The lieutenant re-opened his book. "I'm waiting."

"I saw John Folck leave. Folck is a shoe salesman at Barr's Department Store."

"What is your acquaintance with Folck?"

"I interviewed him for a story on winter shoes." Jemmy started to add that Folck was a friend of a friend named Sassy Patterson, but reconsidered.

"What did this Folck person do in the alley?"

"Put something—I couldn't tell what—in his pocket and walked toward the street."

"Did he appear sneaky?"

"No—just in a hurry."

"Is there anything else you recall?"

Jemmy considered a few seconds before she spoke. "No. I believe that's everything. Are we finished?"

"I have just one more question. Would you do me the honor of accompanying me to the confetti battle tomorrow evening at the Hebrew fair?"

Jemmy blinked twice. "Are you asking to escort me on behalf of the police?"

The lieutenant grinned. "Not at all. I'm asking on behalf of yours truly, Sorley O'Rourke."

"Isn't it illegal for you to consort with suspects in a murder case?"

"Illegal? No, I don't think so. Besides, I don't consider you a suspect. You're a witness."

"Perhaps it's not illegal, but isn't it immoral for police to consort with witnesses in a murder case?"

"Last Sunday I let you get away without even knowing my name. By thunder, I've been kicking myself ever since. So, may I call for you at eight?"

"I am already engaged for the Confetti War."

Jemmy had to look at O'Rourke with new eyes. He'd turned into a prospective suitor. The lieutenant was quite good looking, in a black Irish sort of way. He was tall, at least five feet ten inches tall, and well-muscled. Glossy, black curls crowned his head. Jemmy looked at them in envy. She could have such curls only by sleeping on rag curlers.

He smelled of horses and leather. Jemmy found the scent manly and agreeable.

O'Rourke had one feature even more striking than his hair. His steely-gray eyes probably caused people to confess when he grilled them. They carried the menace of lead shot.

Then, too, something she couldn't quite identify bespoke intimidation. Lieutenant O'Rourke scared her. Jemmy decided to keep him at arm's length, the way she would carry a slops bucket on the verge of overflowing.

Jemmy couldn't leave for the Benigas home until after three. At the trolley stop, she jotted notes until something tickled her leg. Movement under her skirt made her jump back. Mabel's scruffy cat sneezed. It stood on the board sidewalk with its long, white eyebrows quivering.

Jemmy flicked an arm towards the creature. "Shoo. Scat. Go away."

The cat seemed to think the words were an invitation. It trotted under Jemmy's skirt. Jemmy hopped back.

The cat blinked its eyes and trotted toward Jemmy's skirt

again. "Oh, no, you don't." Jemmy scooped up the cat and slipped the animal into her satchel. "Don't you make a mess in my handbag."

At the Benigas home, the maid answered her knock and invited her in from the cold. "Miss Pervia and her mother have already left for her concert in Cincinnati. Would you like to speak to Mr. Benigas?"

"When did Pervia leave?"

"I don't recall, but I do know her train was scheduled to depart at 4:02."

"Thank you. Perhaps I can still catch her."

As Jemmy raced to the nearest trolley stop, she calculated the minutes. Yes, she should be able to get to Union Station by four. She could tell Pervia that the big bare knuckles fight would be held at Uhrig's Cave at midnight. *Why would Pervia want to know if she had already planned to be out of town?* Well, she'd ask Pervia if she had time.

Jemmy ran the last block down Market Street to Union Station. Breathless, she searched the departures board. She raced to track eleven as the last customers boarded the eastbound 4:02. Pervia was not among them.

Despite protests from passengers, she pushed herself to the front of the boarding line. The conductor said, "Miss, would you please go to the end of the boarding line."

"I apologize for my rudeness, but I'm not a passenger. My sister is on her way to Cincinnati, but she forgot her medicine. May I take it to her? I'll be back in a few seconds."

The conductor said, "For Cincinnati, she should be in the first or second car on the right."

Jemmy brushed past passengers stowing their belongings, but Pervia wasn't there. Frantic by now, she hurried up and down the aisles and back down the steps to the conductor. "Please, sir, can you tell me if Miss Benigas has come on board?"

"Sorry, Miss. I don't even know how many people are on board until we leave the station. You must get off the train now or become one of the passengers."

"But my sister's medicine. I—"

"Calm yourself. Give me the medicine. If she's on board, I'll see she gets it."

"But I couldn't find her."

"She might have gone to the dining car. She very probably is on board." He held out his hand.

Jemmy fumbled in her reticule but could find nothing to give him to cover her lie. The best she could do was say, "Heavens in a handbag! I seem to have forgotten the medicine, too."

He chuckled. "Forgetfulness must run in the family. Not to worry. Cincinnati is a fine city. I'm sure your sister will be able to find whatever medicine she requires."

The conductor put his hands round her waist and set Jemmy firmly on the platform. He took his stepstool and climbed up on the lowest train step to fasten a chain across the exit. He waved the all-clear, and the train chugged out of its berth.

Jemmy watched until the caboose proved the train was well and truly gone. *I still don't know why Pervia wanted to meet Handsome Harry Benson. I don't even know if Pervia and Benson were supposed to meet on Wednesday at all. Perhaps Pervia was stringing me along. Perhaps she didn't want to tell me why she was at Union Station, so she made up an excuse.*

Filled with many questions and few answers, Jemmy started for the nearest trolley stop to go home but changed her mind and her direction. *I may find a few answers on Lucas Place. I think I'll pay a call on Sassy Patterson. At half past four in the afternoon, she should be out of bed. That will make a nice change.*

The maid opened the front door with "Good afternoon, Miss McBustle. Would you care to wait in the morning room while I see whether Miss Patterson is at home?"

"What a stylish greeting. You must have been practicing."

The girl beamed. "Mrs. P. said if I didn't learn how to answer the door, I would find myself on the other side of it."

"Is Sassy in her room?"

"Yes, go on up—but don't tell Mrs. P."

"If I see Mrs. P., I'll praise the elegance of your door performance. By the way, could you be so kind as to give my cat a little milk or water?"

The maid took Mabel's cat with one hand and held it well away from her skirts. "Never seen such an ugly cat afore. I've heard tell some things is so ugly, they get cute. Don't work for this cat, though."

Sassy's room looked as though it had been ransacked by looters. The armoire doors hung open. Bureau drawers dripped undergarments like white icing trickling down a chocolate cake. Wearing only drawers, chemise, and corset, Sassy was trying to shut an enormous steamer trunk. "Come help me, Jemmy. I can't close my trunk."

Even when Jemmy threw her shoulder into the task, the girls still couldn't make the lock hasp reach. "You'll have to remove some items."

"But I couldn't possibly. I need every stitch that's inside."

"Perhaps you have another valise."

"I'm already using everything from the cellar."

"You could tie your clothing in a bed sheet and stick it on a pole, like hobos do."

"I'm in no mood for your humor. Just push a little harder, Skeezuck."

The pair finally managed to shut the trunk and lock it. Jemmy asked, "Where are you going?"

"Do you promise not to tell?"

Jemmy put her hand over the claddagh that had once belonged on her father's watch fob. "I do solemnly swear not to reveal Sassy's destination."

"Hot Springs, Arkansas."

"People generally go there when the racing season is over for one of two reasons—to get married or to take the waters to cure their ills. I don't suppose you've recently come down with the rheumatiz."

"Right the first time."

"May I ask who is the lucky fellow?"

"No, you may not. It's a deep secret. I've sworn not to tell a single living soul."

"If I should happen to guess, that wouldn't be telling, would it?"

"Well, I suppose it wouldn't."

"Let me see. Could it be my wild cousin Duncan who's claimed your heart?"

"My mother would never forgive me if I ran off with the son of a society matron like Mrs. Erwin McBustle. She'd weep for years at the missed opportunity for a grand wedding."

"Couldn't be Peter Ploog, then. He's a rich boy, too."

Sassy rolled a white stocking and stuck her foot inside. "I have no time to play your little game, Skeezuck. I'm already late."

Jemmy snapped her fingers. "I know. Dr. Wangermeier, the coroner. Sassy Patterson is going to wed the man who tends the dead."

Sassy flashed out an irritated, "Don't be ridiculous. I'd rather drink carbolic acid."

Sassy Patterson was about as likely to commit suicide as the hellion Heathcliff Smoot was to become a priest. However, if her parents were pushing her to wed the old doctor, Sassy would surely find a way to avoid such a match.

"It can't be Harry Benson. He won't be in any shape to travel after tonight."

237

Sassy paused while lacing a boot. "What do you mean?"

"He's to fight tonight—bare knuckles at Uhrig's Cave. Didn't you know?" Jemmy shivered at the thought of going down in a cave—even one decked out in all the comforts one could wish.

Sassy reached for her bodice. "Of course, I knew. The boxing match just slipped my mind for a moment."

"Well, who is it? Whom do you plan to marry?"

Sassy fastened the hooks on the aluminum-gray skirt of her gabardine traveling suit. "Heigho, my dearie. Ask me no questions, I'll tell you no lies."

"I certainly hope you don't mean to marry Tony von Phul or John Folck."

Sassy slipped her last cuff button through its buttonhole. "Why would you say that?"

"Ask me no questions, I'll tell you no lies."

Sassy shrugged into her suit jacket. "Don't worry about Sassy Patterson, Skeezucks. You'll upset your digestion. Just wish me luck."

Jemmy tried wheedling. "I'm your best friend. Can't you tell me?"

Sassy tried on her hat at the armoire mirror. " 'Fraid not. I promised."

Jemmy tried pouting. "You've no call to be mean to me. If I were running away with the love of my life, I'd tell you his name."

Sassy buttoned her jacket. "Fat chance of that. You're married to the *Illuminator*. What man can measure up to a front-page story?"

Jemmy tried extortion. "If you don't tell me, I'll tell your mother."

Sassy donned her fur cape. "Mother is not home."

Jemmy tried anger. "If you don't tell me, I'll never speak to you again!"

Sassy shook out her fur muff. "I'll miss you, Skeezucks. Of course, I'll be far away, so I think I can manage my grief."

The maid and the carriage driver arrived to breeze out with the baggage. Sassy gave Jemmy a peck on the cheek and swished off in a swirl of cranberry wool and white fox fur.

Jemmy looked around at the snarl of clothes and decided a search would not turn up anything useful.

If she hurried, she might catch a glimpse of Sassy's intended. She rushed downstairs and raced toward the porte cochere.

Chapter Twenty-Six

Friday Evening, November 25, 1898

The carriage pulled away just as Jemmy arrived at the porte cochere. Sassy's steamer trunk strapped to the back bounced jauntily over a pothole. The wheels jounced over snow mounds like a game of ball and jacks hitting the pavement.

Jemmy ran to catch a glimpse of the people inside when the carriage turned the corner. The streetlamps allowed only a glimpse of white fur.

She trudged back to the Patterson home to retrieve Mabel's cat. The maid said, "Miss McBustle, I hope you'll leave the cat here. Cook wouldn't allow a filthy beast in her clean kitchen, so I took the little calico to the butler's pantry and gave her a good wash. She ain't all dried yet, and it would be bad to have her out in the cold. Maybe you could come get her tomorrow. I promise to feed her up good and let her sleep in my room."

Jemmy was too tired to argue. In truth, though, she was a little disappointed the cat wouldn't be coming home with her.

Jemmy didn't reach Bricktop until well after suppertime. She paused with one hand on the front door. *Going home used to be nice. This week, every day has brought nothing but new calamity.* She paused to brace herself, took a deep breath, and opened the door.

For once, no one rushed to clobber her with bad news of new flu victims. As she hung her coat and hat on the hall tree, she listened for rumblings of trouble. The only sounds came from the kitchen, and they seemed normal enough. Someone actually laughed. The pungent odor of boiled cabbage filled her nostrils.

Cabbage is only good in German-style cole slaw. Cooked, it stinks up the house for days. Cabbage has the consistency of old rubber boots and the color of tobacco spit. Worst of all, it tastes the way pond scum smells. I hate cooked cabbage!

Even so, Jemmy practically skipped her way to the kitchen. Once there, she stared in disbelief. Three people were washing dishes, but none of them should have been working at Bricktop.

Lucy Leimgruber searched through cabinets to discover where to stash cleaned dishes. Arms elbow deep in a dishpan of soapy water, Hal was scrubbing a big pot and sloshing suds into the sink. Mrs. Hendershot said, "Gently, dear boy. You're dripping dirty water on clean dishes."

Nana Hendershot handed Lucy a porcelain lid as she spoke to Jemmy. "Welcome home, dear. You're just in time to show Lucy where the soup tureen goes."

Hal turned his head and snarled, "Got here just in time to watch us finish cleaning up."

Lucy bristled. "What a thing to say. I washed nearly every dish. I would be scrubbing that pot right now if you had the sense to put the frying pan somewhere other than on top of the coffee cups."

"That was supposed to be a joke."

"Broken china is no joke."

"I didn't break a single one."

"Not this time, no, but—"

Nana Hendershot piped in with, "Please don't argue. After all, no harm was done."

"Beg pardon, Jemima." Lucy reached for a plate. "We're giving you a poor homecoming. We have leftover corned beef hash—still warm, I think. I'll dish some up."

"That would be lovely. Can someone tell me what happened? Why are you working away in our kitchen?"

Lucy said, "Nana sent word to the newspaper that all of the McBustles and the help, too, were down with the flu."

"Randy, too? Is she sick as well?"

Nana Hendershot said, "Poor thing. She asked me to touch her arm. Hot as a stone in the sun, it was."

"We couldn't let Nana go hungry, so Hal and I came to help. I brought a round of corned beef I'd already cooked. I stretched it with onions and potatoes to make a decent supper."

Hal dropped his whining to give her a compliment. "The best corned beef hash I've ever tasted. The cabbage is not bad either."

Jemmy took her first mouthful. "Hal's right. The hash is delicious. He may not be right about much, but he's right about that."

Hal handed the scoured pot to Nana. "Finished. Now may I take off this apron?"

When Hal turned around, Jemmy clamped her jaws shut to keep from laughing. He wore Merry's dainty bib apron. The pink gingham sported embroidered cats playing with colorful balls of yarn. He looked like a red-headed grizzly bear in a pinafore.

Lucy said, "You're not quite finished. Empty the dishpan and wipe it out."

Hal growled but did as ordered.

The doorbell interrupted this almost-happy domestic scene. Jemmy couldn't think who it might be, though she should have known. She wiped her mouth and dashed to the front door.

On the porch stood Autley Flinchpaugh, hat in hand. The part in the center of his slicked-down hair gleamed white and perfectly straight. "I know I'm early. I wanted the opportunity to speak with your parents."

242

For the first time ever, Jemmy felt thankful her father was not around. "Please come in."

He thrust something wrapped in newspaper at her. "It's a Christmas cactus. My mother grows them."

Jemmy shucked off the paper. Inside three green spiny ovals about the size of children's hands sprouted three minuscule fingers.

Autley said, "I know it doesn't look like much now. Give it a month, and you'll see. The flowers are all the lovelier for blooming on such homely stems."

Autley might also have been talking about himself. Jemmy's heart went out to him. If Hal hadn't interrupted, she might have spilled some highly interesting beans.

Hal's voice stopped her cold. "Flinchpaugh, what are you doing here?"

"I've come to pay my respects to Miss McBustle's parents."

Hal chuckled. "Your bad timing is only outdone by your bad intelligence. Miss McBustle's father died in the big tornado of '96, and her mother is indisposed—a victim of the influenza that's going round."

Jemmy thrust the potted cactus into Hal's hands. "Mr. Dwyer, I am perfectly capable of speaking for myself."

Hal pretended astonishment. "Whoever could imagine that?"

Jemmy faked a smile at Autley. "I'll just put on my hat and coat."

Hal spoke in a lord-of-the-manner voice. "Explain yourself. Where do you think you are going with this strange man, young lady?"

"Ignore Hal, Mr. Flinchpaugh. He's Irish. Drinkers—you know."

"You're Irish, too, my girl."

"Scots-Irish. It's not the same."

Hal leaned toward Autley. "The Scots-Irish are the real drink-

243

ers. Two kinds of whiskey named after them—Scotch and Irish."

"Try not to be insulting while I go to the kitchen for a moment."

Jemmy hustled herself to the kitchen to give a final thanks to Lucy and Nana Hendershot. When she returned, the two men were glaring at each other but not speaking.

Jemmy pulled on her galoshes and whisked Autley out the door. A smallish, dark horse and runabout were tethered at the front gate. "I didn't know you had a carriage."

"This one is hired, but I've saved enough money to purchase one. Though I rather imagine—I rather hope—I shall need to spend the money elsewhere."

Autley helped her into the runabout. Jemmy heard the front door bang shut. Half in and half out of his coat, Hal came bounding down the walk with Lucy close behind. "Wait for me."

Autley stopped short and turned to face him. "Naturally, Hal, we'd love your companionship, but the runabout has room for only two."

"Nonsense. Jemmy can sit on my lap. That poor excuse of a horse looks strong enough to pull three."

Jemmy tossed in, "What about Miss Leimgruber? Are you deserting the young lady?"

"Not at all. Lucy has promised to spend the night with Mrs. Hendershot. Isn't that right, Lucy?"

Lucy's raised eyebrows spoke volumes of surprise about the supposed promise. She put up a brave front, though. "I'll be happy to spend the night on a pallet in Nana's room if that's what is needed."

"See there, Flinchpaugh. It's all settled." Hal clambered into the runabout and shoved Jemmy over. Autley stepped up on the running board and looked in vain for a place to sit. He had told the truth when he said the runabout had room for two, but not three.

Hal yanked Jemmy onto his lap. "See there, Flinchpaugh. Plenty of room."

Autley clapped his hat on his head so roughly that it covered his eyes. He jerked it off and scrambled inside the carriage.

Arms straight at her sides and hands balled into fists, Lucy stood by the gate as Autley maneuvered the runabout into the street.

Jemmy fidgeted in a futile effort to find comfort on Hal's bony knees.

"Sit still. You wiggle more than a catfish on a fishing hook."

"Well, excuse me for being a pest. Please recall that no one asked you to come along to be annoyed by a wiggling girl on your lap."

"I felt duty bound to come." He turned to Autley. "This girl gets into nothing but trouble when I'm not with her."

Even in the flickering light of a streetlamp, Jemmy saw Autley's face bloom red with embarrassment. *Heavens in a handbag! Autley must think Hal is the father of the child he thinks I'm going to have.*

Heavens in a handbag! Autley asked to see my parents. I think he means to take this defiled and discarded flower off Mother's hands. Autley Flinchpaugh wants to marry me!

As the trio set off toward Uhrig's Cave, Jemmy's mind flitted from the Sproat case to Harry Benson to Pervia Benigas to Mabel Dewoskin to Frank James to Hal and Lucy's new-found devotion to Mrs. Hendershot. Underlying all this mental chaos was the knowledge she'd soon, very soon, have to do something about Autley Flinchpaugh's clumsy attempts to make an honest woman of her.

Jemmy had been paying no attention at all to the words passing between Hal and Autley, even though they grew more heated. But then the carriage came to a full stop before the trio had traveled a single block.

Hal shoved Jemmy off his lap and clambered out one side of the runabout. At the same time, Autley wrapped the reins around the brake handle and jumped down from the opposite side.

Jemmy stared in amazement as both men tossed their overcoats at her and started unbuttoning their jackets. Not until then did it dawn on her they were about to come to blows. In a few more seconds, jackets and hats came flying into the runabout. Then both men loosened ties and unbuttoned cuffs in that final ritual before the serious work of grappling one another could begin.

"Gentlemen, perhaps you haven't noticed, but we've missed our destination. The boxing match is to be held at Uhrig's Cave."

Neither male paid her the slightest bit of attention. Breathless from running down St. Ange Street, Lucy grabbed Hal's elbow. With a jerk of his arm, he flicked her off like a housefly. She would have splatted on the ground if she hadn't caromed off the fence and found something to hold onto.

In a streetlamp's dim pool of light, Autley and Hal circled each other with fists raised. Both looked grimly intent as they sized each other up.

Jemmy called out, "Lucy, come into the runabout. You'll catch your death of cold if you stand out there watching these hooligans waltzing around."

Jemmy offered a hand to steady Lucy as she climbed on board.

Lucy asked, "What are they fighting about?"

Jemmy pulled Hal's overcoat around Lucy's shivering shoulders. "I have no idea. I know Autley didn't want Hal to come with us."

"On that point, the two of us agree."

"On that point, three of the four of us agree."

"But that's no reason to resort to violence."

"For men as pigheaded as those two, maybe it is."

"Do you think they'll truly hurt each other?"

"So far, all they've done is dance around looking mean."

"Is there anything we can do to stop them?"

Jemmy brightened. "I can think of one thing." She unwrapped the reins from the brake. "If we leave them here squabbling like schoolyard bullies, I think they'll come after us."

Lucy covered a giggle with her hand. "Let's."

"One teensy problem, though. I've never driven a horse before. Well, just the one time. That worked out well enough, if I do say so myself. I've seen boys drive horses. If they can, so can I."

She flapped the reins harder than she'd intended. The little dark horse reared in the gig shaft and took off at bone-rattling speed. It was all Jemmy could do to pull the left rein and guide the beast. They negotiated the Chouteau intersection on one wheel and came near to overturning.

Lucy's scream must have caught the men's attention. Jemmy yelled over the clatter of horse hoofs on the road. "Can you see what they're doing now?"

Head turned to see round the carriage side, Lucy bubbled with delight. "It worked, Jemmy. It worked. They're coming after us. You can slow down, now."

"I'm not sure I know how to do that."

"Are we in a runaway carriage?"

"Whoa, horse. Whoa."

"I think the horse is calming a little."

"I wish I knew the creature's name. It seems silly to keep calling him, 'Horse.' "

"Are you sure it's a him?"

"The only thing I'm sure of is that those two will be hopping mad when they reach us."

"What should we do?"

"I think we'd better keep them running for a time."

"What a brilliant idea! A nice run in the cold November air should cool them down."

"And wear them out."

By the time the little dark horse jolted the ladies to the Fourteenth Street viaduct over the rail yards, Jemmy had very nearly figured out how to drive the runabout.

Lucy said, "Perhaps we should stop here and wait for them. They're so far back, I can barely see them. I think they stopped running. No, they've started again."

"You know what, Lucy? I don't think I want to be here when they catch up. If they can still run, they're not exhausted enough to forget their quarrel, whatever it was." Jemmy urged the horse forward, slower this time.

"What do you mean to do?"

"Drive the two of us to the big event."

"What's the big event?"

"A no-holds-barred bare-knuckles fight."

"I had no idea such fights still existed."

"Polite society may frown upon it, but I suppose there will always be an appetite for blood sport. I'm beginning to think it's part of human nature—at least for men."

"But what about Hal and Mr. Flinchpaugh? Won't they worry if we just take off and leave them?"

"They'll find us. They know where we're going."

"But won't they be angry if we just up and leave them running after us?"

"They'll be angry either way, but if they have to walk all those blocks to Washington and Jefferson Streets, they'll be more tired than angry. At least, I hope they'll be more tired than angry."

"It sounds awfully mean to leave them running down the street. They don't even have their jackets, much less their overcoats."

"They'll stay warm enough if they run." Jemmy looked at Lucy. "Any time you want, I'll stop the runabout, and you can get out."

"I can't walk. I'd ruin my good boots. I can't afford Snow Queen boots on a shop girl's pay even with my employee discount."

A quick glance out the back told Jemmy the men were catching up. "Quick, throw something out." Jemmy urged the little horse into a trot.

"Throw out what?"

"A hat, a jacket, anything."

Lucy tossed a hat into a snow bank under a streetlight. "Oh, I see. They both veered off the street to collect the hat. Good thinking, Jemmy."

"If you see them gaining on us, throw out something else. We can't let them catch us. The big fight is the best chance I have to get to the bottom of Quisenberry Sproat's death."

CHAPTER TWENTY-SEVEN

Friday Night, November 25, 1898

When she saw the battered Uhrig's Cave sign, Jemmy shook her head. *I can't believe I'm going down into another cave voluntarily.*

Jemmy set her jaw and determined to enter. She entrusted the horse and runabout to a young man who promised to care for the rig for fifty cents. Jemmy gave him her last quarter with a promise her young man would supply the other quarter when they redeemed horse and carriage.

The pair of girls owned not a single cent when they reached the entrance. Jemmy showed the ticket taker her press credentials, but the man refused them. "I'll wager them papers is faked. I heered of one or two lady newshounds, but I never heered of no lady without no man to protect her sent out to cover no boxing match in the middle of the night."

"Our escorts will be arriving shortly. They'll be happy to pay our way."

"You two don't look right to me." He pointed at Lucy. "That gal ain't even wearin' no proper coat."

Jemmy had to agree. In Hal's much-too-big overcoat, Lucy looked like a five-year-old playing dress-up-like-papa. All she lacked was a pipe and a drawn-on mustache.

"Move on off to the side."

"My good man, why are you being knavish to these ladies? Where's your chivalry, sir?" The Tom Loker–Simon Legree actor from the Crystal Palace Theatre strode alongside the queue.

In black overcoat and fedora hat with white silk scarf around his neck, he looked his usual glamorous self.

"I don't know nothin' 'bout chivarees, but I know my job. I don't let in no freeloaders. Nor do I believe some young gal who says she reports on sportin' events."

"How dare you call them freeloaders? They are my guests. Didn't they tell you I was settling the disposition of our conveyance? You're extremely rude to keep these delicate flowers waiting out in the cold."

Loker-Legree handed the man three one-dollar bills. The ticket taker dipped his head. "Sorry, ladies. I was just tryin' to stay on the right side of the boss."

Loker-Legree ushered the pair into the cave. Jemmy asked, "Is the admission price a whole dollar? That's twice as much as Buffalo Bill Cody charges for his gigantic Wild West Show—and that show has a cast of six hundred."

"The circumstances here require certain discreet inducements to insure the security and uninterrupted pleasure of the attendees." He nodded in the direction of a pair of fellows in police uniforms. "I think you follow my meaning."

Lucy piped in, "Do you mean the management has to bribe officials to look the other way while they break the law? That's the most—"

Jemmy cut her off. "Lucy, I'd like you to meet our savior, Mr. . . . I'm overcome with embarrassment. The only name I can think of is Tom Loker, but of course that's the name of the character you play in *Uncle Tom's Cabin*."

"I am a person of many names—role names, stage names. I sometimes forget my real name myself. But Tom will do, Tom Rafferty. I'm pleased to meet any friend of Miss McBustle."

"Well Mister Tom Rafferty, Miss Lucine Leimgruber and I are most grateful you came along when you did. Call on me at the *Illuminator* any day so I may reimburse you for our entrance fee."

"Nonsense. How could I wish for anything better than to find myself escort of two lovely ladies?"

Lucy said, "We're deeply in your debt, Mr. Rafferty. We'd love to keep you company, but that won't be possible. We really do have beaux who will be arriving shortly."

"Mr. Rafferty, would you be so kind as to excuse us for a moment?" Jemmy took Lucy's elbow and whispered into her ear. "I need to find Handsome Harry Benson. Could you stay by the entrance and distract Hal and Mr. Flinchpaugh when they arrive?"

Lucy's jaw dropped. "You want me to face them alone?"

"No, I was wrong to suggest it." *Lucy must think I'm a selfish monster with no feelings for anyone.* "I'm sure Mr. Rafferty and the pair of us can get lost in this great crowd for a while. I hope we won't have to see Hal and Autley for hours—or at least as long as I need to find Handsome Harry."

With a *whuff* of relief, Lucy nodded. "I hope you make your conversation short. Hal and Mr. Flinchpaugh are already angry as hornets. If they don't find us right away, they'll be fretting with worry as well."

"The sooner I find Harry, the sooner we will be able to face the wrath of the righteous. I'm sure you anticipate that moment as eagerly as I do."

"May I treat you ladies to a pre-bout libation?"

"We'd be most pleased to acc—" Jemmy slipped on a bit of moss trod slick by many feet.

Tom caught her and wrapped her arm around his. Jemmy batted her eyes at him, "I seem to be at sixes and sevens when I'm around you."

"In all sincerity, I hope you're falling for me in a more metaphoric sense of the word."

"It's not beyond the realm of possibility. We'd be more than pleased to accept your kind offer. Wouldn't we, Lucy?"

Tom offered his other arm to Lucy, and the three strolled into Uhrig's grand auditorium—an immense cavern that seated three thousand. Jemmy scanned the main room, where a roped boxing ring had been set up on a platform in the middle of rows of chairs reaching back in ever-enlarging squares.

Tom guided the ladies through a brick arch to a smaller dining room filled with laughing guests at tables covered with checkered tablecloths.

As a waiter seated them, Tom said, "Bring us three Simon Legrees." The waiter nodded and hustled off.

"What's a Simon Legree?"

"All the rage at the moment. I confess to popularizing it myself—and to making a tidy bit on the side. You see, I invented the Simon Legree. At least that's what I'm calling it for the run of *Uncle Tom's Cabin*. When I move on to another show, I'll change the name and the garnish to complement the new play.

"When we arrive in a new city, I make a point of speaking to the men who tend bar in the best watering holes in town. I give them the recipe and supply them with the special cordial which I've arranged to have concocted locally. It's the secret syrup that makes the drink unique."

"And you manufacture the syrup. How clever you must be."

"I see you understand the ways of the world. I love the life of an actor, but none of us have guarantees of a new role when a company dissolves. We need to have a second income. Also, our expenses are heavy—at least for the way I wish to live."

The waiter brought three tumblers of a bright red liquid with a licorice-whip stirrer. When Lucy took a sip, her eyelids shot up in surprise. Her head darted about frantically for some way to spit it out. Eventually, she braced herself and swallowed. "That drink is liquoritous. I never drink anything stronger than white wine."

"Waiter, Miss Lucy has changed her mind. Bring her a glass of white port."

"And you, Miss Jemima, do you like my creation?"

"I find it quite pleasing on the palate. Somehow it reminds me of Thanksgiving. What's in it?"

"Rafferty's Cranberry Cordial, Kentucky bourbon whiskey, seltzer water, and a licorice whip."

"How very clever. I only wish I could savor it with you, but I must excuse myself for a time."

Lucy rose to accompany her. "No, Lucy, please sit. Eat your licorice stick and keep Mr. Rafferty company. I won't be long."

Jemmy made a mental note to ask Tom if his local cordial maker might have been Mabel Dewoskin. It would stand to reason. As an actor, he would know a woman who lived in a hotel that catered to theatrical folk. She'd have to broach the topic carefully now that Mabel was dead. She found herself wishing she could prove Tom Loker Rafferty innocent. *What a shame if the killer should turn out to be such a fine-looking, well-spoken young man.*

Still, her immediate challenge was finding Harry Benson. She walked briskly toward the ring in hopes of seeing a face she recognized. Her heart beat faster when she spied Benson's manager. He crisscrossed the canvas-covered ring floor. From time to time, he'd bounce up on his toes, then fling himself at the ropes. He looked like an oversized tyke playing Red Rover who'd just been called to "Come over."

As Jemmy approached, he was making circling gestures toward two men at the corner of the ring. The pair tightened the top rope with a turnbuckle.

"Mr. Medley, may I have a word?"

"If it isn't the little lady who stirs up trouble. I forget the name."

"Miss Jemima McBustle. Would you be so kind as to tell me where to find Mr. Benson?"

Amos Medley didn't try to hide his lecherous smirk. "Try his hotel room tomorrow or the day after. Right now he has a fight to think about. I won't have him disturbed."

"Let me assure you I'm not interested in Mr. Benson as a suitor. I am a journalist seeking to interview him for my newspaper, the St. Louis *Illuminator*."

"I don't care if you're Nelly Bly or Queen Victoria, Harry has no time for females—young or old, rich or poor, newswoman or new pussy."

Jemmy had never heard the word "pussy" used to describe anything but a housecat. For a moment she stood puzzled. When she put two and two together, she blushed red as a mess of measles. She used the only weapon she had—sarcasm.

In mock gratitude, Jemmy sank in a deep curtsy. "I do thank you for your estimable assistance and your clever repartee. May I quote you?"

Before he could answer, she trounced away in a huff. "The man is about as helpful as a bowlful of termites."

She stopped to take stock of her surroundings. A man carrying a stack of towels emerged from an arch on the far side of the cave. Jemmy recognized him as Dcke Whicher. *Harry must be down that corridor.* Jemmy took a step in that direction but didn't get very far.

"You stop right there, Jemima McBustle. You have a lot to answer for." Hal grabbed her shoulder to spin her around. "What's the big idea of leaving us out in the cold? I've a good mind to take you across my knee."

"Not likely, since you failed to bring along the Mongolian Horde."

Autley Flinchpaugh whined, "You threw my new derby in a puddle. It'll never be the same again. And where's the runabout?

It's rented. I'll have to pay for it if you smashed it up."

"The rig and horse are fine. You owe the boy a quarter for looking after it."

"If he doesn't steal it, that is."

"Later, Flinchpaugh. Right now I want answers from our little miss runaway, here."

"Hal, Autley, please lower your voices. We're attracting a crowd."

Hal propelled Jemmy by the arm past curiosity seekers. Before long, she found herself backed into the base of a brick arch.

"Now, why did you humiliate us? What have the two of us ever done to deserve such misery? You left us running after you without so much as a coat to keep out the cold."

Jemmy fumed over Hal's rough treatment. "I have no intention of telling you anything at all so long as you're bruising my arm. You're supposed to be my bodyguard. You're supposed to keep me from harm, not attack me."

Hal shoved her against a wall before he let her elbow drop. He placed both his hands on the wall and trapped her between them. "I'm listening."

"Try to look at things from our point of view—Lucy's and mine."

"I'm not interested in points of view. I want answers."

Jemmy waved a hand to fend off Hal's cabbage breath. "Lucy and I saw the pair of you get ready to fight when you tore off your jackets. We were afraid you'd hurt one another. It seemed the best way to stop you two from coming to blows."

"All right. Fair enough. But your plan worked. We stopped—but you didn't. You kept on going. In fact, you whipped up the horse to go faster, so we couldn't catch up. Why did you do that?"

"I'll tell you the answer to that when you tell me why you

and Mr. Flinchpaugh wanted to fight in the first place."

"If you must know, Mr. Flinchpaugh made a perfectly ridiculous—"

"Stop right there, Dwyer." Autley pulled one of Hal's hands
away from the wall. "We should not be discussing this in public."

"Let go of me. My partner, Miss McBustle, and I may have
our differences; but I'll be damned if I believe for one minute
she'd"—he struggled to find the right word—"she'd do what
you said."

Jemmy cringed when she understood what Hal meant. The
pigeons were coming home to roost and were dive-bombing her
head along the way. She tried to speak—own up to her lies—but
she was too late. The two men had already begun squaring off
for another set-to.

Autley tossed off his ruined derby. "Let me warn you. I was
the best boxer in my weight class at Southside Turner Hall."

Hal set his porkpie hat on the cave floor. "Oh, yes. You were
so excellent at fisticuffs, you let someone break your nose."

Autley removed his water-spotted overcoat. "You've no call to
get personal."

Hal laid his soggy jacket on the floor by his hat. "I'm about
to get personal with that broken nose. Probably do it some
good. Bust it from the other side and straighten it out."

Autley dumped his mud-splotched jacket on top of his
overcoat. "You Irish are all dirt and duck. Got no stomach for
doing right or participating in an honest fight, either."

Hal said, "That's just wishful thinking on your part."
Simultaneously, the pair rolled up shirtsleeves and tugged at
their ties. "We Irish were born with war in our bellies."

Autley said, "Lots of babies are born with hair on their heads.
They soon lose it." The pair circled each other warily.

Hal said, "I haven't lost my taste for wiping up the floor with
a lout like you."

"Where are the rest of the Irish louts? I've heard the Irish travel in packs like stray dogs."

"I don't need a pack to whup a runt like you."

"You'll need every yellow dog from Kerry Patch."

"I'll make you wish you'd never been whelped."

Autley lunged at Hal, and the pair grappled. A crowd gathered to make bets on which one would win.

Jemmy saw her chance to escape and took it.

CHAPTER TWENTY-EIGHT

Friday Night, November 25, 1898

"A fiver on the little ugly guy. He looks like a real scrapper to me."

"I'll take your five and bet five more that Big Red takes him in less than ten minutes."

"You're on, if you'll make it twenty."

"Twenty bucks or twenty minutes?"

"Both, if you're game enough."

"Done and done."

Jemmy slipped through the crowd as people made wagers on Big Red and Little Ugly. She set a course for the arch where she'd seen Deke Wicher. She didn't get far.

A man's booming voice called, "Where are you going in such a hurry, Miss McBustle?" She slid on the damp floor as she turned toward the sound. Lieutenant O'Rourke's arm shot out to steady her. "The cave floor is uneven and slick. By thunder, I'd hate for you to injure yourself."

"I appreciate the advice, but my footing was fine until you distracted me."

"I would apologize, except I don't feel the least bit sorry. Surprise is the best way I've come across to speak to you."

A whispered female voice dripped sarcasm in Jemmy's good ear like lemon juice on a bite of fish. "If it isn't my faithful classmate—the one who promised to inform me of the location for this bout of fisticuffs." Pervia Benigas pursed her lips as if daring Jemmy to answer.

"I went to your home as soon as I was able. When I discovered where you had gone, I rushed to Union Station. I even searched the train. Of course, you weren't there. I kept my promise. It's not my fault you weren't where everyone told me you'd be."

"Nonetheless, I feel no obligation to share certain information with you. A promise attempted is not a promise fulfilled."

"No matter. I'll put the question to our favorite pugilist, Handsome Harry Benson. Perhaps he will be more forthcoming than you."

"Mr. Benson won't tell you a thing. I suggest you don't bother him. It would be as useless an exercise as dashing about train stations trying to find people who don't want to be found."

"Why are you here? Shouldn't you be practicing? Has your concert for tomorrow night been cancelled?"

"I won't be in Cincinnati in time to choose a piano, but Pervia Benigas never misses a concert."

"Ladies, please allow me to accompany you home. It seems clear that neither of you is likely to enjoy tonight's boxing match."

"I have no intention of leaving. If you'll excuse me, Miss Benigas, Lieutenant O'Rourke. I'll leave you to continue your evening together."

Lieutenant O'Rourke's brow furrowed. "An unaccompanied young lady is not safe in a mob such as this. Please allow me to escort you wherever you wish."

"Please don't bother. I have an escort. In fact I have two. I'm sure your Miss Benigas deserves your full attention."

Suddenly, Jemmy noticed Pervia Benigas had disappeared. *That exasperating woman! I bet she's off to convince Handsome Harry not to talk to me.*

Sassy Patterson's voice sounded like cream on peach cobbler.

"Jemima McBustle, why didn't you tell me you were attending this sporting event? Could it be because you have such a handsome escort?"

"Miss Patterson, may I present Lieutenant O'Rourke of the St. Louis police."

Sassy offered a dainty gloved hand. "I'm always delighted to meet a gallant officer of the police corps."

"Lieutenant O'Rourke—Miss Isabel Patterson and her fiancé, Mr. John Folck." Jemmy placed a tad too much emphasis on the word *fiancé*.

O'Rourke bowed low over Sassy's hand. "Pleased to make your acquaintance, Miss Patterson." He nodded in Folck's direction. "You, too, Mr. Folck."

Folck acknowledged the introduction with an impatient dip of his head.

Jemmy entwined her arm around the lieutenant's and purred at Sassy, "I can't imagine why you're still in St. Louis. I was under the impression you planned to be off in a carriage. I would have thought you'd be halfway to Hot Springs for your honeymoon this very evening."

Sassy scowled. "I fully expected to be on the train for Excelsior Springs and sipping champagne by now. However, our plans changed. An acquaintance—I wouldn't consider this person a friend of John's—persuaded him to make a sizable wager on the outcome of this bout. Apparently, if our man does not win, we shall have no funds for a wedding trip." She looked ice picks in Folck's direction. "We'd have to postpone our wedding."

Lieutenant O'Rourke beamed. "By thunder, I can't imagine any man who would engage in such folly. It's simply beyond belief. Were I a fellow with Folck's luck, I would not—for a single second—delay the possibility of claiming such a lovely lady as my wife."

261

Folck spoke up at last. "And if the challenger wins, we'll be set. I expect to make enough money not only for a wedding trip but also to start my own business."

Sassy rounded on him. "If you win, that is. If you do not, I may change my mind about marrying you. After all, a young lady in my position can't hitch her star to a gambler who loses."

Jemmy enjoyed watching the lovers' spat. To see Sassy crossed by a suitor was not something she'd ever expected to witness. Her guilty pleasure lasted less than a minute.

Hal's voice bellowed loud enough to make her cringe. "So there you are. I will not be left out in the cold like some worn-out shoe you'd toss in a ditch."

"Neither you nor Mr. Flinchpaugh looks much the worse for your skirmish. I'll wager neither of you exchanged even one pair of punches."

Flinchpaugh said, "It wasn't a fight because it wasn't fair. This gorilla has arms a foot longer than mine. I would have put him down with a single uppercut if he hadn't stuck his big paw on my head and held me there."

"Stop whining, Flinchpaugh. When you discovered Jemmy wasn't watching, you lost your taste for trading blows right fast."

Flinchpaugh turned toward Hal with clinched fists. "Are you accusing me of trying to show off?"

"If the shoe fits . . ."

Hal moved toe to toe with Autley. He looked down his nose at Flinchpaugh, who did what he'd been boiling up to do—hit Hal in the solar plexus.

Hal crumpled in half like a cookie broken in the middle. He wheezed, "I think you broke my stomach."

"I warned you."

Hal rolled around, moaning, on the cave floor.

"I told you I'm a boxing champion."

Hal moaned some more and wobbled onto hands and knees.

Flinchpaugh took a step toward Jemmy and held out his hand. Jemmy hid behind Lieutenant O'Rourke. Flinchpaugh circled round in an attempt to catch Jemmy's hand. Jemmy circled, too, as she kept the lieutenant's body between herself and Autley.

O'Rourke began to laugh. "By thunder, Flinchpaugh—I assume that's your name—I'm beginning to get dizzy. Do you think we might end this game of ring-around-the-rosy?"

Autley stretched himself to his full height. "I claim my rights as escort." He extended his hand. "Miss McBustle, please come with me."

Jemmy took a few seconds to ponder—a few seconds too long. O'Rourke chuckled deep in his throat. "I don't know what you've done to upset Miss McBustle, but she's hiding from you. I guess that means she doesn't care to accompany you this evening."

Autley stood with jaws clamped shut. Tension rose from his head like steam from a teakettle.

O'Rourke stiffened and stood up straight. "I'm beginning to understand. By thunder, if you've made unwelcome advances, you'd best keep your distance."

"I assure you I've done no such thing. If anyone made unwelcome advances upon Miss McBustle, it's that big fellow there on the floor."

"Her actions tell me otherwise. Appears to me Miss McBustle has discovered you're a brawler and doesn't like what she sees."

Hal struggled to his knees. "Now wait a minute, Lieutenant. You don't know the first thing about why Flinchpaugh and I got lathered up. It was all her fault."

"If you don't mind, I'll let her explain what happened. Ladies may have a completely different view of events than brawling boy-os."

Hal rose to his feet with one hand on his stomach. "Mr. Flinchpaugh and I would like you to remove yourself from our business."

"The pair of you seem bent on making your quarrel my business."

As words flew hotter and hotter among the three men, Jemmy retreated. The angry voices drew yet another crowd. Her last vision was of Sassy's radiant face. Clearly, Sassy loved a good argument, especially one that could erupt into a good fight.

Jemmy managed to sneak away during the fracas. The voice of Big Ed Butler calling spectators to their seats echoed in her bad ear. The fisticuffs bout would start soon. She had a few minutes at best to find Handsome Harry.

She picked up her skirts and headed for the arch. She paused at the entryway and wrung her hands. *How did I wind up here? I promised myself I'd never set foot in a cave again. Yet, here I am, about to trot down a corridor that leads who knows where.*

Inside the archway, the floor became even more slippery. She kept one hand on the rough-hewn wall in hopes of staying upright.

Noises from the crowd faded as she slid along the wall's rugged surface. Some thirty feet down the corridor she came to another brick arch. Inside she discovered an unoccupied room. It reeked of Watkins liniment. The place overflowed with chairs, clothes trunks, and boxes of medical supplies. Stacks of Turkish towels perched at the ends of two sheet-covered tables.

Jemmy was too late. Harry had already left for the ring. Her spirits fell. She didn't have long to feel sorry for herself.

The sound of a woman screaming roared and echoed through the cave.

Jemmy sank to the floor in horror. Electric fear jolted up her spine. A second scream sent her scurrying under the nearest sheet-covered table.

Jemmy heard scuffling feet and a woman's muffled cries pass by the changing room. When the sounds faded, she slipped out from her hiding place and sneaked into the hall.

To her left lay the cave's main room, where clanging bells and the noise of the crowd announced the bout had begun. That way promised safety.

But how long would it take her to gather her little army and convince them she needed them all? They would harangue her—probably for many precious minutes—or start fighting again. Meanwhile some villain would be performing unspeakable acts on a poor, defenseless female in the dank recess of Uhrig's Cave.

Perhaps it could be done. Persuading Lieutenant O'Rourke to come with her would be as easy as batting an eyelash. Flinchpaugh would be eager to show how tough he could be. Hal had to come; after all, he was her bodyguard.

Or she could go the other direction—the direction of the scuffling. *Yes, my story is that way. I feel it in my bones.*

The string of electric lights ended at the archway to a second empty changing room. The way forward was inky dark, but every fiber of her body pulled her in that direction. That way seemed less than inviting—terrifying, even. Still, she felt as if she were a penny coin being pulled along into the black pit by a gigantic magnet.

After all, I might waste hours convincing those stubborn men to accompany me back here. Hal and Autley would probably start another fight. They've already crossed words and fists three times this evening.

She kept her back to the wall and edged along with both hands against its jagged surface. The noise of the crowd in the main room faded until it seemed no louder than the scratching of a mouse in the attic.

The musty smell of the place sent a chill down Jemmy's spine. Her hand recoiled when she touched something soft as an angora baby blanket. *Moss! I just stuck my hand in wet moss.*

After the cave wall turned a different direction, noise from the auditorium came as murmurs, barely louder than the ringing in her bad ear.

Although the cave was clammy cold, Jemmy began to perspire. A feeling of suffocation overwhelmed her. Her chest heaved against her corset stays. She gasped to catch her breath. *Maybe I should go back.*

Memories of a different trip in a tunnel dizzied her. In some ways, this trip was even more daunting. At least there had been a lantern then. Jemmy persuaded herself that no light had penetrated this blackness in a thousand years. She panted as her corset stays kept her breath shallow. *If I go back now, what will happen to the woman who screamed? She could be seconds away from unspeakable evil.*

The wall turned in another direction, and the sounds from the main cave ceased altogether. She had never been more profoundly alone. Relief flowed through her body when she decided to start back. The relief faded when she spied the tiniest glow of light up ahead.

I must return and force Lieutenant O'Rourke to come investigate. No sooner did she think that thought than she took it back. *The lieutenant will get the wrong impression entirely. He won't believe I've discovered a woman in peril way back here in the bowels of this cave. He'll think I'm a forward girl who's smitten with him.*

No, I'll have to bring Hal. He's always complaining that I never let him guard me. He's duty bound to come with me. No sooner did she think it than she took it back. *Hal is already so angry with me that he would finish what he started earlier—shove me up against a wall and scold me for the better part of an hour. By the time he finished, the woman could be dead—or worse.*

Jemmy took a calming breath to still her pounding heart. She edged toward the light. *I'll sneak up and have a look. Perhaps I've misinterpreted what's going on. Perhaps there's no danger at all. If there is danger, perhaps I can do something. If I find everything is all right, I've done no harm by looking. I've done what everyone is always telling me to do—take my time to understand what I'm poking myself into.*

The moment of truth had come. Jemmy could give in to her fear of caves, or she could choke down the terror and keep going.

CHAPTER TWENTY-NINE

Late Friday Night, November 25, 1898

Jemmy felt her way along the damp cave wall. The place smelled like mildew mixed with sour milk. She inched forward toward the point of light. She heard no sounds except the roaring in her bad ear. *Jemima McBustle, calm yourself. Nothing untoward is going on. A quick glimpse will prove no one is being harmed in any way.*

She reached the brick arch opening to the lighted room, but, before she could turn the corner, her foot slipped on the moss of the roughhewn floor. She went down like a sack of beans. As she hurtled forward, she hit her head on the sharp edge of the brick arch. She didn't hear her own shriek as she plummeted into darkness.

Jemmy didn't wake so much as emerge through the half-light inside her skull. Her first woozy thought was, "Why is this bed so lumpy." She tried to move away from the mass that felt like a boulder boring into her back. She gradually came to realize the clump was her own hands: useless—tied together—numb.

A gurgling sound came from somewhere. Her eyelids seemed stuck shut. She managed to open one by a supreme effort of will. She squinted in the dim light and tried to get her bearings. The gurgling sound came again—this time accompanied by scuffling sounds. She peered in its direction.

Panic ran like ice in Jemmy's blood. Images of her own hands trying to claw their way out from sheer rock flooded her brain. She found the strength to force both eyes open despite the pounding ache in her head.

Her gaze met brown brogans in feet attached by rags to a pair of chair rungs. Above the brogans, ropes crisscrossed legs in brown, tweed trousers. Still higher she saw a man's eyes—wide open and urgent above more rags gagging his mouth. Jemmy searched her memory to identify what little she could see of that face. The fellow was trussed up like a rolled pork roast.

Who is that man? I must stop the swimming in my head. Concentrate. Concentrate.

It all seemed too much to take in. *What happened? Why are the pair of us tied up? Who would do such a thing—and why?*

The man tapped the toe of one foot and tried to talk. "RaRa-RaRa."

Jemmy scuffled her feet in an attempt to push herself into sitting position. She failed. Still, she could move her legs. She might be able to run away if she could manage to stand. *Run away from what? Who is that man? What is he trying to say, and who imprisoned us in this cave?*

With a blinding flash, Jemmy knew just where she was—the deep recesses of Uhrig's Cave. A stroke of head pain spurred her brain awake. She had slid on the mossy floor and knocked herself out when her head hit the rock wall. Someone had dragged her unconscious body into this cave room and tied her hands behind her back. *Who was it? Who would want to pull me in here and to overpower this man? Who and why?*

Jemmy's head ached more as she tried to identify the man in the tweed suit. *Is it Loker-Legree? He has a tweed suit.*

But no, this man had dark, straight hair and a mustache. Actor Tom Rafferty was blond and clean-shaven. *If only she could see that face without the rag that divided it in half.*

Jemmy strained to imagine the face the way it ought to look for a minute, then two. At length, little pieces started to congeal—the heavy shoes—the droopy mustache—the dark, limp hair.

Jemmy snapped from her wooziness in one quick stroke of recollection. She recognized the man, but the recollection only brought more questions.

This man is Handsome Harry Benson's manager. What is his name? Jemmy agonized to call up the man's name. She grew angry with herself because it would not come to mind. *Why can't I remember his name? My brain doesn't want to function.*

Jemima Gormlaith McBustle, pull yourself together. You don't have time to worry over names. You've got to get out of here before whoever did this returns. Med—Med—something . . . that's it.

"RaRaRaRa." The man jerked rapidly backward and forward in his chair like a little boy urging his rocking horse to an imaginary finish line. *Medley—Amos Medley. That's his name.*

"RaRaRaRa." Jemmy couldn't identify the words, but the man's meaning was clear enough. He wanted help.

She thought she might be able to loosen his ropes with her teeth. Jemmy snaked her body along the floor in an attempt to reach the man's hands. Each movement scraped her shoulder on the jagged floor as she inched toward him.

One of his hands was tied at the corner post where the seat meets the chair leg. Jemmy couldn't fit her head behind the chair. The knot was out of reach between his chair and the wall—mere inches from the wall. She pulled up her feet and pushed at the front chair leg. The man figured out what she was trying to do and lifted his weight as best he could.

The chair came around with a scrape and bang. Jemmy could see the knot, but it was still too high up. She couldn't reach the bindings with her teeth—not even when she ground her shoulder against rock till it bled. Even when she managed to prop herself up against the wall, she still couldn't reach the knot.

Jemmy had one more thing to try, though she wasn't at all sure it would work. If her corset would let her bend enough, she might be able to scoot her body through her hands. She stretched her arms as far as possible and began passing her rump through the loop.

When she was halfway through her hoop of arms, when she could all but taste the freedom having her arms in front would bring, a wave of panic struck. Something was pulling at the rope. It took an agonizing minute to discover the rope was caught in a crevice in the floor. She spent another precious minute freeing the rope's tail. Every movement brought another jab of her corset. The stays knifed her flesh and stifled every breath until she believed she would faint.

After what seemed hours, she managed to slip her hands past her feet in a swish of petticoats. Her hands were now in front. She shook them to bring back the feeling and began to pick at the boxing manager's knot.

As if by magic, the knot floated apart. Jemmy had to curl her body aside when the man began a furious assault on the loosened ropes. He twisted his body and banged the chair against the floor until he could pull himself free.

He yanked off his gag and stretched his mouth. He rubbed at the red marks along his jowls. Jemmy held up her fettered hands. He pulled her to her feet, but before he could untie her, a sound behind him made him turn.

Pervia Benigas came rushing on them like a hellcat. She raised a carriage whip and began slashing at Medley's back. *So Pervia Benigas is the killer.* Jemmy couldn't have been more amazed if the whip wielder were Archbishop Kain, all decked out in miter hat and white gloves.

Medley cringed. He wheeled around to face Pervia and

271

presented his shoulder to her barrage of blows. When he moved toward her, Pervia spun around. She raced toward the arch some thirty feet away. Before she got there, Medley caught her skirt. She turned back toward him and began beating his hand with the whip handle. When he let go, she slashed at his face. He put up his arms to deflect the blows. The lashes fell on his tweed jacket instead of his flesh.

While the pair kept up their battle, Jemmy pressed her back against the wall and sidled along it. When she stood directly behind Pervia, she took a deep breath and lunged. With hands still tied together, all she could manage was to give Pervia a good shove.

Jemmy's catching Pervia off guard gave Medley the chance he needed. He grabbed one of Pervia's wrists. He smacked at her other hand until she dropped the whip. Then he picked her up bodily. She thrashed and screamed like a banshee on Halloween, but her strength couldn't match his. He carted her across the room and slammed her down in the chair that had so recently been his own prison.

She fought and struggled to no avail as he trussed her up like a holiday turkey. Jemmy picked at the knots on her hands with her teeth as she watched the manager subdue Pervia.

All of a sudden, Pervia took notice of Jemmy. "Stupid, stupid girl! Look what you've done—set a murderer free."

"Poisoning Miss McBustle against me won't work. Anyone can see that you're the killer."

He turned toward Jemmy. "You're my witness. She was trying to cut me with that poisoned whip."

"Don't believe him, Jemmy. The greedy bastard killed Quisenberry Sproat. Do you know why? For money, that's why. That's why he killed my lovely boy."

"This woman is deranged. Why would I harm Sproat? He was my best boxer—my meal ticket. Give me one reason why I would want to kill him."

"He found out you were cheating him. I proved it. I have connections in this town. I showed him the numbers—the expenses for the fights—how much you made off of his sweat and blood."

"I had off-the-books expenses that don't show up on ledgers. I swear I treated him fairly."

"Off-the-books expenses like whores and paregoric for you and those other two so-called crew?"

"The paregoric was for Sproat's mother. As for the boys, yes, I paid for them out of my end. That's what good managers do."

"Jemmy, you can't believe a word this viper says. He knew Q.B. was going to leave him high and dry, but he'd already set up tonight's bare-knuckles fight. It cost him plenty to rent this place and bribe the police and everything that goes with an illegal fight. Without a big name like Q.B. to fight, old Amos here would be just about broke."

Jemmy dropped the ropes and rubbed her sore wrists.

Pervia turned to Medley. "I know what happened. You tried to change his mind—get him to fight—but he refused. He told me so himself."

"Don't fall for this tripe. Gasbags here is trying to pull the wool over your eyes. I knew Sproat was leaving. Of course, I knew. Why else would I have called Harry Benson? May I point out that he arrived before Sproat died?"

Pervia's eyes narrowed to slits. "I know that temper of yours. You went backstage to beat Q.B. with a whip. When he didn't meet me at my carriage before the play a week ago Thursday, I went to his dressing room. I found him lying on the floor groaning. He named you."

Medley said, "What a ridiculous thing to say. Sproat was a boxer in tiptop condition. Do you think he'd let me lay open his back with a whip?"

"He'd been unconscious. Before you beat him, you hit him over the head."

"Miss McBustle, I certainly hope you're not being taken in by this woman's mad rantings. She's just trying to cover up her own guilt. Look what she did to me and to you. Tied us both up."

"Liar—you tied Jemmy."

"She's the murderer. You can believe that."

"I would never kill Q.B. I loved him. I planned to marry him. Don't you see? I had to stop Q.B. from fighting. He was ruining his hands."

"Stop talking such drivel." Medley finished tying the knot and stepped back. "I'll give you a taste of your own gag if I can find it." He glanced around at the floor.

Jemmy's face flushed as a slow realization crept up her neck. Something in Pervia's words rang true. *How did Medley know the whip was poisoned unless he put the poison there himself?*

Tears trickled down Pervia's face. "I can't stand the thought of Q.B. breaking his fingers in a bare-knuckles fight. It's criminal to treat precious hands like mere instruments of brutality. Hands are the essence of humanity. Hands separate humans from beasts."

Jemmy began a slow retreat toward the arched doorway. She might have succeeded if she hadn't stooped to pick up the whip handle.

Medley's head shot up. "What are you doing, Miss McBustle? Mustn't touch the whip. Belladonna—nasty way to die."

"So you said earlier. I was just going to take it to the police as evidence against Pervia."

Medley took one step toward her. "Give it to me. I wouldn't want you to accidentally harm yourself."

Jemmy got a better grip on the whip handle. With her free hand she grabbed her skirts and took to her heels. She raced through the doorway and down the hall as fast as her legs would churn.

She slid on the slippery floor over and over again. She couldn't count the times her hip slammed into a rock wall or her shoulder ached from hitting an outcropping in the rough limestone. Grit and moss underfoot made the going even more treacherous. She could see practically nothing.

She knew Medley was gaining on her. She had a weapon. But what use was a whip, even a poisoned one, in such tight quarters?

Just one possibility presented itself. If it failed, she shuddered to think what would become of her.

CHAPTER THIRTY

Late Friday Night, November 25, 1898

Jemmy slowed down. She had no room to swing the whip. Still, it might be of some use if Medley were close enough. She flattened herself against the wall. She laid the whip leathers on the floor and gripped the whip handle in both hands. *Heaven help me if this plan doesn't work.*

Every fiber of her body quivered with the desire to run. Sweat popped from her forehead despite the cold. Medley's huffing breath grew louder as he stumbled along the corridor. She could hear his hands smacking against the rock. Each *thwack* brought another obscenity erupting from his mouth.

In seconds, his footfalls placed him mere feet away. He muttered, "Shoulda killed the smart-ass bitch when I had the chance."

Then she felt his foot hit the whip tail. She yanked the handle. Her elbow rammed into the cave wall. Pain shot down her arm like flame on straw. The plan worked.

Medley hit the floor with a strangled cry. Jemmy surged forward. She left him there howling and scrabbling to get back on his feet.

Skirts gathered in one hand, Jemmy stumbled toward the glimmer of electric lights. Chest heaving against her stays, she ran. Lack of oxygen made her light-headed. *Heavens in a handbag—how's a person supposed to breathe? I've a good mind to scandalize the world and stop wearing corsets altogether.*

Behind her, she could hear Medley grumbling and gaining ground as she rounded the last corner by the boxers' changing rooms. At the entrance into the great auditorium, human-like shadows blocked the way. *Who are those people?*

She stopped herself in mid-flight. *Maybe those fellows are Medley's corner men. No, they must still be at the bare-knuckles fight. But what if the fight is over?*

Indecision pulled her in two different directions. She hadn't heard Medley sneak up behind her. "I've got you now, Miss McBitch."

Medley grabbed Jemmy's right arm and twisted it to the middle of her back. He clamped his other around her waist and lifted her bodily off the cave floor. "You'll not be telling tales out of school against me now."

Jemmy squealed like a stepped-on rat.

"Jemmy, is that you?" The voice of Hal Dwyer had never sounded so good. A rush of energy surged to her feet in her heavy Snow Queen boots. She aimed kick after ferocious kick in the direction of Medley's legs. She landed a solid hit on his shin. "Kick me again and I'll slam your head right into that rock."

Voices from the hall grew louder. "We're coming, Jemmy."

"Take heart, Miss McBustle."

"Who can run on this wet floor?"

"I damned near fall down every time I take a step."

Footfalls and scuffles from the rescuers caught Medley's attention. He shoved Jemmy in their direction. Surrounded by friends, she fell in a heap on the cave floor.

Hal wheezed, "Are you all right, Jemmy?"

She pointed back down the dark corridor and choked out the words, "Pervia—save Pervia Benigas." With lanterns raised, Hal and Lieutenant O'Rourke stepped over Jemmy and disappeared around the corner into the dim hall.

"Of course, she's not all right. Her shoulder is bleeding." Autley Flinchpaugh bent down to Jemmy. "Do you think you can stand? If I help, do you think you can stand?"

Tom Rafferty brushed him aside and fell to one knee. He pulled Jemmy to sitting position, then scooped her up in his arms. Autley stood by in awkward silence.

"Move your bones, Flinchpaugh. Can't you see you're blocking the way?"

Lucy's voice offered, "I'll just get your lantern off the floor so you don't knock it over."

"Thank you, Miss Leimgruber. Now if Flinchpaugh would please get out of the way."

Jemmy regained her breath well enough to walk, but if Tom wanted to carry her, well . . .

The pair squeezed by Flinchpaugh. Tom carried her to the first changing room. He laid Jemmy down gently on a sheet-covered table. "How do you feel? Is anything broken?"

"I don't believe so."

"Let me tend her, Mr. Rafferty." The ever-practical Lucy had already dipped water from the barrel into a pan. She scuttled about piling first-aid supplies on the table.

Tom caressed Jemmy's cheek with one hand and smoothed her hair with the other. Lucy washed Jemmy's scraped shoulder and treated other abrasions with iodine. Bits of skin peeping through her torn shirtwaist gleamed red-orange under the single light bulb of the room.

"I can't find any other damage. I think the patient will live."

Tom crooned to Jemmy. "Do you think you can sit up?"

Autley Flinchpaugh took Jemmy's hand to pull her upright. "I thank you for your pains, Mr. Rafferty, but I'll take over now."

Flinchpaugh is becoming a nuisance. The time had come for

Jemmy to do something about him. She did. She pretended to faint.

"Look what you've done! You made her faint. She wasn't ready to sit up. Stand aside, man." Tom maneuvered Flinchpaugh to the foot of the table. He took Jemmy's hand and rubbed it. "Lie still, Jemmy. You're going to be fine."

Tom looked at Lucy, who was patting Jemmy's other hand. "Do you think she might have a concussion?"

Lucy dropped the hand and began exploring Jemmy's head with her fingers. "Oh, my. She has a grand lump on her head. I hope it's not brain fever. When the brain swells, nothing will do but to drill holes."

"We'd best get her to the hospital." Tom scooped her up like a bouquet of flowers.

CHAPTER THIRTY-ONE

Late Friday Night, November 25, 1898
Tom carried Jemmy, but the pair didn't get as far as the doorway. The sound of obscenities echoed from the hall. Medley burst through the archway with O'Rourke pushing from behind.

Jemmy couldn't hold in a little scream. She abandoned the fainting pretense and threw her arms around Tom's neck.

"Shut your yap, Medley, or by thunder I'll slap you senseless." O'Rourke let go of Medley's manacled hands and shoved him against the wall. He drew his truncheon and smacked it once across his palm. Medley scowled but stopped cussing under his breath.

O'Rourke called back over his shoulder, "Is Miss McBustle all right?"

Lucy said, "Nasty lump on her head. Perhaps a concussion. She should see a doctor."

Medley piped up. "I didn't do nothing to her head." O'Rourke raised his blackjack and took a step toward his prisoner. Medley cringed while he spoke. "It's not my doing. Ask the other one. Ask Pervia."

All heads turned to Pervia and Hal in the archway.

O'Rourke asked, "Is Medley here telling the truth, Miss Benigas?"

"Isn't anyone interested in whether I'm all right? Does anyone care whether I might have a concussion?"

Hal helped Pervia cross the room and lifted her up to sit atop the sheet-covered table. On the way, he glared at Tom, who was still carrying Jemmy in his arms.

Tom offered, "I didn't want her to catch a chill."

"Gentlemen usually give ladies their coats when ladies are cold."

Tom set Jemmy back on the table. He removed his jacket and wrapped it around her shoulders. He chafed her hands, then held them between his.

O'Rourke asked again, "Is Medley telling the truth, Miss Benigas?"

"You might give me a minute to catch my breath. But the answer is 'Yes.' I heard her screech outside that hole where Medley had me tied up. Jemmy must have fallen and hit her head all on her own."

O'Rourke said, "Miss Benigas, Do you feel up to telling us what's going on? It's clear this Medley fellow had you tied up in the bowels of the earth. I can't think of any good reason a good man would do such a thing. He must have had some evil purpose."

Medley defended himself. "I was about to go find the police. You should thank me for catching a killer. She's the one—that Pervia woman. She poisoned Quisenberry Sproat and Mabel Dewoskin, too."

O'Rourke said, "Do you think me a fool? Police business is always conducted in the public holdover, not the entrails of a cave. I daresay you must have a bit more strength than a woman. Surely you could deliver one female to the authorities without roping her to a chair."

Medley whined, "If you'll just hear me out."

"One more word from you, and I'll give *you* a concussion." O'Rourke smacked his hand with his blackjack—twice. "Now, Miss Benigas, can you tell us what all this is about?"

"I persuaded Q.B.—Mr. Sproat—to quit the boxing racket.

He and I wanted to start a new kind of business. Mr. Sproat would teach fisticuffs while I played piano. We believed music would help students achieve concentration and coordination. When Amos Medley realized he was losing his star boxer, he hit the ceiling. Then he hit my beautiful boy over the head and horsewhipped him to death."

Pervia hissed at Medley. "You monster—why did you use a poisoned whip? Wasn't a lashing enough?" Pervia would have jumped down from the table if Hal had not prevented her.

O'Rourke said, "Sorry to put you through this, miss, but what do you know about this other death—the death of Mabel Dewoskin?"

"Q.B. bought cordials for his mother from the Dewoskin woman. She made all kinds of potions and looked like a witch straight out of *Macbeth*. I imagine he got the poison from her and wanted to make sure she couldn't tell anyone."

Medley started to speak. O'Rourke beaned him with the blackjack. "I'm a man of my word, by thunder. Two warnings is enough."

To Pervia, O'Rourke said, "What proof do you have that Medley killed either person?"

"None for Mabel, but I know Medley whipped Q.B. My beautiful boy told me as much. After he died, I spoke to people backstage at the Crystal Palace Theatre. A grip and the costume mistress both saw him go into Q.B.'s dressing room with the whip. I didn't know how Q.B. was murdered until tonight. Medley himself said the whip was poisoned with belladonna. How could he know unless he was the poisoner? Jemmy heard him say it. Didn't you, Jemmy?"

Jemmy nodded and began to shake. Tom Rafferty put his arms around her and pulled her against his chest.

Lucy clucked her tongue. "I have nothing to treat these rope burns on Pervia's body. Her wrists need salve. So do Miss Mc-

Bustle's, but I can't find any in the kit."

Hal turned to Autley. "Make yourself useful, Flinchpaugh. Find the lady some salve. Try the changing room we passed on the way."

"Get it yourself. I don't take orders from you, Mr. Harold Dwyer."

"The salve is not for me. It's for Jemmy and Miss Benigas. Don't you care that two ladies are in pain, and you could do something to help?"

"It's your idea. Go hunt for salve yourself. Nobody is stopping you."

"I used to think you were a decent fellow. What's caused you to get so contrary and—yes, I'll tell it like I see it—so downright mean?"

Autley marched to Hal and looked up at him. "So I'm mean, am I? A fine thing for you to say, you disgusting pig."

"I'd be obliged if you'd take that back."

"I can't think why I should. You're a repulsive brute and a contemptible cad." Autley slapped Hal's face, and the pair began grappling on the floor—for the fourth time in as many hours.

O'Rourke poked at Hal's back with his blackjack. "Stop that rolling around on the floor, you two. By thunder, we have serious work to do. We have ladies to take to hospital and a felon to take to jail. Your quarrel will have to wait."

Hal and Autley paid no heed.

O'Rourke called out, "Rafferty, lend a hand. Help me separate these two imbeciles."

Tom pulled his jacket tighter about Jemmy shoulders before he left her to aid the lieutenant.

Jemmy shivered at the blast of cold that replaced Tom's warm arms.

O'Rourke grabbed Hal's arms and twisted them behind him. He dragged Hal to the side and dropped him on the floor. "I'd manacle you if I carried a second pair." Hal scrambled to his feet and moved out of range of O'Rourke's blackjack.

Tom glided around the table and offered a hand to pull Autley to his feet. Autley slapped it aside. "I can get up on my own hook." Tom shrugged and returned to his place beside Jemmy.

When Tom once again put his arms around Jemmy, Autley objected. "Kindly remove your person from contact with Miss McBustle."

"I'll do no such thing unless she asks me herself."

Autley balled his hand into a fist. "I ask you again to remove your arms from Miss McBustle."

"She stops shivering when I hold her. Surely you don't want her to swoon again."

Autley limped around the foot of the table. "If Miss McBustle needs to be warmed by someone, that someone should be me."

Rafferty blinked and chuckled. "What cause, pray tell, have you to give orders on Miss McBustle's behalf?"

"I intend to marry Miss McBustle."

Jemmy winced. *Oh, Flinchpaugh, do you have to force the issue now—now when I'm so weak, so tired. Please just go away.*

Hal stopped dusting moss off his trousers. "You say Jemmy promised to marry you?"

Hal would have to meddle. Why does he always have to butt in at the wrong time?

"She hasn't promised as yet. Not exactly. I wanted to ask for her hand, but circumstances prevented me. I haven't made an official proposal, but I have the highest expectations."

Arms still around Jemmy, Tom said, "Why do you believe the lovely Miss McBustle would deign to marry you?"

"Because *he* won't." Autley pointed to Hal.

Dismay darted through Jemmy. *Heavens in a handbag, I can't face this now. Maybe I should pretend to faint again.*

The room fell silent for what seemed like an hour.

All waited for some response from Hal, but Hal stood silent, with mouth shut and eyes the size of duck eggs.

Lucy stuck her hands on her hips. "Mr. Dwyer, I'd be much obliged if you'd explain what this man means."

Hal finally found his voice. "I don't know what that fighting banty rooster is talking about."

"I suppose she hasn't told you." Autley nodded in Jemmy's direction.

Hal's voice fairly exploded with exasperation. "Told me what?"

"That she is having your baby."

"My *what?*"

All eyes turned toward Jemmy. She pulled herself away from the warmth of Tom's arms and faced the group, but no words came—just a creeping blush up her cheeks.

The room erupted in an explosion of voices. Jemmy could only catch a few words here and there.

"Harold Dwyer, have you been toying—"

"By thunder, this is a—"

"If Jemmy told you that I—"

Autley got down on one knee, "Miss McBustle, I regret the circumstances . . ."

Jemmy could feel Tom's warm breath as he spoke into her good ear. "You seem to have caused quite a—"

Pervia Benigas began a low pitched laugh that sounded remarkably like a coonhound baying at the moon.

At length, O'Rourke pulled out his whistle and produced a mighty blow. The sound screeched across the hard limestone. Jemmy covered her good ear in fear of losing her hearing. Conversation stopped as heads turned toward O'Rourke. "One at a time, please."

Hal raised his hand. O'Rourke nodded.

"Jemmy, Flinchpaugh accused me of putting you in the family way. You tell him right now that I did no such thing."

"No, Hal did not put me in the family way."

Autley said, "But you led me to believe that he was the father."

O'Rourke said, "Let me understand this, Flinchpaugh. You were willing to marry Miss McBustle even though she was, well . . ."

Autley nodded.

Hal said, "So that's why you've been attacking me every whipstitch. You think I shirked my duty to this fallen woman."

Autley nodded.

"I'm sorry, Flinchpaugh. If I'd known your reasons, I would have been easier on you." Hal turned toward Jemmy. "If I'm not the father, then who is? Is it O'Rourke? He's been making moony eyes at you. Maybe he did more than ogle."

"You forget yourself, Dwyer. I've never even seen Miss McBustle except in great crowds of people. And, believe me, if I fathered a child—Miss McBustle's or anyone else's—I'd stand to my responsibility. By thunder, with Miss McBustle, I'd count myself fortunate."

Pervia threw in her opinion. "We're all on tenterhooks, Jemmy. Do tell your whelp's parentage. Of course, I wouldn't be surprised to find out it's the milkman who made you *enceinte.*"

Hal pointed to Tom Rafferty. "Then it must be this actor fellow."

With a bemused look on his face, Tom didn't deny or confirm. "Well, Miss McBustle, you seem to have dropped another china plate. Shall I catch it for you?"

Jemmy blinked twice. *Did Tom Rafferty just propose? No time to think about that. I have to tell these people something.* She pushed herself away from Tom's arms and set her jaw. She turned toward the expectant faces.

Anticipation thickened in the room until Lucy broke the tension. "Please, Miss McBustle, put us out of this misery of not knowing."

Jemmy took a deep breath and raised her chin. "I am not a fallen woman. I am not in the family way. Such a thing is not only unthinkable, it's impossible. I am a virgin."

The room erupted again in an avalanche of people talking at the same time.

"Hal dearest, I apologize for suggesting—"

"By thunder, I'm relieved to hear—"

"Lucy, I've never given you any reason to think—"

Tom whispered in Jemmy's ear. "As always, everything you do surprises and delights me."

Pervia filled the room with baying laughter.

Autley's voice rose above the din. "Miss McBustle. I demand to know why you told me you were with child."

"I protest. I did no such thing. You drew that conclusion all by yourself."

"Yet you did nothing to set me straight. A lie is still a lie even if it's a lie of omission."

Hal jumped in. "Buck up, man, she gave you only a little taste of what I have to put up with every single day."

"Dwyer, can't you keep your mouth shut for ten minutes while I try to find out why this woman has so abused me?"

Hal and Autley moved toward each other as if they were going to mix it up all over again.

Lucy raced to put herself between them. "Harold, dear, let the man have his say. Surely you want to know what's been going on. Even if you don't, hush up and listen, because I do."

Silence descended yet again.

Pervia broke it. "Do put the little troll out of his torment, Jemima. Confess to us all just how black your greedy little heart is."

287

Jemmy lowered her head. "Mr. Flinchpaugh, I am deeply sorry for the way this has turned out. I was very wrong to play on your emotions. I never wished to hurt you."

"Then why did you do it?"

"I needed your help, and it seemed the best way. I was going to tell you as soon as I could—not in front of everybody, like this—in private."

"You needed my contacts to help you get the story."

"You knew as much days ago. That's why I came to you in the first place."

"You could have told me the truth before I made a fool of myself at your home today."

"You're right, of course. I should have. I was in such a hurry to get the story that I . . . Well, you're a journalist. Surely you've cut a few corners to get a story."

Autley turned on his heel and walked toward the archway. "I've never deliberately humiliated another journalist—not to get a story, nor for any reason at all."

"I'll make it up to you. I promise. I'll find a way." Her voice rose higher as he limped into the hall without a single backward look. "I will make it up. You'll see."

Jemmy slipped down from the table and followed Autley into the hall. "Please, Mr. Flinchpaugh. Autley, will you stop and let me explain."

"I'll hear no more of your lies."

"But where are you going?"

"Where I should have been an hour ago. I have a boxing match to cover."

Autley reached the opening to the grand auditorium and disappeared. Jemmy started to run after him but tripped. Fortunately, Tom steadied her, then swooped her into his arms. "I think you'll be safer if I carry you."

Tom led the way down the hall with Pervia and Lucy close

behind. O'Rourke and Hal shoved Medley in front of them as they brought up the rear.

Hal stuck out a leg to trip the prisoner. Medley yelped when his face hit the rock wall.

O'Rourke said, "Leave off, Dwyer. He'll blame me for that bloody nose."

"He deserves that and more for ruining my only means of transportation. He threw an iron bar into the spokes of my tandem bicycle's wheel."

"Next you'll accuse me of blowing up the *Maine* in Havana Harbor and assassinating President Garfield."

"Are you saying you didn't try to kill Jemmy and me?"

"Never even saw you until today."

Once in the grand auditorium, O'Rourke blew three short blasts on his whistle. A half-dozen policemen came to his aid. He spat out orders.

"You, stand guard at the entrance to the hall leading to the boxers' changing rooms.

"You, find a telephone and tell headquarters to send a wagon. And see if Detective Captain Fergus Connolly can come at once to Uhrig's Cave.

"You two, take custody of Amos Medley. When the wagon gets here, go with him to headquarters and charge him with murder. He's a big fellow, and strong. You be careful he doesn't get away. I'll have your badges if you let him. In fact, if he so much as looks like he's about to run, you cosh him a good one.

"Mr. Dwyer and Mr. Rafferty, I thank you for all your help. I'd be obliged if you'd take Miss Benigas and Miss McBustle for medical assistance. I have to go back where Medley had the ladies tied up to see if I can find anything useful in the way of evidence."

Jemmy urged, "Hal, do you think you might stay here and . . ."

289

Hal got the message. "Yes. Mr. Connolly is my uncle. I'd like to be here when he comes."

"And Hal, be sure to stop by your mother's cousin's saloon in the morning for a telephone message from me."

Hal nodded.

O'Rourke said, "I suppose Miss Lucy and Mr. Rafferty can manage Miss Benigas and Miss McBustle. I'll have the ambulance boys take you."

Tom said, "Don't bother. My brougham sits four quite comfortably."

At St. Pius hospital, both Pervia and Jemmy were pronounced only a little the worse for wear and sent home with sulfurated salve and orders to rest.

Tom discharged Pervia at Lucas Place and Lucy at her home on Sidney Street before escorting Jemmy to her door. "Miss McBustle, when I offered to catch the china plate you seemed about to drop, I hope you . . ."

CHAPTER THIRTY-TWO

Saturday, November 26, 1898

Jemmy woke at dawn with achy shoulders and skin scraped raw in a dozen places. The mere act of getting out of bed took a good five minutes. She wrapped herself in a quilt and dragged herself to her desk. Before eight o'clock, she'd finished the first story in her "Death of a Boxing Legend" series and sent recovered-from-the-flu sister Nervy off to the *Illuminator.*

She cowered at the thought of putting her bruised body into a corset, but she had places to go and people to see.

Once downstairs, Jemmy telephoned the Boatmen's Bank president. They set the time for turning over Frank James's letter at 12:15, a few minutes after the bank closed for the day.

Mother tried to dissuade her. "Jemmy, you need rest. I insist you go back to bed."

"I hope you don't mind if I make another telephone call. I must let Hal know when to meet me at the bank."

Mother hovered over Jemmy while she ate oatmeal and drank Postum. "Truly, Mother, I'm fine—just a little bruised." *Thank Heavens in a handbag she can't see my skin. It's the color of black plums on one shoulder and Hal's chartreuse bike on the other.*

"I worry about you. That newspaper job puts you in harm's way. I'll be glad when you leave it. Though, of course, I'll still fret when you leave for Europe with your Aunt Delilah. A trip across the Atlantic has its own dangers."

"I see Auntie Dee told you her plans, but . . ."

When Jemmy didn't finish the sentence, Mother prompted, "But what?"

"Nothing. I'm overjoyed that you and my sisters feel well again."

"Yes, the girls have recovered completely. In fact, the family's health is nearly normal, which means today is cleaning day."

Jemmy moaned.

Mother hastened to add, "Not that I expect you to help. The rest of us need to get back our energy. We'll feel all the better for doing your chores along with our own. So you go return to bed and give your body time to mend."

"Believe me, Mother. I long to do exactly that, but I have responsibilities."

"Now, Jemima—"

"Mother, you cannot treat me like a child."

Mother gazed at her eldest daughter for a silent moment before she said, "I thought when you became a woman I wouldn't worry about you. I see I was wrong. Still, I suppose you must do what you must do."

Jemmy winced when she stuck her arm through her coat sleeve. Mother held the coat and guided her other arm.

Jemmy looked around for her father's muffler—then remembered she'd given it away.

Mother took her own pale-yellow scarf of soft wool from its peg. She wrapped it around her daughter's neck.

"Aren't you going to scold me for losing another muffler— Father's muffler?"

Mother smiled as she shook her head.

"You must think me careless and ungrateful."

"No, just stubborn like your father."

"Such forgiveness—I don't deserve such a sweet mother as you."

The pair found a new relationship in those few minutes.

Jemmy took streetcars to Lucas Place. Once again, she found Pervia gone. The Benigas housekeeper said, "Miss Pervia took the first train east this morning. She has a concert in Cincinnati tonight. She thought you might be stopping by. She left orders with me to take good care of you. If you'll follow me, please."

"I appreciate the offer, but—"

"Please, miss, do come into the drawing room. Miss Pervia was most specific that I shouldn't present you her letter until you were sitting by the fire drinking your coffee."

Jemmy grew agitated waiting for the woman to return. She rubbed her hands by the fire and stamped her feet a little—and not just to warm them. *I'm all goosebumps. What did Pervia write in her letter?*

November 26, 1898
Dear Jemima,

You wanted to know why I was meeting Harry Benson at Union Station. I had three reasons. The first was to convince Harry not to fight with bare knuckles. I felt certain Medley would force him into a low-down-drag-out, and that's exactly what that evil man did.

The second reason was suspicion. I couldn't prove the manager killed Q.B. because my beautiful boy refused to go through with the illegal match. I believed then and now that Medley was the murderer. I wanted to warn Mr. Benson. What happened to my Q.B. could also happen to him.

The third reason was that Mr. Benson pledged investment in the dream Q.B. and I had of a musical boxing school. He promised to turn over his share of the rental money and the signed lease. I caught you snooping, so I passed up our meeting. For all I knew at the time, you might have been the killer's spy.

I apologize for tying you up last night. I thought you

were party to Medley's swindle. Had I not bound your hands, you wouldn't have thought me wicked or set Medley free. I hate to think what that evil man would have done if you hadn't sent Mr. Dwyer and Lieutenant O'Rourke to help me.

Please accept my deepest apologies.

Perhaps we can be better friends when I return from my concert tour.

Yours most sincerely,
Miss Pervia Benigas

Pervia's letter explained a few details of interest to the police and answered the question Jemmy had come to ask.

Jemmy nibbled macaroons in the warmth of Pervia's drawing room fire. *How pleasant it is to simply sit in quiet comfort. I could do this every day if I married well. I would have nothing more taxing on my schedule than writing dinner menus and deciding which jewelry to wear. I could be a lady of leisure if I married well.*

Stop it, Jemima. You would be so bored you'd have to do something desperate—like take up tatting. Thank heavens in a handbag I don't have to decide right this minute. She put on her wraps and braved the cold morning air.

Since she was in the neighborhood, she dropped by the Patterson home. The untutored maid answered the door with the ugly orphan calico cat in her arms.

"Miss McBustle, I'm so glad to see you. You must take this poor kitty. It's not safe here."

"What happened?"

The maid led Jemmy into the foyer and peeked around the portieres. "If it please you, come with me." The girl led Jemmy to the butler's pantry and closed the door.

"We've had a shedload of trouble round here this morning. Mr. Patterson had no more than left for the day when Mr. von Phul come round poundin' on the door, hollerin' for Miss Sassy.

Mrs. Patterson, she goes up to Miss Sassy's room and starts a-screamin'. 'She's gone. Isabel is gone. Her room is a mess, with clothes thrown all about. Someone stole her away. Kidnapped my precious Isabel.' Mrs. P. had a right breakdown in Miss Sassy's bedroom—cryin' and callin' out for Mr. von Phul.

"Well, cook hollers for me and for the old gardener to tell her what we knew about yesterday afternoon. I didn't want to stick my bones in the business. But the old man, he pipes right up and tells as how Miss Sassy had him fetch up the steamer trunk from the cellar, and how Miss Sassy goes off all gussied up in some strange carriage with some strange man.

"Well, Mr. Tony, he throws a right fit, he does—face as red as a sunburned albino. Starts kicking Miss Sassy's unmentionables what didn't get packed. And that's what happened to poor kitty here. Kitty was all wound up snug in a pair of Miss Sassy's drawers, and Mr. von Phul kicked drawers and cat clean across the room.

"Poor kitty can't hardly walk. Mr. Tony broke something inside. I just know it."

"Do they know where Sassy went?"

"Indeed they do. She left a note saying she was off to Hot Springs to marry Mr. John Folck."

"Is Mr. von Phul still here?"

"No, he stormed out sayin' he'd find her and bring her back if'n he could get to Hot Springs before Folck done her mischief."

"I never imagined that Sassy would marry a shoe salesman—a poor and ugly shoe salesman, at that."

"So you know this Folck feller. I seen him once. He looked the kind of feller Miss Sassy wouldn't speak to if he owed her money. And you say he's a shoe salesman. My, my."

"I'm as surprised as you are. I can't imagine what she sees in him."

The girl handed the calico to Jemmy. "Please take her. She needs more help than I can give. In fact, I wouldn't be surprised if Mrs. P. gives me my walking papers—for helping with the baggage and for not telling her Miss Sassy took off with a man."

The calico had grown a trifle less bony, thanks to the young maid's kindness, but one of its back legs was surely broken. Jemmy eased it into her satchel. "I don't know what can be done for the kitty, but I'll try. Does it have a name?"

"No, ma'am. I ain't had no time to think of one."

Jemmy took herself and the nameless cat to Boatmen's Bank. By the time Jemmy arrived, Hal had already set up his camera. The president stood, beaming, at the vault door. Exchanging excited chatter, the entire smiling staff waited in the hall. None went home, even though they'd finished their half day's work.

Jemmy read aloud Frank James's conditions for opening the letter.

"This envelope to remain sealed until Quisenberry Sproat's true killer is discovered, at which time it is to be opened by Miss Jemima McBustle *in private.*"

With great ceremony, the president himself escorted Jemmy to a private cubicle. The brass rings rattled on the brass bar as he pulled green velvet curtains shut behind her.

Jemmy's fingers trembled as she broke the seal and drew forth the letter. She turned it over in her hands, once—twice—three times. The page was blank. Frank James had written not a single word on either side.

She put her hand over her mouth to keep from laughing. *You sly boots. You never knew the killer's name. This is no more than a grand grab for publicity, and I'm supposed to supply you with it. Well, well, well.*

Frank James had presented Jemmy with interesting choices. She could walk out with the blank piece of paper and show everyone that Frank James's boast was a fraud. She could write a name on the paper—a wrong name that would discredit Frank. Or she could write Medley's name and add even more luster to the James legend.

Jemmy pondered for ten seconds or so. She could imitate Frank James's handwriting well enough. The flowing ovals could have come straight from *Spenserian Key to Practical Penmanship*—the very book Mary Institute used to teach cursive writing. He'd written the words in pencil. What journalist doesn't carry a pencil?

No question about it. One scenario will make for a much better story. She wrote something on the paper, then emerged from the cubicle with a big smile on her face.

"Ladies and gentlemen of Boatmen's Bank, I have in my possession something that will astound you."

She posed with the paper held aloft so long, the crowd became restless. Hal directed Jemmy and the bank's president into several positions before he was ready to capture the moment for posterity.

The spectators buzzed with excitement.

"What does the paper say?"

"Did Frank James really know the killer's name?"

"I wish she'd hurry up and read it."

"How long is she going to stand there and keep us waiting?"

Hal ducked under the black cloth at the back of his camera. When he finally pushed the plunger, the crowd let out a sigh of relief.

Most solemnly, Jemmy read the words on the paper.

CHAPTER THIRTY-THREE

Saturday, November 26, 1898

"Sproat's manager." Jemmy handed the paper to the bank president to verify.

He nodded his head. " 'Sproat's manager.' That's what the paper says." He obligingly posed for another picture. Murmurs spread among the bank employees.

"Imagine that. Frank James knew who the killer was."

"Knew or guessed. Takes a criminal to know one."

"Why didn't he tell the police straight off?"

"I'll bet he did. They just didn't believe him."

"Maybe they did believe him but didn't have enough proof."

"Maybe the whole business with the letter was some fancy way to trap that boxing manager."

"I don't suppose we'll ever know. Frank didn't tell the secrets of the James gang. I don't think he's apt to tell this secret either."

"Shoot, anybody with half a brain could've figured it out in twenty minutes."

A great wave of gratification swept through the bank. The crowd was pleased to be among the first to have their curiosity satisfied. Hal was pleased with his photographs. The bank president was pleased with free publicity.

Jemmy was not only pleased; she had the perfect headline for her second story in her "Death of a Boxing Legend" series.

By the time she and Hal reached the *Illuminator*, she had finished writing the piece in her head. "Frank James Identifies

Quisenberry Sproat's Killer" would sell more than a few papers. Hamm couldn't possibly fire her—at least not until after the hubbub died down.

Bruised from the night before and bleary-eyed from lack of sleep, Jemmy nodded off on the trolley ride home. She would have fallen from the bench were it not for a kindly lady who propped her up and offered to wake her at her stop. Trudging up the steps to Bricktop, she fully intended to take her mother's advice and crawl into bed.

Mother met her at the door. "Jemima, you have visitors in the parlor. A Mr. Rafferty and Lieutenant O'Rourke."

Lieutenant O'Rourke might wish to see her on police business, but Tom Rafferty couldn't have that excuse.

Mother spoke in low tones. "They both brought flowers. Your sister has been entertaining them for more than an hour."

Heavens in a handbag. Only Sassy Patterson wants more than one suitor at a time. The only grown man who'd courted Jemmy in the last month had done so from a hospital bed in Sedalia. She had not seen him since.

Why did these two have to arrive on the same afternoon? I am too exhausted to deal with the pair of them. Help arrived from an unexpected direction. "Miaouw." The ugly calico, which had been silent and respectful for hours, suddenly popped her head out of Jemmy's satchel.

Jemmy crooned, "You poor kitty. I bet you smell that ham baking in the oven."

The cat tilted its head as if to say, "I've been the perfect cat for hours. Are you going to feed me or talk till I starve?"

"I must tend you right away. Those fellows will simply have to wait, won't they?"

After depositing her wraps, Jemmy gently scooped the calico out of her satchel and carried her into the parlor. Both men started to rise. "Don't get up, gentlemen, please. I can't greet you properly until after I've done what I can for this poor cat. It may take some time. Tony von Phul kicked her all the way across a room. She has a broken leg and perhaps internal injuries as well. This may take rather a lot of time. I'll quite understand if you're unable to wait." Jemmy beamed at her sister. "Minerva, dear sister, please continue your conversation. I'm sure the gentlemen are fascinated."

The two men locked stares and sat back down.

Nervy said, "Gentlemen, perhaps you'd like to see the fever charts I made to illustrate my influenza experiment. I assure you, they're most instructive."

Jemmy ducked out into the hall and headed for the kitchen. When sister Merry saw the cat, she dropped the sterling silver demitasse spoon she was polishing. "What a darling cat. I'll bet she's hungry." Merry fetched cream from the icebox. Gerta the cook stopped peeling potatoes long enough to say, "Milk would do as well. Your mama be much put out if she run short of coffee cream on Sunday morning."

"I'll replace the cream with milk. If the boarders notice, I'll tell them their cream went to save this sweet kitty."

Jemmy put the calico down to lap the cream. When Merry saw the cat couldn't stand on all fours, she began to weep. "Oh, the poor little thing. What happened to it?"

"A big brute of a man kicked her across the room and broke her leg."

"I'll get Nervy. She has a big animal husbandry book. She will know what to do."

When Merry returned with Nervy, Jemmy asked, "What are the men doing?"

"Most of the time, they pretend not to hate each other. I asked Mrs. Hendershot to entertain them." Strains of "Beautiful Dreamer" floated from the piano in the parlor.

Nervy said, "Merry, hold the cat's head. I don't want her to bite me when I touch that leg."

Merry took the cat's head in her lap and held the upper body. She nodded to Nervy.

"You'd best get a good clamp on that jaw."

"Kitty won't bite the hand that feeds her." Merry pursed her lips and cooed at the calico. "Oooo wouldn't bite me, would oooo, kitty?"

"What's kitty's name, Jemmy?"

Without hesitation, Jemmy said, "Flinchpaw—after her broken leg." *Every time I see this poor calico cat, I'll remember how beastly I was to a nice man. Autley, I meant it when I said I'd make it up to you.*

Nervy's fingers probed the cat's leg and gave it a quick jerk. Kitty yelped, "*M-r-r-r-o-w.*" Merry held it close to keep it from bolting. It didn't bite her, not even once.

Nervy pronounced the leg a clean break. "I'll get a bandage to hold it in place. I think she'll be fine."

Jemmy had no more excuses. She had to face her pair of swains. At the piano in the parlor Mrs. Hendershot sang "Annie Laurie" slightly off key. The would-be beaus had decamped. Nana Hendershot hadn't noticed.

Jemmy heaved a sigh. At least she didn't have to face them. Both had left flowers and their cards with notes on the back.

The lieutenant's read, "Dear Miss McBustle, I regret I had to leave. I'm on duty tonight at the Jewish fair and hope I might see you there."

Tom Rafferty's read, "Dearest Jemmy, I regret I could not stay. I have a 6:30 call at the theatre, but I shall return after the play in hopes you'll accompany me to the Confetti War at the Jewish festival."

CHAPTER THIRTY-FOUR

Saturday Night, November 26, 1898

When Hal arrived to take Jemmy to the big finale of the Jewish fair, she was still asleep. By the time she made herself presentable, Hal had worked himself into a snit. "Well, it's about time. If we don't hurry, we'll miss the Confetti War."

"Don't yell at me, Hal. I am sore and bruised and dog-tired. The last thing I need is to hear you grumble."

"I think I deserve a good grumble. I've spent two days cleaning up your messes and fighting Autley Flinchpaugh on your account. The last thing I need is to hear you beg for sympathy."

"Let's change the subject—speak about something pleasant."

"Like what?"

"Like this. I'm glad we could take streetcars instead of your wobbly old puke-green tandem."

"That puke-green tandem has been saving us money—and getting you where you want to go. I just hope it can be repaired. I don't like my chances of getting a new one from Hamm." The pair groused and fussed all the way to the fair. "Medley said he didn't damage the tandem, but he could have lied. Do you think I might get him to pay for the repairs?"

"When horseflies plant turnips."

While Hal unpacked his camera, Jemmy surveyed the gaiety inside the Coliseum. In her gray gabardine, she felt underdressed among the gentlemen in tuxedos and ladies in ball gowns. The new electric lights brought flecks of brilliance from diamonds on necks, fingers, and wrists. Ladies wearing taffeta and velvet in all colors of the garden bloomed like flowers.

Young boys and girls handed out coiled paper streamers from baskets decorated with ribbons. As the band struck up the "St. Louis Fair Schottische," Jemmy envied the dancers swirling onto the dance floor. She wished she could join them but settled for seeking the president of the fair.

"Miss McBustle, I'm glad to see you came, by thunder." A familiar voice with an Irish lilt caught her ear. "I wish I weren't on duty. I'd find great pleasure in waltzing you across the dance floor."

"Lieutenant O'Rourke, I'm on duty as well. I'm covering the fair for the *Illuminator*. I'm not dressed for dancing—as you see."

"By thunder, you're as lovely in plain as the rest are in fancy dress. Would you walk with me? I'm expected to circulate around the hall."

One of the two Little Eva actresses from *Uncle Tom's Cabin* tugged at O'Rourke's sleeve. "Pardon me, Captain, I am in need of assistance."

Jemmy blinked twice. The girl looked all grown up and sophisticated in her evening finery. *Heavens in a handbag, she's thirty if she's a day. On stage, she looks about ten.*

"Duty calls, Miss McBustle. Please don't leave before we have a chance to talk." The tiny actress took O'Rourke's arm and moved him off toward an avenue of booths.

Another voice, suave and compelling, caressed her good ear. "Will you do me the favor of granting me the next waltz, Miss McBustle?"

Jemmy turned her head to see Tom Rafferty looking resplendent in his black cutaway with vest of gleaming white brocade. His tawny waves of hair reflected glints of gold in the bright lights. When she tried to turn the rest of her body to face him, her boot heel tangled in her skirt. He caught her flailing arms and kept her upright while she extricated her foot from her ripped hem.

"A few stitches will make the gabardine good as new. I'm glad I wore something sturdy instead of silk. Still, I feel a bit self-conscious among all these lovely gowns. Are you sure you wouldn't prefer dancing with a lady dressed in satin?"

"I'm sure you'd look equally charming in burlap bags, as long as you emptied the potatoes first."

"You pay outrageous compliments, Mr. Rafferty. How's a girl supposed to believe anything you say?"

"I hope you won't find what I wish to ask you tonight too . . ."

"Here comes Hal. We have to find Mr. Lesser to tell us where we might get the best view of the Confetti War."

Hal smiled at Tom as if the actor were making him a gift of a five-year-old fruitcake. "Rafferty, I thought you'd still be at the theatre." The pair shook hands with all the warmth of January water in a baptismal font.

"I left before curtain call. I was unable to converse with Miss McBustle this afternoon, but it's imperative that I see her today."

"Well, you've seen her. We've got work to do. Come on, Jemmy. Where do you want me to set up?"

"I have to go now. Perhaps we can talk later, Mr. Rafferty."

"I look forward to a moment alone with you. There's a very particular question I'd like to ask."

"Jemmy, get a move on. I see Lesser by the burlesque booth."

Heavens in a handbag! Is Tom going to ask me to marry him?

For the next hour, excitement kept Jemmy's mind bouncing back and forth from the merits to the demerits of marrying Tom Rafferty—not that he was about to propose, of course.

Every thought she birthed both pleased and vexed her.

My family want me to marry, but they'd be appalled if I married an actor. *They believe theatre people are sinful—somewhere on the scale between Jack the Ripper and men who tuck their napkins down their shirt collars.*

Hal tapped her on the shoulder. "Are you listening to me?"

"Did you say something, Hal?"

"I said, do you want to stand beside President Lesser when he drops the flag to start the Confetti War?"

"I don't know. Would that make a good picture?"

Traveling from town to town would be exciting; but a nomadic existence seems unsettling and so confined—even if we could afford grand hotel suites. If we had children, how could I launder the diapers?

Hal shook Jemmy's shoulder. "Do you want your picture taken with President Lesser?"

"What?"

"Do you or don't you?"

"Do what?"

"Do you want your picture taken with Lesser? It's not a hard choice. I'm not asking you to pick out a china pattern."

"What, where?"

Hal shoved her in the right direction and picked up his camera gear.

Being Tom's wife would make me the envy of droves of women, but having a husband so admired would make me jealous. What if I were great with child? Would I have to hide in a hotel room for months on end?

"Not that way. Lesser is on the reviewing stand."

"The what?"

"The reviewing platform—with the bunting in front. What's the matter with you?"

Jemmy's feet moved in the right direction, but her mind didn't.

Being alone with Tom would be glorious, but the thought of being far from my family scares me. What if I took sick? Nothing is more comforting than Mother's care.

"Aren't you going to say something to President Lesser?"

"Say something?"

"Pardon us, President Lesser, my partner would like her picture taken with you. Please ignore her gaping mouth and vacant eyes. She always wears this expression to important celebrations."

Hal twirled her by the shoulders and backed her into place. "Mr. Lesser, could you hold the flag a little higher. No, not in front of Jemmy's face."

I wouldn't have to work, but I love the newspaper. How could I leave St. Louis? I haven't even exposed the Combine for their dirty deeds.

Hal shook the fair president's hand. "Thank you, Mr. Lesser. Might I ask where you think would be the best place to photograph the Confetti War."

"I believe by the east door would show the hall off to best advantage."

"Thank you again. I'm sure you'll enjoy our coverage of the fair. Tell everyone you know to buy an *Illuminator* on Monday."

He's an eager suitor now, but what about later? Would he tire of me when my looks fade? How would he treat me when my hair is gray and I grow a second chin?

"What's got into you?" Hal muttered into Jemmy's good ear.

In his presence I'm cursed by clumsiness. Tom enjoys rescuing me now, but he might tire of caring for such a lumbering fool. And what if I stopped being ungainly? Would he find me ordinary and boring?

Hal gave Jemmy a little shove toward the east door. "I don't understand you. You never let me talk."

"Are you talking?"

"According to you, I always say something stupid."

"Sorry?"

"You say a snail with brain damage makes more sense than I do."

Tom Rafferty is easily the handsomest man in the state, but look what happened the last time I nearly married the handsomest man in the state. I don't want to end up in a mental institution.

In a huff, Hal marched off alone toward the east door of the Coliseum. He muttered, "Females—now I have two headstrong young females to answer to—not to mention an Irish mother."

For every reason to marry Jemmy could think of, at least two reasons not to wed popped into her head.

The band played a fanfare to announce the start of the Confetti War. *Where did Hal go?*

All of a sudden, Tom was at her side. He swept her, stumbling, out to the middle of the dance floor. "This seemed like the perfect time to wrest you away from your job."

New Year's Eve was more than a month away, but the Jewish fair borrowed that occasion's most colorful tradition. Fairgoers bombarded each other with little coils of paper. The hall blossomed with colored streamers thrown at friends and strangers alike. Tom draped a spiral of white paper around Jemmy's neck. "I wish this paper were pearls, for that's what you deserve."

"Paper is all the vogue tonight."

"You look better in paper than other ladies do in diamonds."

"More outrageous compliments. I swear, you could turn a girl's head."

"I mean my words most wholeheartedly. In fact, there is something which, in all sincerity, I wish to discuss with you."

"I'm hanging on your every word."

"Perhaps you know that tomorrow's matinee is the end of our St. Louis run of *Uncle Tom's Cabin*. From here we perform in Denver, then Indianapolis, then someplace else for the next six months—and the tour keeps getting extended.

"I am gainfully employed, and I'm a good actor. I'll have

steady work as long as I live. My success has enabled me to put a little money by, so you see I'm not a pauper, nor am ever likely to be one.

"I've found no other woman like you, Miss McBustle. When you're in the room, I find myself gazing at you and dreaming we might find great pleasure in each other's company. If you wished, with my tutoring, I believe you could be an actress without peer. Together we could be the Madame Sarah Bernhardt and the Joseph Jefferson of the new century. In short, Miss McBustle, will you come with me to Denver?"

"Are you proposing marriage, Mr. Rafferty?"

Tom's head snapped up. Shock lit his face. He reminded Jemmy of a barking dog doused by a pail of water from a second-story window.

For the first time, he fumbled his words. "I hadn't really— that is—you said you are a virgin but . . . you work at a newspaper so I thought . . ."

"I don't understand what you mean, Mr. Rafferty."

He stood erect and pulled down his vest. "Of course I'll marry you, Miss McBustle, if that's what you want."

Jemmy blinked back her tears and held her lower lip between her teeth to keep it from trembling. "I've had more elegant proposals."

He took her hand as he slipped to one knee right in the middle of the Confetti War. A purple streamer landed on his head in the shape of a flower garland crown. "Miss Jemima McBustle, will you do me the honor of becoming my wife?"

ABOUT THE AUTHOR

Fedora Amis has won numerous awards including Outstanding Teacher of Speech in Missouri, membership in three halls of fame—state and national speech organizations and her own high school alma mater. Her non-fiction publication includes educational magazine articles as well as books on speaking and logic. Her Victorian whodunit, *Jack the Ripper in St. Louis,* won the Mayhaven Fiction Award. *Mayhem at Buffalo Bill's Wild West* was a finalist in the Missouri Writers' Guild "Show Me" contest. In St. Louis, she performs as real historical people and imagined characters from the 1800s.

She has one son, Skimmer, who partners with Fedora in writing science fiction, fantasy, and magical realism.

"Why do I write? I love words. Kind words are the greatest gifts we humans give each other."

The employees of Five Star Publishing hope you have enjoyed this book.

Our Five Star novels explore little-known chapters from America's history, stories told from unique perspectives that will entertain a broad range of readers.

Other Five Star books are available at your local library, bookstore, all major book distributors, and directly from Five Star/Gale.

<u>Connect with Five Star Publishing</u>

Visit us on Facebook:
   https://www.facebook.com/FiveStarCengage

Email:
   FiveStar@cengage.com

For information about titles and placing orders:
   (800) 223-1244
   gale.orders@cengage.com

To share your comments, write to us:
   Five Star Publishing
   Attn: Publisher
   10 Water St., Suite 310
   Waterville, ME 04901